Clay: a football novel

by Tom Van Heest

For Sam, Priscilla, and Matthew

...a father's greatest treasure

Winners never quit and quitters never win!

Chapter One

Friday, 8:00 a.m.

Pete O'Connor could not believe he was actually suiting up for the four-way scrimmage. He arrived at the Juddville Jaguar locker room two hours before game time.

How spectacular he felt as he pulled on his white practice pants and a brand new pair of white game socks. As he laced up his Nike cleats, adrenaline surged through his upper body. He put on his old New Haven Dragon tee-shirt; it must have been four or five years old it was so tattered.

Sitting alone on a badly-painted blue bench in the locker room, Pete reviewed his blocking assignments for offensive left guard. Though the assignments were quite simple, he wanted to make sure his performance in the scrimmage was flawless. As a matter of fact, Pete had one goal in mind for today's scrimmage: total domination.

Experience had taught him this: the players who were mentally prepared, didn't have to over-think their responsibilities in the heat of the competition; they just let their natural instincts take over.

When Coach Allen called a 34 trap, he would take his bucket step, scrape behind the center, and pulverize the opposing defensive tackle, driving him a minimum of three to four strides backwards, knocking him flat on his buttocks. Quickness was key, and playing on the line at a bodyweight of less than 200 pounds necessitated that he take full advantage of his speed.

Pete saw it this way: two weeks ago he was a running back, and if he couldn't beat every single one of his opponents off the ball on the line of scrimmage, he had no business wearing a Juddville football uniform.

After reviewing the offensive playbook three times, Pete opened up his bottle of orange Gatorade and took a big sip. He looked at the clock on the locker room wall. It read 8:15. His teammates would be showing up anytime now. He figured the first one to show would be quarterback David Riley.

Naturally, Pete was taken completely by surprise when Roger Collins walked through the door. Roger was currently suspended from participating in any athletic competitions. If there was one conclusion that Pete had formed about Roger, it was that he was completely unpredictable. He was a tough person to read.

As a result, Pete never knew how to act around him. One moment he wanted to tear his head off for deserting him out at Lakeside Park; the next moment, Pete wanted to kiss his feet for coming forward with information clearing him of unwarranted criminal charges.

"Hey, Pete. I figured I would find you here. Just wanted to come and wish you luck."

Pete was unsure of how to respond, so he offered up an obligatory, "Thanks."

Roger sat down next to Pete, clearing his throat before continuing. "I sure wish I could play today... There's no way I could have ever kept silent, though. Anyways, we're a heckuva lot better off with me sitting out instead of you."

Pete turned to his teammate, looking him straight in the eyes. "Well, I wouldn't be playing today if it wasn't for you. I appreciate what you did. I know it couldn't have been easy."

"Dude, I'm just sorry I didn't come forward sooner. You don't know how bad I felt seeing all those ridiculous stories that were coming out on TV and in the newspaper. I thought only the American Enquirer came out with stories like that."

"Well, I'm going to dedicate my first pancake to you, Roger. I hope Coach Allen calls a 34 trap the first play."

The next player to walk into the locker room was sophomore running back Mike Owens.

"Hey guys," said Mike, setting his duffle bag down on the bench in front of his locker. After three quick spins the lock opened, and Mike sat down, kicking off his shoes.

"Awfully quiet this morning, rookie," said Roger Collins. "You're not nervous are you?"

"Not really," responded Mike, unconvincingly.

"You'll do fine, Mike. Keep two hands on the ball," advised Roger, "and just remember this: if you do happen to commit the unforgivable and fumble the ball, Coach will bench you a minimum of four games."

"Seriously?" asked the gullible running back, obviously a bit wet behind the ears.

"I think Roger might be exaggerating," offered Pete, "but I would do everything in your power to avoid turning the ball over — even if it is only a scrimmage."

The next players to surface were right guard, Steve Wilcox; center, Craig Daniels; and behemoth right tackle, Gary Oxstance.

Steve was the first to speak, "Hey Mikey, notice how we've got most of the offensive line here already. Where are the rest of the Prima Donnas?"

Mike lifted his head up, embarrassed that he had missed the first half of Steve's comment. His brain was in a complete fog.

"Ease up on the rookie," cautioned Roger, "I think he's a little nervous; I bet his girlfriend's going to be up in the stands."

—

4

"Nervous?" Gary interjected, "What does he have to worry about? He's got the easiest job in the world. All he's got to do is take the ball from David and run straight through a 10 foot alley. If you don't make it to the end zone at least a dozen times today, you'd have to be slower than Big Larry."

"Who you calling slow, fat boy," said Mammoth Moore as he strolled through the door. "You know I could beat you in the forty by a full second if I wanted to, Ox."

"Maybe if there was a bucket of the Colonel's Extra Crispy waiting at the finish line."

"Make it two buckets and you're on. This is one race none of you anorexics will want to miss," promised Larry.

For the next few minutes, the boastful trench men predicted how many times they were going to pancake their opponents. The next player to enter the locker room was so quiet, his presence almost went unnoticed. Yet the high-octane pre-game atmosphere gave way to a sudden chill.

"Guard your lockers, boys," warned Steve, stepping directly in the path of the unwelcomed one. "Take one step towards my boy Pete's locker, and I'll drop kick you twice as far as I kicked that loser friend of yours."

Adam Foster's eyes were glued to his toes. Words usually didn't come easy to him, but he proceeded to repeat his dispassionate speech from the previous day:

"I'm sorry for what I did. I really am. I totally screwed up. It ain't going to happen again."

Gary the Ox cut to the chase, "None of us really gets why you acted the way you did, Adam. But most of us think your ass should have been kicked off this team. But we all respect Coach Abraham's authority around here. So if Coach says you deserve another chance, so be it. Just don't expect us to forget about it, though. It's going to take a heckuva a long time for us to accept you as our teammate."

The next person to enter the room was Coach Abraham. After surveying the situation, he ordered the former Billington Bulldog to follow him.

"The first thing we need you to do, Foster, is fill up the water bottles. Then we need to fill up two big water jugs — one for both sidelines since we are hosting this 4-way scrimmage. We'll also need two dozen bags of ice. Put a dozen in each of the coolers. Bring the water and ice out to the field first. Then come back for the equipment kit and ball bag, and don't forget the first aid kit."

After Coach Abraham and Adam left the room, Steve quipped, "If we're lucky, maybe Adam will enjoy being water boy so much that he'll want the position permanently."

"I sure hope not," said Roger. "I'd like to pummel him at least 100 more times out on the practice field before he decides to pack up his bags and move back to Billington."

Steve responded, "What are you talking about Collins? You and Foster are in the same boat right now, aren't you? You're lucky Coach Abraham isn't making you help Adam fill the water bottles right now."

"You know what I think, boys," said Gary, "We've got the two cutest water boys in the state."

Roger's face turned to deep purple, having no option but to accept the ridicule in silence.

Meanwhile Coach Abraham had returned to his coaching office, eyes staring at his offensive and defensive depth charts, his mind miles and miles away from football.

His gaze shifted to a family picture, hanging on the wall, ordinarily overshadowed by the numerous Juddville team photos and a few prestigious photos taken next to a handful of legendary college coaches over the last 25 years. Keith's most cherished photo was the one taken alongside the late Coach Rhino Roberts who set the all-time college victory mark at 465. But now that cherished photo seemed to have lost its luster, for just above this particular photo was a photo taken the previous summer on his 25th wedding anniversary. Keith couldn't help but notice the unabashed smile upon his face, yet the contrasting blank expressions of his wife and daughters Mary and Julia were inescapable.

It made him wonder why, in fact, he was smiling. Was it for the milestone he and Carol had achieved together as husband and wife? Was it for the job well-done raising two gorgeous and successful daughters? No, it had nothing to do with family; it was his football smirk—the by-product of an extreme confidence in Juddville's prospects for making a run all the way to a state championship. And the latter had most certainly come true. Yet his family had surely taken a pounding in the process.

A sharp knock on the door jolted Coach Abraham out of his pregame reverie. Keith jolted to his feet and opened the door.

"Hey Coach. I didn't mean to disturb you," apologized Coach Oliver.

"Are you kidding me, Gary? You can knock on this door anytime. What can I do for you?"

"Weren't we planning on going over the depth charts one last time?"

"Oh, that's right. I'm sorry. Completely slipped my mind. So who do we have starting at left guard today?"

"Ha, you're joking."

"Simpson or McDonald?"

"If that's the case Coach, you'll have to be the one to break the news to Pete."

"Pete? Who's Pete? Do we have a Pete on this team?"

"All right, Coach. I can see this is going no where. Let's shift to defense. I don't remembering you ever cracking jokes during pregame when I was a player."

"Maybe I should have, Gary... Maybe I should have. Anyways, Coach Oliver, I was thinking that since I have been out of commission for most of the week, I'm going to put you in charge of the depth chart for the linemen. It'll be a good experience for you. Go with your ones for the first 10 to 15 minutes of each scrimmage and then substitute in your twos and threes for the last 5 to 10 minutes. If someone's getting blown out in the trenches, feel free to put in someone who can get the job done."

"All right, Coach. I think I can handle that. I guess I'll take a walk through the locker room. Make sure all of our players are here and accounted for. I'd also like to see how they're preparing themselves mentally for their first taste of competition."

"That's a great idea."

"See you out on the field, Coach Abraham."

"Coach 'em up, Gary."

Shocked? Baffled? No words could aptly describe rookie Coach Oliver's thoughts right now. The responsibility of deciding who would be playing in the trenches on *his* shoulders? His mind was racing so quickly he didn't have time to ponder whether he appreciated this opportunity or not. One thing was for sure: he would have preferred more advanced notice than just an hour and a half before the start of the scrimmage.

Nevertheless, Coach Oliver had his first offensive line already in mind. Unfortunately, there were very few linemen on the second team that were even remotely close to "battle-ready". Simpson and McDonald had shown their worth during the Monday and Tuesday practices when Pete was temporarily suspended. Simpson had the brains to play on the line, and McDonald had the brawn. Put the two together and you would have a decent lineman.

Defense was a bigger mystery. Up to this point, McDonald had proven to be a pretty formidable nose tackle, as long as he didn't jump offsides before the ball was snapped. In time, he would learn to focus on the movement of the ball that was only three inches in front of him — instead of listening to the deceptive inflection of the quarterback's cadence.

At one defensive tackle, Coach Oliver wanted to try Larry Moore. His 6'2", 285 pound frame would certainly fill up a lot of space on one side of the line of scrimmage. If Big Larry could only learn to play low, and just submarine when he felt a double-team coming, Coach Oliver was confident that Larry could one day develop into an all-conference player. Moreover, if he could trim about twenty pounds, he would become a potentially lethal defensive weapon.

Even though Larry possessed a blue collar work ethic on the practice field, his eating accomplishments were obscene. The average human being could probably force down two Quarter Pounders with cheese in one sitting, but who would ever entertain the idea of shoving four of them down in less than five minutes? Only to be chased down with a large order of fries and large chocolate shake? Coach Abraham would have to lengthen practice time to eight hours in order to offset Larry's ridiculously-high caloric intake.

Other defensive tackles that would be sharing time with the red unit were junior Jimmy Smith and senior Gary Osborne. The Ox was by far the best offensive tackle, but his conditioning was suspect. Playing one way was going to be enough of a challenge, so expecting the Ox to play on defense too was almost entirely out of the question. Yet, he could play in certain situations like short yardage or goal line if need be.

Coach Oliver assumed that Coach Abraham had his outside and inside linebacker depth charts completed. Gary didn't feel like he would be able to offer much help there. Obviously, Wilcox and superhuman O'Connor would assume the inside linebacker positions, but as for outside backers, Gary hadn't a clue.

Slipping his head into his helmet, Pete was now complete. He paced up and down the length of the locker room. He felt like jumping up and down and celebrating though he had done nothing yet to celebrate. Just to be able to go out on this field again had him nearly overdosing on euphoria.

Earlier in the week, he was beginning to think he might never play another game on Raymond Sanders Field. Now that he had a second chance, he promised himself that he would make the most of this opportunity. How many times had Coach Abraham and Allen gone on and on about how they should enjoy this time in their life and how they shouldn't waste even one down of playing time? Pete had heard that speech so often last season, he could just about repeat it verbatim.

But now he understood. He could blow out a knee or break a collar bone and his senior season would be over just like that. Having been forced to sit out of two full practice days—forbidden from even standing on the sidelines—Pete had experienced a taste of what his life would be like without football, and it had been unnerving, driving him frighteningly close to a mental breakdown.

Circumstances had obviously changed for the better. Consequently, Pete had resolved to avoid hanging out at Lakeside Park or any other place that might bring him trouble. Yet, one danger zone was his trailer park. Fate had compelled him to live in the same residence as Josh Evans though that was no longer a concern now that Josh was back in jail for flashing a switchblade in the brief skirmish with a couple of Pete's teammates. Nevertheless, Pete was quite sure that one day he and Josh would have some unfinished business to settle.

Fortunately, Pete had the good sense to realize that worrying about some thug in prison right now was just plain foolishness; instead, he should be getting super pumped about the prospect of bulldozing players of a different color jersey.

So he let out a hearty chuckle, snapped on his chin strap, and slapped his helmet with both hands, followed by both fists to the sternum. It was a ritual he had utilized all the way back to his youth football days. It wasn't quite Tarzan, but it usually did the trick.

Pete was biting down on his mouthpiece so hard; he nearly bit right through the plastic. This was going to be so much fun it ought to be illegal.

No one had seen Coach Allen yet.

Under normal circumstances, Coach Allen would have been sitting next to his quarterback, reviewing the game plan in front of the grease board, or going over alignment and coverage adjustments with the defensive backs.

Coach Abraham was still camped out in the coaching office, content to let his assistants make the call for when to gather the troops for battle. Coach Oliver and the handful of returning seniors were starting to grow a little bit uneasy about the delay in their pregame routine.

If the truth be known, Coach Allen had arrived 15 minutes ago. Not wanting to make a scene—or a spill, for that matter—Jim had opted for the boys' bathroom next to the cafeteria. Unfortunately, the Denver omelette he had devoured for breakfast was finding its way back up, and the green pepper and onions did not leave a very pleasant taste during their second tour through his mouth. By this time, however, he was quite certain that his stomach was sufficiently emptied, but he had to make sure.

—

Nothing would be more embarrassing than to get sick in front of the team right before a competition—even if it was only just a scrimmage. What kind of message would that send to the team? Feeling a bit relieved, he got up from his knees and flushed the toilet.

Good riddance! Now it's time to put up or shut up, Jim thought to himself.

Chapter Two

When Coach Allen entered the coaching office at approximately 8:55 a.m., he found Coach Abraham sitting on a chair staring straight ahead with a dazed and confused look on his face. He recovered quickly, however, hopping to his feet and grabbing his clipboard and whistle from the cluttered desk behind him.

"Ready to roll, Jim?"

"It's time to see what we've got."

"I tell you what, Coach. If we score once every five plays, no one'll remember how we played defensively."

"Come on, Keith. You know defense always has the advantage in these scrimmages. It always takes more time for the offense to gel than the defense."

"We'll see. I know I'm anxious to see how our juniors hit. Sometimes you get kids who play a lot more aggressively during games than in practice. I sure hope that's the case with this group."

"Only time will tell."

"Alright let's go send them out," said Coach Abraham.

Jim grabbed the door knob to lead the way out and paused.

"Something wrong, Jim?"

"Not really... any chance you have any gum or breath mints?"

"Actually I do," grabbing a pack of wintergreen gum from the middle drawer of his desk.

Twenty-seven Juddville Jaguars were dressed for kill in their black mesh practice jerseys and white practice pants. Traditionally, teams chose to wait until their first official game before donning their game jerseys and pants. Although they wanted players to compete in the scrimmage as if it was a game, they didn't want to elevate it to game-like status—after all, they didn't keep score at scrimmages. Furthermore, coaches knew their opponents would be filming their scrimmage, and they didn't want to provide them with player numbers for their scouting reports. In fact, players have been known to exchange their jerseys with a teammate prior to the scrimmage with the intention of confusing their future opponents.

Quite noticeable were the two Juddville players not suited up for action; one looked embarrassed and discontent while the other had a permanent scowl etched on his face. Scouts could only speculate as to why two players not hobbling around in crutches or not wearing a cast on their arm might not be suited up.

"Who's ready to play some football?" inquired Coach Abraham.

A chorus of "**I am.**"

"Let's try that again. Who is ready to play some football? Juddville style… as a team."

"**We are!**"

"That's better. We always do things as a team around here. Never as individuals. We are going to march out to Raymond Sanders Field, side-by-side in two straight lines. No one talking. Everyone concentrating on how they're going to play.

"When you get to the North end zone, line up along the goal line, and we'll have our captains count you off into five lines. Then I want you to run up the side line, cross the field at the fifty, and down the other sideline. The first six will form lines on the 5 yard line; the next six on the 10 yard line, and so on. I'm sure that all of the three other teams are not here yet, so we should have half of the field to start out with for our pregame warm up."

The captains for the scrimmage had been voted on after Thursday's practice. No one was surprised that Pete O'Connor was elected; the other captains were Steve Wilcox, David Riley, and Jeff Nash. Wilcox and Nash were both two-way starters, and Riley was currently the starting quarterback. The under-sized signal caller showed great leadership potential and demonstrated good ball handling mechanics, but the strength of his arm was seriously in question.

Nevertheless, the captains did a great job leading the Jaguars in stretching; the team looked poised and prepared for their first taste of competition. By the time they were half-way through their form-running, all three of their opponents had arrived. With about 20 minutes left until the start of the scrimmage, the team split into their defensive position groups for tackling technique and ball drills. After 10 minutes they divided into two offensive huddles to run a few plays against "air".

Excitement was mounting as the four scrimmage teams gathered into their own huddles for the final minutes of warm-ups. David Riley received a play from Coach Allen and kneeled down inside the red offensive huddle.

"Alright fellas, this is our bread and butter. 36 Trap on two. Ready... Break!"

A chorus of battle-hungry voices followed, and the Juddville Offense sprinted up to the line of scrimmage. Craig Daniels crouched over the ball, and the guards, tackles and ends positioned themselves accordingly. Riley squatted under center and began the cadence.

"Blue 29... Blue 29... Set... Go... Go..."

The brand new leather Wilson football was snapped crisply into David's hands. The right offensive guard took a bucket step with his left foot and angled downhill behind the center's buttocks. The left tackle and guard blocked down.

Fullback Mike Owens stepped towards the line of scrimmage with his right foot and lifted his left forearm, making a pocket for receiving the handoff. The quarterback took a six o'clock reverse pivot step with his right foot, handed the ball off to his fullback, and took another step with his left, riding an exaggerated fake handoff to right halfback Jeff Nash. Then David snapped his hands out, placing them on his left hip before sprinting for the left sideline.

The coaching staff kept a watchful eye on their areas of responsibility.

Coach Oliver belted out, "Make sure you call for help from the left guard if you have a nose tackle over you, Craig. We have to make sure we clean out the middle."

Coach Allen complimented his backfield, "Excellent mechanics, David. Great job carrying out your fake, Jeff. Michael, way to lower your shoulder as you hit the hole. Not bad at all. If we execute like this today, no one will be able to find the ball."

Coach Abraham nodded his head approvingly.

The white offense ran the mirror play, the 34 trap. Junior quarterback, Don Jacobs bobbled the snap, and was unable to regain control of the ball in enough time to hand off the ball to the full back, so he did the wise thing and followed him through the hole.

"Come on Jacobs. We've got to stay under center long enough to receive the snap. You can't pull out early," reminded Coach Allen.

Both offensive units ran four more plays and were then dismissed to water up at the trough that had been set up in the grass next to the concessions building. The other three teams were wrapping up their warm-ups, waiting for the announcement for the beginning of the scrimmage.

"Well, Keith. This is the moment of truth. In about two hours we'll have a pretty good idea whether or not we've got a team this year. You guys sure did a great job preparing the offensive line. I hope our backfield can deliver," said Coach Allen.

"You know the old saying, Coach," said Coach Oliver, "When the line rocks, the backs roll. We can make our backfield look All-World or make them look like All-nothing. It sure makes a big difference having O'Connor in there... just in the huddle alone."

"I noticed that too," Coach Abraham interjected, "Pete looks like a blood-thirsty gladiator. I venture to say he's going to leave a mark or two on our opponents today."

"I am so happy that he's just able to play. To be honest with you guys, I really thought we were going to lose him. When it became clear that Dr. Jones and the school board weren't going to offer their support, I thought he was done. I'm still not sure how I feel about Roger Collins anymore. I don't know whether I should hug him for coming forward or strangle him for being such a coward in the first place," confided Coach Allen.

Meanwhile, Keith's attention had drifted from the football field up into the stands. Ten rows down from the top, on the fifty yard line, at the end of the row he had hoped to see Carol, perhaps accompanied by his daughter Julia. But her customary seat was vacant. He had purposely opted not to ask his wife if she would be coming to the scrimmage this morning. His fears were now confirmed. He certainly couldn't blame them for staying home. They would most definitely draw a few inadvertent stares and whispers.

Unfortunately, there was someone else in that vicinity. Dr. Jones, proud superintendent of Juddville Schools was chatting with the board president, Mrs. Valerie Snow. Aware that Coach Abraham's eyes were upon him, he gave Keith an impossible-to-interpret thumbs up. Keith turned his back to the stands, refusing to even acknowledge the presence of the school chief. He imagined how wonderful it might feel to push Dr. Jones off the back of the bleachers right now. Fortunately, only God was aware of his thoughts. The presence of Mrs. Snow seemed most unusual, however; why would she be at the scrimmage when none of her kids played football?

13

The Juddville Jaguars returned from the water trough eager to begin the scrimmage. The late August sun was beginning to heat up the field, and the players were glad to begin playing before the temperature reached its peak.

Coach Abraham was at midfield going over last minute details with the three other head coaches. When he returned to the Juddville huddle, he informed them that they would be going on offense first against the Mapleview Vikings.

The Vikings were expected to be the weak-sister of the scrimmage. In the past, a banner season for them would be three wins. As part of the Grand River Conference, their competition was inferior. Not even one team from their conference had won a playoff game in over a decade. Mapleview was a well-to-do community that was satisfied to excel in swimming, tennis, and science competitions. Friday night football was just a place to socialize with friends, and if the game didn't go Mapleview's way, at least they could enjoy the outstanding half-time performance by their state-ranked band.

The Vikings chose to go on defense first, so Juddville would have the first opportunity to put the ball in the end zone. On the north end of the field, the Jaguars were huddled on the 50 yard line waiting for their opponents to give the go ahead.

Finally, Mapleview broke from their huddle. From the looks of things, it looked like they were running an even-front defense — most likely a 6-2, the defense of choice for so many of their opponents.

Coach Allen gave the first play to his quarterback. David knelt inside the huddle to call the play.

"Okay, boys, let's show them whose field we're playing on. 22 halfback power pass. On two... Ready... Break!"

The O line sprinted to the 40 yard line, eager for the chance to hit fresh meat. David crouched under center and nervously began his cadence.

"Blue 34... Blue 34... Set... Go... Go..."

Daniels snapped the ball into the quarterback's hands. David received the ball, and pivoted counter-clockwise as Owens sprinted by for the fake, colliding head on with their defensive tackle. Riley took another step to Rob Bast, holding the ball out and riding his fake long enough to draw the attention of Mapleview's playside outside backer and safety. Then he pulled the ball out and took two quick drop steps.

As David looked downfield he saw Jeff Nash twenty yards downfield, wide open. But the signal caller doubted he could throw the ball that far. As his mind was considering what action to take, Pete O'Connor had pulled in front of him, joining Bast in a double-team block on the outside linebacker.

14

David sprinted full-throttle towards the sideline, hesitant to throw the short out pattern to tight end Dan Hardings who was being closely defended by the corner. Instead, the quarterback tucked the ball under his arm pit and ran for his life.

Ten yards down the field, David was brought down by the backside linebacker, catching him from behind. David hopped to his feet and sprinted back to the huddle, confident that he had made the right decision given the circumstances.

Coach Allen pulled him aside for a brief pow wow. "Why didn't you throw it deep? Nash was wide-open. He could have walked into the end zone."

Choosing not to incriminate himself, David just shrugged his shoulders, and said, "I thought I'd take the safe option."

"Well, I've got no problem with that, generally speaking. But it's 1st down, and it's a scrimmage. When you get a golden opportunity to throw a TD pass around here, you should probably take it. Alright... enough said. Next play. This one should make Pete happy: 34 trap."

Riley returned to the huddle with his tail stuck between his legs. His mind in a tizzy.

I really blew that one. If I would have thrown to Jeff, it would have been a duck for sure. Then I would be sitting on the sidelines.

The Jaguar linemen grunted in appreciation when they heard the next play. Pete O'Connor's heart was about to burst right through his shoulder pads. He couldn't help but steal a look at the player he was about to light up in a few short seconds.

On the first go, the center snapped the ball, and Pete was shot out from a cannon. He bucket stepped with his right, lowered his hips, and exploded up and through the opposing tackle.

Pete rocked him so hard he flew backwards into the defensive end, earning a rare two-for-one deal. The center cleared away the backside tackle as Wilcox and Osborn manhandled the inside linebackers.

The result? Owens received an early gift-wrapped Christmas present. All he had to do was take the ball into his hands and run straight up the middle of the field to the end zone. The only player who had a shot at him was the safety, but Hardings had released inside — untouched — and had no problem getting to the funnel in advance of Owens.

Mike showed everyone in Raymond Sander's Stadium why he had been brought up to the varsity as a sophomore. His blazing 4.5 speed left no doubters as the Juddville faithful rose to their feet in applause.

No one was standing taller than Mike Owens, Sr. "That's my boy. That's my boy. He's got his daddy's speed. Look at him go!"

Jamming his fingers into his mouth, he whistled so loud that the dozen or so people sitting closest to him had to cover their ears, prompting a couple of scouts from Billington to get up from their seats and move down to the next section of bleachers.

Standing on her feet—four rows lower—was Cindy O'Connor. Jumping up and down, clapping her hands, tears spilling down her sun-warmed face, she was grateful that her boy had been given a second chance to play the game he so dearly loved. No one had to tell her why a simple running play up the middle had resulted in a touchdown; she knew which player had decleated two Mapleview players with one mighty blow. And she wasn't the least bit surprised to see that one of the players was still down.

After about a minute of quiet, the wounded player was helped up to his feet. Both teams clapped respectfully, and the scrimmage resumed.

Normally, Mrs. O'Connor slept in on Fridays—especially after working overtime until 3:00 a.m.—but Pete wasn't the only one in the family whose adrenaline was pumping this morning. Her mind was bombarded by a barrage of emotions.

Hadn't her baby just been facing assault charges? Earlier this week she had been convinced that the two men in her life would be behind bars. In a remarkable turn of events, Pete's reputation had been restored, and he was back on the field leading the Mighty Jaguars. Yet she was hesitant to allow herself the luxury of being happy. Was there another unexpected helping of misery waiting in the wings?

During the next fifteen minutes, the Jaguars reached the end zone six times. Two scores were on inside traps, two on halfback powers, one was a wingback counter, and the last one was a quarterback bootleg that David had opted to run rather than throw to the wide open tight end streaking across the field on a drag route. The momentum was so heavily slanted in the direction of Juddville, even the red offense got in on the scoring. First year player, Tommy Schultz, ran 40 yards untouched, straight up the middle, courtesy of a phenomenal trap block by left guard Greg McDonald. Boyish Coach Oliver was so excited when the reserve offense returned to the huddle; he actually picked McDonald up off the ground.

After a three minute water break, Juddville switched over to the defensive side of the ball. Mapleview ran a basic I formation; their favorite running plays were the toss sweep, fullback dive and the inside ISO. They liked to throw out of a pro set with a flanker and a split end. Their quarterback had a decent arm, their tailback had good speed but lacked power, and their line was definitely a work in progress.

The first play from scrimmage was a toss sweep to the right. Mike Owens—replacing the suspended Roger Collins—had difficulty shedding the flanker's block, but managed to maintain enough of an angle to contain the tailback while Pete O'Connor—who had been sprinting for the sideline the second he saw the quarterback pitch the ball—flew up to meet the running back just as he made his cut.

The ball carrier ended up on his back, barely able to retain possession of the ball. As Pete hopped up to his feet, the runner curled up into a ball, gasping for his next breath after having the wind knocked out of him.

Standard procedure during a scrimmage allowed coaches the freedom to stand on the playing field as long as they stayed out of the way. Consequently, Coach Abraham was in a position to immediately sprint up from his position 20 yards behind the play to congratulate Pete.

"Way to fly to the ball, Pete," said Keith. Then he looked in the direction of Mike, "Owens, you've got to get rid of that receiver sooner, so you can get across the line of scrimmage. A lot of backs in our league could have easily made it around you on that play."

"I've never played corner, Coach."

"We're not interested in excuses, Mike," interjected Coach Allen, from his position fifteen yards behind the defense. "If you don't think you can do the job, I'm sure I can find someone else who wants to play."

The next play was a fullback dive. Pete read the guard's eyes prior to the snap; somehow he could sense that his opponent was planning to fire out at him. On the snap of the ball, Pete stepped forward, and his instincts served him well, for the guard was shooting straight towards him. Two quick steps to the line of scrimmage and Pete coiled his legs for lift off.

In perfect harmony, his legs, hips, chest, shoulders, and triceps wielded a crushing blow into the thorax of the oncoming guard. His adversary was driven back a step, creating an opening to the inside where the quarterback was in the process of handing off the ball.

One diagonal step to the right and Pete was barreling into the mesh point. His helmet went straight for the ball as his arms ripped around the midsection of the fullback, securing the tackle. The ball squirted loose, and nose tackle, Greg McDonald, pounced on the ball, picking it up and sprinting untouched to the 50 yard line as a Mapleview coach blew the play dead.

Although Coach Abraham was even more ecstatic over Pete's *second* defensive hit, he held his emotions in check, not wanting to appear as if he was rubbing it in the faces of their weaker opponents. Nevertheless, he couldn't help but feel good about what he was seeing from his defense so far. And the irony was that he hadn't even called a single stunt; they were just playing their basic 5-2 Cover 2.

Over the course of the next 12 plays, the Vikings offense managed a net gain of 21 yards while turning the ball over an additional three times. The last turnover was an acrobatic interception by Schultz who soared above the Mapleview receiver to pull down a badly under-thrown fade.

Fully aware that the competition level of the next two opponents would be much greater than Mapleview, Coach Abraham opted to substitute his white defense earlier than planned.

"Coach Oliver, let's put in the white D. Jim, you got another group of secondary you want to look at?"

"Sure, Coach. We probably should have let our seconds play these guys for the entire 40 minutes. They're terrible. And I thought *we* were down this year."

The white defense continued to dominate the Viking offense. They swarmed all over the tailback on an off-tackle power. On the next play, reserve linebacker, Rob Bast, ran down the tailback on a toss sweep, grabbing him by the jersey and throwing him out of bounds.

"That's a middle school tackle, Rob. We hit with our shoulder pads on the varsity," instructed Coach Abraham.

On the next play, Mapleview had a quarterback/center exchange malfunction, resulting in a fourth turnover. Backup nose tackle Joey Miller pounced on the loose ball, holding the ball proudly up to the sky as he emerged from the pile.

The final play took a little longer for Mapleview to call from their huddle. When they finally broke to the line of scrimmage, they had a wing back on the right and a split end to their left.

On the snap of the ball, the quarterback reverse-pivoted, faked to the fullback on his right and handed the ball off to the wingback running behind the formation to the left. The wingback, in turn, handed the ball to the split end on a reverse. The quarterback was his lead blocker, and he managed to execute a decent hook block on the cornerback, leaving only safety David Riley to make a play. David came up to make the tackle, diving at his feet, but coming up with nothing but grass as the Viking scurried for a touchdown.

"What the *heck* was that?" asked Coach Allen, deeply disturbed by the lack of aggressiveness in his starting quarterback.

Mapleview's entire team was sprinting to the end zone to congratulate their teammate who had scored their first touchdown of the season. Judging by the inordinate amount of enthusiasm, one might have thought that Mapleview had just won a state championship.

The Jaguar quarterback was quickly met by Coach Allen, engaging his quarterback in a private conference for the next five minutes. Jim was doing all of the talking, and David, all the listening. Many eyes were upon them, but Coach Allen didn't grant his audience the performance they were expecting. He seemed relatively calm, his hands folded together behind him. While the team watered up for the second round of the scrimmage, the conversation continued. Finally, the quarterback was dismissed to get water while Jim rejoined Coach Abraham and Coach Oliver.

As they began discussing strategy for the next session, Coach Abraham's gaze lifted once again into the bleachers. Still no sign of Carol and Julia, but on the positive side, his fair-weather friend Dr. Jones and companion Mrs. Snow must have seen enough football, for they were already gone. The temperature had already climbed to 80 degrees; the aluminum bleachers—void of any shade whatsoever—were occupied by only diehard Jaguar fans bound by duty to endure the extreme heat.

Next up were the Watertown Wildcats. This was the scrimmage that was causing Coach Allen the most worry. Two years ago, Juddville had faced Watertown in the second round of the playoffs, and Jim was quite certain that their coaches hadn't forgotten the drubbing they had received at the hands of the Jaguars. On that blistery cold Saturday two years ago, the Wildcats were annihilated 42 to 7. Even Juddville's white offense got in on the scoring. When one team gets up by 35 points or more in the second half, the mercy rule goes into effect—which means a running clock, except for timeouts, injuries, penalties, or a score. It was generally an embarrassment for a team to be mercied, but in the playoffs it was downright humiliating.

Today would be their first opportunity for vengeance. Watertown chose to go on defense first. Coach Allen remembered that Watertown had run a 4-3 defense their previous meeting. After the thrashing they had received two years ago, perhaps they had made a change.

When Juddville broke out of their huddle and began to trot towards the line of scrimmage, even Coach Allen had difficulty identifying their defense. It looked like an even front—there was no one covering the center—but they had two pinching tackles in A Gap. Stacked behind them were two inside line backers. Their defensive ends were in the gaps between Juddville's tackles and tight ends. A foot outside of the tight ends and up on the line of scrimmage were the outside linebackers. The corners were stacked three yards behind the outside linebackers, shaded slightly to the outside. It almost looked like a 6-4, with 10 players in the box, and a single safety lined up 10 yards deep over the center.

They must have been scouting us while we were scrimmaging Mapleview. They know we can't throw the ball, thought Coach Allen.

—

19

The first play was a 34 trap. As David received the snap on the second "Go", Daniels was slow out of his stance and did not get a good piece of the back side tackle shaded to the inside of Pete. As a result, Pete's trap route was pushed backwards, preventing him from getting his head into the 4 hole. When Mike received the handoff, he saw no opening up the middle and decided to look for greener pastures towards the sideline. He stiff-armed the outside linebacker who was coming up on the play, and then from out of no where, the corner came up aggressively, upending the sophomore running back, knocking him flat on his back, in front of the Juddville bench.

"Oohs" and "ahs" erupted from the stands, similar to what one might hear during the Grand Finale of a Fourth of July fireworks. Mike, Jr. rolled over on his side in agony.

In perfect synchronicity, Mike, Sr. rose to his feet, screaming, "What the heck was that? My boy ain't going to last very long with that kind of blocking, Coach Abraham!"

After a few moments of anxiety, Mike finally got up on his feet and reluctantly returned to the Juddville huddle.

Coach Allen purposefully downplayed his starting fullback's condition.

Not going to baby him, thought Jim. *There will be a lot more hits like that coming his way. Better toughen up or hang 'em up.*

Nevertheless, Jim did opt to give the ball to someone else on the next play, calling for a 22 halfback power. Again, the result was not pretty. The same defensive tackle who disrupted the first play went untouched, dragging Rob Bast down from behind just as he was about to reach a wide open running lane.

"Owens," screamed Coach Allen, loud enough for his daddy to hear up in the stands, "do you know whose man made that tackle? After the fake, you have to fill for the pulling guard!"

"Yes, sir."

"Come on, Mike. All you have to do is get a piece of him, and we're off to the races."

Mike, Sr. had taken three steps down the aisle of the bleachers before thinking better of it. "Just wait till I talk to Abraham after the game," he announced to his pot bellied friend who opted to remain seated with his box of buttery popcorn nearly emptied.

"What are you going to tell 'em, Mike? Your boy's not tough enough to play fullback?"

"What do you know, moron?" responded Mike. "All you ever played was offensive tackle!"

"That's right... in the trenches... where only the *strong* survive."

———

"Well, my boy's a highly-skilled athlete. He's going to play Division I football one day. He can't afford to be thrown to the wolves like that."

"Why not? It'll be good preparation for him. Don't you think there'll be *wolves* in college?"

Meanwhile, Coach Allen walked over to the offensive huddle. Taking a knee next to his quarterback, he looked into the faces of his players.

"You boys a little *scared*?"

"No, sir," responding in unison.

"I didn't think so. Let's not forget whose field we're playing on. We've got to spread things out a little. We're going to run the 11 Keep with David. Michael, you've got to get a good fill on the defensive tackle. Hit him low and take his feet out from underneath him. Bast, you've got to sell your fake. If you don't get tackled, I'm going to tell your girlfriend you're a sissy. Nash, you hook the outside backer, and Pete'll be all alone on the corner. Then it's clear sailing to the end zone, David."

Coach Allen dismissed himself from the huddle as Riley called the play. The line bolted from the huddle with a sense of urgency.

"Blue 28… Blue 28… Set… Go… Go…"

The ball was snapped crisply into David's hands. He reverse pivoted to his left. Mike sprinted by and dove at the knees of the defensive tackle. One down… ten players to go. David turned his back to the line of scrimmage and found Bast. He held out the ball to him, holding it in his bread basket for a count, drawing the attention of the inside linebacker and defensive end who were crashing down into the middle of Juddville's T formation. Rob's fake was so good he was tackled by two defenders. Nash sustained his hook block on the outside backer just long enough for Pete and David to get to the outside.

David hid the ball behind his right hip as he bolted for the sideline. A step in front of him was Pete. The cornerback had already converged upon the line of scrimmage, determined not to get hooked.

Pete had other plans, however. Crouching low, his legs and hips thrusting in unison, he delivered a blow with his hands into the midsection of the unsuspecting cornerback. Pete lifted him backwards onto his heels and absolutely flattened him, coming close to leaving a permanent imprint of the Wildcat corner's numbers in the well-groomed turf. Still on his feet, Pete peeled back to the inside and picked up the outside linebacker who had broken free from Jeff. Now all David had to do was sprint straight down the sideline for 6.

He's at the 25… the 20… the 15… the 10…

Much to the dismay of every blue-blooded Jaguar fan in Raymond Sanders Stadium, the back side cornerback ran down their quarterback, pushing him out of bounds at the 5 yard line. The Jaguar faithful were not the only ones to react in horror. Coach Allen removed his sweat soaked hat and turned his head sharply towards Coach Abraham knowing with absolute certainty that both he and Keith were having the exact same thought.

You have got to be kidding? Katie could've scored on that play, thought Jim. *Is he carrying a piano on his back?*

Choosing not to say something that might come back to haunt him, Coach Allen chose to bite his tongue and go on to the next play.

Juddville broke from the huddle only to discover the defense even more bunched up in the middle.

"Let's punch it in right now," said Pete to his fellow trench men as they approached the line of scrimmage.

"Red 18… Red 18… Set…"

A quick count. The ball met David's hands squarely; Daniels drove Pete's tackle away from the middle of their formation as Pete scraped behind him and executed a perfect trap block, hitting the tackle low, taking his feet out from beneath him. The linebackers were both stunting through B gap leaving a tight but secure hole inside.

Everything was proceeding according to design except for the quarterback who had mysteriously bobbled the ball and was unable to handoff the ball in time to fullback Owens. Quickly regaining control of the ball, David saw a rapidly-shrinking running lane before him. Lowering his head, he followed Mike into the end zone, diving across the goal line a half a second before being sideswiped by a Watertown defensive back.

Standing all alone in the end zone, Mike held up his hands in disappointment as the rest of his Juddville teammates sprinted by him to congratulate David.

Coach Allen again was forced to bite his tongue. He wanted to give his quarterback a good tongue lashing for botching the handoff, but at least he had the presence of mind to tuck the ball way and deliver the ball into the end zone.

"That should have been your touchdown, Mike," shouted Mr. Owens, impervious to the disparaging thoughts and looks of reproach from those around him.

The rest of the offensive scrimmage versus the Wildcats didn't fare too well, however. The red offense failed to earn a first down in the next eight plays. Coach Allen was so frustrated that he substituted the white offense early; unfortunately, they had even less success as they were unable to earn positive yardage in four attempts.

For a brief moment, Jim was relieved to turn over the reins to Coach Abraham and his defense. That was until Watertown unveiled their star halfback who was already attracting a lot of attention from Division I football schools. The Wildcats — like Mapleview before them — also ran out of the I-backfield, but the difference was number 32. This kid must run a 4.5 forty or faster.

On the first play, Watertown pitched the ball to #32, and he sprinted immediately for the right sideline. Mike Owens came up to turn him in, but the back faked like he was going to cut up the field and then suddenly turned his hips back to the outside. Mike dove at his ankles and came up empty. Both Schultz and Jacobs tried to pursue him, but once he kicked it into high gear, no one had a prayer of catching him.

Coach Allen had been getting a drink of water from a water bottle on the sideline. He sprinted directly onto the field where Mike was just getting to his feet.

"Do you see what happens when you don't do your job? The defense had no chance to make a play... especially against a running back with that kind of speed. I don't think you can stay with him, can you, Mike? I'm going to have to put someone else in to do the job."

Unfortunately, Jim had forgotten to consider his depth chart before speaking so quickly. Because of the suspensions of Roger Collins and Adam Foster, his next available defensive back on the depth chart was David Riley. Nevertheless, for at least a play or two, he was going to with the slower-footed, less aggressive senior.

"David, get in there at corner for Mike," commanded Coach Allen. "Nash, I want you to move to left corner. And when the ball is on our left hash, I want you to switch back to the right side. In other words, Jeff, you're now our wide side corner. Secondary, if we get burned for another touchdown around the end, we're going to have one heckuva practice on Monday. Do you hear me?"

"Yes, sir," they responded timidly.

On the next play, Watertown came back with another pitch sweep. As soon as the ball was pitched, Pete was in hot pursuit, parallel with the line of scrimmage. This time Jeff Nash came across the line of scrimmage and took on the fullback's lead block, forcing the tailback to cut inside. The moment #32 made his cut up field, Pete was ready to pounce.

Watertown Wildcat meet Juddville Terminator.

Pete rocked the elite runningback so hard, he coughed up the football. Safety Tommy Schultz scooped up the ball and ran to the 50 yard line. A Wildcat coach blew the whistle in order to prevent any interference with the scrimmage on the south half of the field.

Coach Allen turned towards the sideline and observed Mike trying to obtain sympathy from a few of his teammates.

With a voice that lacked neither clarity nor volume, Jim shouted to his sophomore back, "Do you see what happens when the corner does his job?"

No one anticipated the uprising that ensued.

Chapter Three

Suddenly, a boisterous voice erupted, "Don't you dare talk to my boy like that, Coach Allen." The entire Jaguar team turned as one towards the bleachers behind them. Sprinting down the steps was the star sophomore running back's father, and he was livid. Within a few seconds both hands were clutching the fence that surrounded the perimeter of the field. He awkwardly lifted himself up and over the fence and was quickly advancing towards Coach Allen.

Jim squared up with his unwelcomed adversary, staring him straight in the eyes.

Coach Abraham called out to his assistant, "Jim, let me take care of this. I need you out on the field helping Coach Oliver."

Jim heard nothing of Keith's words, however; his mind was fully engaged upon the one who had dared to challenge his authority in front of his players and a large proportion of the Juddville faithful.

Fight or flight?

Oh how he yearned to stand up to his challenger even though it defied everything he had ever learned in his education training. However, if he acted on his primal instincts, it would surely result in at minimum a written reprimand in his personnel file. The worst case scenario would be a forced leave of absence possibly leading to dismissal.

Fortunately, Keith made the choice for him, grabbing hold of his arm and tugging him back towards the middle of the field.

"We can't have both of us in trouble with the administration, Jim. These kids need you. This guy is not worth it. Let me handle it."

Reluctantly, Coach Allen submitted to the authority of his head coach and trusted friend. "Tell him to keep his rear end up in the bleachers where it belongs."

"Don't worry, Jim. I'll do better than that. He'll be leaving the stadium, or I will be calling the police."

As Keith turned around to approach Mr. Owens he thought to himself, *Now would be a good time to have an administrator in the vicinity.*

Then he corrected himself, *No, it would be much better if I handle this instead.*

24

"Mike, you're out of line here. You have no place coming out on the field like this."

"No, *your coach* is the one who's out of line. He's been harassing my son, and I'm not going to stand for it."

"Listen to me real carefully, Mike, before you embarrass yourself and your son any further."

Both scrimmages had now stopped play. The showdown had commanded the attention of every player, coach, and fan.

"You need to walk calmly out of this stadium right now," pointing emphatically to the gate of Raymond Sanders Stadium, "or I will have you banned from these premises for the rest of the season."

"What? You can't do that."

"Watch me."

Mike Owens, Sr. took a few moments to mull over Coach Abraham's words. Then he called out to his son.

"Mike, you're coming with me. You're done playing for this idiot."

"No, Dad. He's right. And Coach Allen was right, too. He was only trying to make me a better player. You're embarrassing me right now, Dad... You should leave."

Mike, Sr. was infuriated. He didn't know what to say. His face was beet red, and he had a look of defeat about him. He had been backed unexpectedly into a corner. Worse yet, he was suddenly aware that the eyes of a large contingency of Juddville fans were zoomed in on him at this very moment; his reputation and ego were at stake.

Not having much choice now but to bow to the wishes of his son and of Coach Abraham, Mike Sr. turned and walked down the sidelines, across the track, and through the gates of Raymond Sanders Stadium.

Coach Allen walked over to the sideline and put his hand on the shoulder of his sophomore running back and said, "Mike, I'm sorry for calling you out like that; I have to remind myself that you're new to this, and that you're only a sophomore. I would like to get you back in there as soon as you're ready. The only way you're going to get better is by playing, right?"

After an awkward moment of silence, Mike mumbled, "Sure... let me get a quick water first, and then I'll be ready."

The next play Owens was back on the field. Watertown abandoned their outside running game for a few plays, trying to run off-tackle behind its fullback, followed by a weak inside trap that Pete saw coming a mile away. The next play was designed to test the ability of the secondary to defend the pass.

The quarterback received the snap and took a quick three-step drop, set his feet and threw the ball to the wide receiver on a slant route. Mike was on the receiver quickly, wrapping up his feet, trying desperately to drag him down while maintaining his grip on the receiver's right foot.

The receiver was wriggling in desperation like a perch trying to break free from a hook. His sights were focused upfield towards the end zone... which was why he never saw Pete coming.

The first indicator was a sharp pain piercing the small of his back. The second was a fist violently tomahawking the ball out of his possession.

Tommy Schultz was the next one to the scene, diving onto the ball, a half a second before the Wildcat tight end who had been trailing the play. Lifting the ball high above his head, Tommy was basking in pleasure.

This time it was a Watertown coach to step up to the stage. Sprinting twenty yards downfield from his position at midfield, he threw his cap to the ground and proceeded to rip his receiver a new one.

"I've told you a million of times to cover up that ball with both hands when you're in traffic. You've got to protect the gold!"

Coach Allen critiqued the technique of the Wildcat coach. He always found it amusing to observe one of his peers in the heat of the moment. Most of the time, they fell way short of his legendary performances.

The next play was so predictable. In an attempt to save face and regain the upper hand, the Watertown coach would most certainly return to his bread and butter: the toss sweep.

Coach Abraham brought the secondary together to give them specific instructions.

"Let's go Cover 1 Sting. Tommy, man-up on the tight end, but disguise it from your centerfield alignment. I want Jacobs blitzing from the edge."

A smile broke out on the face of the strong safety. Blitzing a defensive back was a risky move. If he was blitzing into the point of attack, he would most likely neutralize the running play. But if the quarterback was throwing a quick pass or rolling out in the opposite direction, he could burn the secondary for a touchdown.

On this occasion, however, Coach Abraham was almost certain of the next play. And he was right. The quarterback received the snap, reverse-pivoted, and pitched the ball to his star tailback who was sprinting towards the right sideline.

The ball carrier received the ball into his hands and looked to his right. He saw Don advancing upon him from an outside-in pursuit angle.

Realizing that he would not be able to get to the outside, the frantic ball carrier stopped abruptly and reversed back towards the opposite side of the field. The Jaguar defense was in hot pursuit.

In order to reach the opposite sideline, he would have to bow back at least 5 yards. He made it to the center of the field without much problem; now all he had to do was make it around outside linebacker, Chad Williams, who was trying to cut him off.

Unfortunately, Chad didn't have the proper depth nor speed to contain him. After a net 70 yards of sprinting, the Watertown running back had broken free from Juddville's defense and was racing for the end zone. After he crossed the goal line, he had to wait a few seconds for his teammates to catch up to him to celebrate.

Coach Abraham was the first to respond.

"Simpson, get in there for Williams."

Taking the young outside linebacker aside, Keith explained to him, "Your role is to pursue cautiously, and to stay at an equal depth with the ball. That way we won't get burned on the cut back, the counter, the reverse, or the bootleg. Everybody's got a responsibility on defense. All it takes is one broken assignment, and the whole defense is in trouble."

By the end of the defensive session against the Wildcats, Juddville had given up two touchdowns, but they had caused two turnovers—one of them resulting in a score. Overall, the defense hadn't played as badly as Coach Abraham had feared, given the turbulent circumstances of the past week.

After a short water break, the team huddled on their sideline at the 50. Coach Abraham could see that most of the players didn't have much left in the tank. The linemen were still huffing and puffing, and the running backs and receivers were beginning to look sluggish.

Little did they know Rapids City was waiting anxiously in the wings. The Eagles had observed how easily Juddville had dismantled Mapleview, so they had opted to play their firsts against Watertown and let their seconds play the entire scrimmage against Mapleview. Therefore, their starters were rested and ready for the Jaguars.

The Eagles had requested to start out on defense, so Coach Allen huddled his offense on the 50 yard line.

"I expect to see a 4-4 defense in this last scrimmage, men. Remember we need to down block on our halfback power and outside running plays. The inside trap will be very tight, and if they're blitzing linebackers into A gap, we'll trap the backer instead of the tackle. This team is well-coached, and they won't telegraph their stunts. You've got to step aggressively to your gap and block the first man that appears.

"Alright, let's start out with a 22 halfback power, David," said Coach Allen, as he stepped out from the huddle.

David repeated the play to his teammates, calling it on one.

Despite their fatigue, the Jaguars hustled up to the line of scrimmage. Riley surveyed the defense. A 4-4, just as Coach Allen predicted. Four linebackers were stacked behind four defensive linemen.

"White 15... White 15... Set... Go!"

Craig snapped the ball into Riley's hands. David pivoted counter-clockwise. Mike sprinted by, receiving the fake handoff for an inside trap, and then he cut straight up the field, getting tackled by two Rapid City players. David took another step from the line of scrimmage and found left halfback Rob Bast. He tucked the ball into his cradle, handed off the ball, pulled his hands out abruptly and sprinted towards the sideline, hiding his hands behind his right hip as if he still had the ball.

Right end, Dan Hardings had blocked the defensive end down into B gap and right tackle Gary Osborne got a good jump off the snap and was on the inside linebacker like white on rice. Pete pulled to his right, taking three quick steps, dipping his inside shoulder to lead up the hole. Unfortunately, there was no hole because right halfback, Jeff Nash had double-teamed with Hardings on the end crashing down, so no one had blocked the outside linebacker.

Adhering to the blocking rules, Pete blocked the first opposite-colored jersey, driving the linebacker out instead of leading up the hole.

Rob cut up the seam, put his shoulder down, and collided with the safety who was coming up for run reinforcement. The safety hit him low and wrapped up his legs, allowing a modest three yard gain.

"What are you doing blocking C gap, Jeff?" asked Coach Allen. "The tight end blocks down; you J-block which ever player's got D gap. If you make the right block on that play, Robert's still running."

"Next play. 36 trap. Let's go on two. See if you can get at least one of them to jump, David."

The young quarterback was beginning to feel dizzy as he looked around the huddle.

"36 trap on two... Ready? Break!"

As he crouched under center, David noticed a sparkle in one of the linebacker's eyes. In addition, it seemed like he was leaning extra-heavily on his inside foot.

Here comes a blitz. thought David.

"Blue 48... Blue 48... Set... (with extra force) Go!"

Crash. The linebacker ran smack into Pete, knocking him on his rear end.

Daniels reached down and lifted Pete up off the ground.

"Great job, Pete. Way to hold your ground. Now we only need two yards for a first down."

Back in the huddle, the spirit of the Juddville troops had been rejuvenated.

"Alright men, let's run the play again. Go on a long count again, David."

Riley called the play on two, and the Jaguars sprinted up to the line.

"Red 19… Red 19… Set… Go… Go!"

David received the ball, turned to his left, and quickly stuck the ball into Mike's mid section. Wilcox had blocked the left tackle while Pete scraped behind him, colliding into the blitzing linebacker.

There was about an 18 inch seam between them. Mike lowered his shoulder and plunged straight ahead like a battering ram. David carried out his fake to Rob and then sprinted to the sideline. The cornerback came up and knocked the empty-handed quarterback flat on his behind.

When David got up on his feet, he noticed that half of the offense was already in the end zone, jumping up and down, celebrating with Mike who was holding the ball above his head.

David wanted to sprint downfield to join them, but he was feeling a bit woozy. Coach Allen was fully aware of his young quarterback's condition.

He walked over to David who was now walking groggily towards the huddle.

"You alright, young man?" asked Coach Allen. "Take a sip of water," handing him a water bottle.

After taking a huge gulp, "I'll be okay."

"Good enough. Next play, run the 48 half back power."

Trotting over to the huddle, waiting a moment for the enthusiasm from the last play to subside, he finally spoke, "Okay, boys, let's keep it rolling. 48 power on one. Ready? Break!"

Quickly under center, David began the cadence.

"Blue 18… Blue 18… Set… Go!"

David turned clockwise, faked to Mike, and then handed off to Nash. This time David faked a bootleg to his right, and the cornerback was ready to pounce on him again, so David took his left hand and stiff-armed him in the face mask. The corner never saw it coming. David's hand slipped under his mask and caught him under the chin.

The Eagle defender had a hissy fit, grabbing David's arm, attempting to throw him to the ground. The Jaguar quarterback would have none of it, ripping his arm loose and sprinting back towards the huddle.

Meanwhile, right guard Wilcox was getting an earful. "You ran right by the stunting linebacker. Three steps and up the hole, but look to your inside first. We had a huge hole there if you would have made your block, Steve," hollered Coach Oliver.

That a boy, Gary. Tell him how it is, thought Coach Allen. *This kid's going to be alright!*

"You okay, David? You and that cornerback looked like two old high school buddies at a 30 year reunion."

The Jaguar signal caller was too fatigued and too embarrassed to offer a reply.

"Well, let's go right back at David's long-lost buddy. What do you say, Pete?"

"Call the play, Coach. I'll knock him into the next zip code."

"Okay, David. 11 QB Keep."

Coach Allen could see a gleam in his quarterback's eyes as he called the play in the huddle. He could already see a swagger beginning to emerge.

As he crouched under center, David could tell that at least one of the inside backers was coming on a blitz.

Secure the ball, make good fakes, and run like there's no tomorrow, David reminded himself.

"White 37… White 37… Set… Go… Go… Go…"

The left inside linebacker stumbled out of his crouch, regaining his balance in just enough time to avoid jumping offsides.

David reverse pivoted to his left, feeling a rush of air going by as Mike carried out his fake; then he took another step towards Rob holding the ball into his bread basket an extra count before snatching the ball out and putting it on his right hip. With his peripheral vision, he observed two defenders crashing into Rob to make a tackle. Out in front of him was Pete sprinting towards the forlorn cornerback. Pete ran right onto his toes, driving his hands into his sternum, and decleating him.

Pancake! David tucked the ball under his arm pit and sprinted towards the side line.

35 yard line.

30, 25, 20, 15, and … smash. The weak side corner caught up to David and knocked him out of bounds.

David popped up on his feet, barely aware of the slight pain in his hip. His teammates were there to congratulate him. So what if he didn't score? At least he got them to the red zone.

An enthusiastic admirer of Pete O'Connor rose up on her two feet, clapping fervently. Now that Pete had been restored to his rightful place—on top of the world of high school football—she knew her chances with him would be next to nothing after having screwed up her chances with him not once but twice. Plain and simple, she had acted foolishly. Nevertheless, she was genuinely happy for him because Pete was one of the last of a dying breed. He was a gentleman, he was "class" personified, one of those rare individuals who understood that life wasn't all about "him".

Unfortunately, Melanie came to this realization way too late. Even still, she couldn't miss the opportunity to catch a sneak peek of this year's Juddville football team. She was a hard core football fan, and her attendance at this scorching Friday morning scrimmage was proof of her devotion. There were very few Juddville girls in attendance; they were no doubt staking out their territory at the local beach. Naturally, Melanie quickly identified Pete's mom. How could you miss the cowbell? But she was too embarrassed to go and talk to her.

On the next play, Coach Allen rolled the dice. His stomach turned queasy as the words rolled off his lips. Though David was fatigued from a long run and was clearly suffering from the August heat and humidity, this was the perfect opportunity to test the makeup of his quarterback.

Rapid City would most definitely be expecting run — probably a trap, since that was how Juddville had scored their previous touchdown. With the ball on the right hash, two thirds of the field was wide open to the left.

Juddville broke from the huddle eager to try one of the newer plays in their arsenal. David crouched under center and began the cadence.

"Red 49... Red 49... Set... Go..."

The ball was snapped crisply into David's hands. Mike sprinted by David, with a very low center of gravity. David reached his hands out to Rob, riding the fake for a half a second, and then snagged the ball out, putting the ball on his hip as he bootlegged out to his left.

Instead of pulling to his right, behind the center, Pete pulled to his left, colliding almost instantaneously with the defensive end crashing into C gap. As he drove his shoulder into his groin, he heard his opponent groan in agony.

David bootlegged out towards the wide open flats, fully-intending to run for the end zone. Out of the corner of his eye, he spied the outside linebacker closing in quickly on him. Left end Bryan Cox was tightly covered by the playside cornerback, but right end Dan Hardings was streaking across the field wide open on a drag.

David ran three more steps, allowing Dan to draw closer into his sights. Just before the Rapids City defender was about to make contact with David, he released the ball. The rotation of the ball was less than perfect — not really much of a spiral at all — but its aim was perfect.

Hardings reached out with his hands, pulling the ball into his chest, tucking the ball under his left arm pit as he ran uncontested into the end zone.

Dan was bombarded by teammates. Wilcox, the center, was the first one there, and he had decided that the most appropriate response was to tackle him. The next to the pile was David — who had come awfully close to becoming part of the Raymond Sanders' Stadium turf. Next was Pete, followed by the rest of Juddville Jaguar offense.

If this demonstration had taken place in a game, it would have certainly drawn an unsportsmanlike conduct penalty, but Coach Allen and Coach Abraham would grant them the opportunity to enjoy this moment for now. Considering all they had been through this week, they deserved an unimpeded opportunity to celebrate.

When they were back in the huddle, Coach Allen made it very clear what would happen if they attempted such a stunt in an actual game. Jim was relieved, for the moment, that they had found a definitive answer for the position of quarterback. Now he would shift gears and use up the remaining minutes of offense, keeping his signal caller out of the limelight—more importantly, out of harm's way. As a result, the Rapids City defense—and any of the scouts from Pennington and Billington videotaping from the top row of the bleachers—would be served up a buffet of inside traps and halfback powers for the remainder of the scrimmage.

At 10:45, most of the spectators were growing antsy to find shade from the terrorizing heat. With only the final 20 minute segment remaining in the scrimmage, Juddville was satisfied that their offense had made a convincing statement to any doubters who had showed up on this day. Now it was time for the defense to have their final say.

Even so, the Rapids City Coaching Staff had not appreciated the over-the-top display of emotion on the part of Juddville following the quarterback bootleg pass to Dan Hardings. As a result, they were prepared to make a statement of their own.

The Eagles ran a UFL-style offense featuring a southpaw quarterback who lined up five yards deep and received a "shotgun" snap from the center. There was only one running back, and he lined up a yard and a half to either side of the QB. The rest of the formation was "spread" across the field with wide receivers lined up about 7 to 8 yards from each sideline and slot receivers lined up just to the inside of the hash marks. They had no tight ends or fullbacks. Not many teams were running this offense in high school, but it was becoming increasingly popular in college and the pros, and so high school football would surely be quick to follow.

The first time Rapids City broke out of the huddle, Juddville's defense was unsure how to react. Coach Allen called out to his secondary to play Cover 2. On the snap of the ball the wide receivers ran fade routes and the slot receivers ran 5 yard outs. The safeties picked up the deep routes and the corners stayed in their flat zones. The slot receivers were open immediately, and Rapids City's quarterback released the ball quickly to his slot receiver on the right.

He caught the ball and proceeded up field before running into cornerback Mike Owens for a seven yard gain. When they broke out of the huddle for the next play, they were again in a 2 by 2 formation — two receivers split out on each side of the ball — but this time the left slot receiver went in motion behind the center, all the way over to the right side of their formation.

Coach Allen screamed, "Trips... trips... Cover 3... Cover 3..."

The Jaguars safeties shifted over to strength, leaving Jeff Nash all alone on the right side of the Jaguar defense. On the snap of the ball, Jeff's man ran a quick slant route to the inside. The quarterback hit him right in the hands, and the speedy wideout turned up field and sprinted straight for the end zone. Jeff dived at his feet in vain, and there was no other Jaguar in the vicinity. The Rapids City Eagles sprinted to the end zone to congratulate their teammate for their first score against the host Jaguars.

Before the next play, Coach Abraham and Allen huddled in the middle of the field with the defense to make a much needed adjustment. The Jaguar Head Coach assumed control.

"Okay, men. We're going to go to our nickel package. Larry, we're going to replace you with a defensive back. But I want you to alternate plays with Jimmy. Greg, you're going to shift from nose to left tackle, shading the inside eye of the guard on our left, so basically, we'll be running a 4-2. Jimmy and Larry — whoever is in at the time — you will line up on the right over their other guard. Cox and Daniels, you'll lineup in an outside shade on their tackles. You can play up, or you can put a hand on the ground like a defensive end. Whatever's most comfortable. David, you're in at right corner. Jeff, you switch sides and play left corner. We'll play three deep in the secondary. Mike, you play center field. Tommy, you play the deep left third of the field; Jacobs, you take the deep right third. This will make us stronger against the pass, but we'll have to play tough with only six in the box against the run. Tackles, you've got A gap; Linebackers, B; and Outside Backers, C. Pete, look to me, for any blitz calls. All right defense, no more scores."

Coach Allen breathed a sigh of relief. His comrade was back. He would have made a similar adjustment if he were calling the shots.

"Good adjustment, Keith. Let's see them try to pass now," said Coach Allen.

"We've got to do something to put more pressure on the quarterback, though," cautioned Coach Abraham.

"Let's see what formation they come out on this play."

The Eagles broke out of the huddle in a trips formation—three receivers on the left and one on their right. On the snap of the ball the quarterback sprinted to his right, away from his trio of receivers. The back that had been lined up to his right, ran in the same direction about 3 yards ahead of him, only one yard deeper. Bryan Cox was the outside backer to this side. He didn't know whether to tackle the quarterback or wait for him to pitch the ball to the halfback.

The quarterback continued to run straight at Bryan who at this point was still unblocked. All of the sudden, the hands of the quarterback flung outwards like he was going to pitch it, and Bryan went for the pitch, angling out towards the halfback.

Unfortunately, the QB had maintained possession of the ball, planted his right foot and cut sharply upfield. Their right offensive tackle had blocked down on Pete, controlling him momentarily. Pete spun off the block and tackled the ball carrier after he had advanced the ball five yards.

"You've got the quarterback, Bryan," yelled Coach Oliver. "You put your helmet on the QB's sternum whether he releases the ball or not. After you stick him once, their offensive coordinator won't run the option the rest of the scrimmage. I guarantee it."

The next play was a half back draw that Greg McDonald sniffed out. After two mediocre running plays, Coach Abraham knew a pass was coming.

"Pete, I want you to blitz A gap. Tell the tackle on your side to go B. If you don't get there in time, get your hands up to deflect the pass."

Coach Abraham's prediction held true. This time Rapids City stayed in their 2 by 2 spread formation. On the snap of the ball, the quarterback received the ball and fired a perfect strike to the left wide out who had taken one step back from the line of scrimmage and turned to face the quarterback.

Quick screen. There was no way Pete could have gotten to the QB in time. The slot receiver sprinted immediately for the cornerback, providing enough interference to keep Mike from getting to the receiver. The halfback sprinted hastily towards the safety.

One quick juke to the left and the wide receiver was off for the races. It happened so quickly, there was very little time for the defense to respond. Mike Owens caught up with receiver at the ten yard line, dragging him down on the eight.

"Let's go man-to-man and blitz from the edge, Keith," suggested Coach Allen.

"Good idea." Keith stood in the middle of the defensive huddle and made the call himself. "All right men. Let's see what you're made of. Riley, you're out. Send Larry back out quickly. We're going 50 Eagle, double slam. DBs, I want you pressing up on the line of scrimmage. Make sure you chuck them at the line. Do not let them break to your inside. O'Connor and Wilcox, you're stacked behind the tackles who are down in B gap, but I want you scraping behind our outside backers who will be crashing hard to their inside gap. You've got contain responsibility inside backers, but we have to get to the quarterback and apply pressure."

The Eagles came out in a trips right formation, so Jacobs came over from his spot on the opposite side of the field and lined up on the middle receiver, leaving Nash all alone on the weak side.

"Watch the quick slant, Jeff," advised Coach Allen.

The quarterback was eyeing the lone receiver to his left.

The ball was snapped on the second hit. The left wide out feinted to his inside and then cut sharply to his outside, fading towards the corner of the end zone.

The quarterback pump-faked and reset his arm to throw.

With a full head of steam, Pete was rushing from the blind side. The Rapids City right tackle had followed Daniels down into B gap, leaving Pete untouched.

Leaving his feet and diving forward, Pete reached out with his left hand and tomahawked the ball loose from the quarterback's hand. The ball bounced to the ground as Pete threw the empty-handed QB to the ground. Two hundred and eighty-five pound Larry Moore was the first on the scene, scooping the ball up like it was a juicy bacon and cheddar burger. Putting the ball under his right arm pit, he began to run full speed towards the opposite end zone.

Three Rapids City offensive linemen were alert to the sudden change of possession and were able to quickly catch up to the over-sized defensive linemen. O'Connor, however, wiped out Larry's closest pursuer, and Wilcox knocked the next closest Eagle on his behind. As Larry approached the 25 yard line, he turned and saw the Eagle center closing in on him. He reached out with his left paw, stiff arming his pursuer to the ground.

The next players on the scene were teammates Mike Owens and Tommy Schultz who provided an escort to the 50 yard line where the Rapids City coach irately blew his whistle—a much appreciated sound to Larry's ears.

The rest of the Jaguar defense caught up to their mammoth teammate to celebrate, not more than 10 yards away from the Eagles coaching staff. Now the Eagles were really irritated.

"Great call, Keith. It really caught them off guard. I would switch back to zone on this play, though."

35

"I don't know. I like bringing pressure."

Coach Abraham signaled for Pete to come over to him for the next call.

"Pete, let's stay in a 50 Eagle, and I want you to fire B gap. Tell the D-line to angle right. Secondary is in Cover 0, but tell them to play off their man 5 yards."

"Yes, sir, Coach."

The Jaguar captain sprinted over to the huddle and relayed the call.

Rapids City came out in a 2 by 2 formation but brought their right slot in motion to the left side of their formation. On the second hit, the center snapped the ball.

The quarterback took two quick steps to his right and saw Pete blitzing straight at him. He quickly pitched the ball out to his halfback. Daniels was converging on the quarterback and could not recover in time to make the play. The lone wide out ran a deep fly route, taking the corner with him, so there was no one to contain the pitch man.

It was a running back's dream: all that green and not a single defender in the vicinity. He raced to the 40, to the 30, and the 20. Finally, Owens broke free of his receiver and managed to drag the ball carrier down on the 17 yard line.

"All right... all right... I should have listened to you, Jim. What do you think down here?"

"Let's go Cover 2 Press. Keep our safeties loose over the top."

"Okay, I think I'll send Pete, and have the other linebackers drop back into their zones. I'll tell Steve to keep his eyes open for a drag or quick post over the middle."

"Good idea, Coach."

Rapids City broke out of their huddle in their base 2 by 2 formation. On a quick count, the slot receivers ran crossing routes across the middle, and the outside receivers ran hitches.

Acutely aware of how deep the safeties were playing, the quarterback opted to release the ball quickly before they had time to react. He did not see the linebackers underneath, however.

Craig Daniels stepped in front of the receiver and lifted his hands up to pick off the ball. Unfortunately, the ball ricocheted off his hands.

"Your hands made out of wood?" asked Steve. "You're going to give us linemen a bad reputation, Craig."

The next play was a halfback draw. The Eagles opened up a huge hole inside, but Pete made a touchdown saving tackle, diving out and tripping up the ball carrier's feet before he was off to the races.

Third and eight from the 15.

"Larry, you're out. Send Riley back in."

It would be impossible for Rapids City not to notice that Juddville was making a substitution. The turf rumbled as Big Larry made his way to the side line.

Coach Abraham eyed each player in the huddle. "This is our last stand, men. Two more stops are all we need. Let's go 4-2 Nickel, but I want to fire both inside linebackers through A gap. That means tackles have B and outside backers (defensive ends) have C. Don't let that QB break contain. Corners, I want you up on the wideouts pressing. We're three deep with our safeties, but I want you playing tight. All they need is eight yards for a first down. Be ready to deliver a hit. Be physical, secondary. Last stand... last stand... Ready? Break!"

Rapids City came out in trips right. David Riley was over the lone wideout on their left.

"Shift over towards the hash, Mike," said Coach Allen. "You've got help over the top, David, get right up tight and press him. But don't let him cross your face."

The quarterback received the snap and took a three step drop. His favorite wide out ran a quick 5 yard hitch. The quarterback pumped. The receiver put his hands up, and then abruptly turned 180 degrees upfield, sprinting for the corner of the end zone.

Feeling pressure from the inside, the quarterback rolled out to his left. Safety Don Jacobs, sensing that the quarterback was going to keep it, began to run up. The receiver who had been chucked and released by Riley blew right by Jacobs and was all alone en route to the end zone. The quarterback lofted a perfect spiral to the left corner of the end zone. The receiver reached out his hands to receive the touchdown strike, but the ball trickled off his fingertips.

The Juddville defense breathed a sigh of relief.

"Jacobs, your responsibility is deep third, not to sack the quarterback. Do you hear me?" shouted Coach Allen. "Do your job, or someone else will be taking your place."

Fourth down.

"What do you think, Jim? Run or Pass?"

"Definitely Pass."

Coach Abraham stepped into the middle of the huddle. "Okay, men. Let's go Cover 1. We'll man up on their receivers and have Mike play centerfield. Pete, you spy the quarterback, and Steve, you've got the halfback. Scratch that. Pete, you take the halfback, and Steve, you've got quarterback—if he rolls out to either side, you're right on top of him. Secondary, play tight, but don't let your man get by you. Finish strong... finish strong... Ready... Break!"

The Eagles broke out in Trips Right, but they sent their inside slot receiver back in motion to the weak side.

"You've got to go with him, Jacobs. Move it!" hollered Coach Allen.

The motion brought them back into a symmetrical 2 by 2 formation. On the snap of the ball the wideouts ran deep posts, and the slots ran wheel routes. The half back stepped towards the line of scrimmage, held his position for a count and a half and then pivoted out towards the left flats. The left guard and center showed pass protection for a brief moment before releasing to the left sideline.

Halfback screen, thought Pete. *I've got to get to the flats.*

The quarterback looked deep and then turned abruptly to his left, dumping the ball off to his wide open halfback. The left guard was out ahead of him and the center was trailing behind. Pete sprinted towards the sideline, deciding that the only way to stop the play was to turn it back into his teammates. In order for that to happen, he would have to take on the guard and find a way to get to the back's feet. Attacking the guard's outside shoulder, Pete drove his hands up underneath his sternum, obtaining the leverage he needed, pumping his legs, and forcing the lead blocker backwards into the unsuspecting running back.

The back lost his bearings and his momentum, and Pete was able to grab a hold of his arm. Mike—who had read the play from his position in the middle of the field was quick to the scene, wrapping up the ball carrier's legs and pummeling him to the ground.

The rest of the Juddville defenders were right behind him. They had stopped Rapids City on the 10 yard line, three yards shy of a first down.

Mike was first on his feet; furthermore, he was the one to initiate the celebration. Pete was slow to his feet, thoroughly exhausted. He was quite sure he had nothing left but fumes in his tank.

As the two teams headed back to midfield for the remaining five minutes of the scrimmage, Pete heard words that were music to his ears.

"White defense… White defense."

The second defensive unit of Juddville defenders charged onto the field as the burned out red defense jogged off the field for a long awaited breather. After a quick water break the defensive starters cheered on their teammates from the sideline, and the reserves prevented Rapid City from any further scores.

Chapter Four

As Coach Allen enjoyed a brief moment of relaxation in the coach's shower—keeping the temperature just a tad above lukewarm—his mind was preoccupied by the singular task of reviewing the debut performance of the Juddville Jaguars.

Objective number one is to get out of the scrimmage without any serious injuries. At this point, Jim was quite sure that they had survived the scrimmage unscathed. Objective number two was to get a basic feeling for the overall makeup and personality of the team. How did this team get juiced up for competition? Were they loud and energetic? Or silent and subdued? For the most part, Coach Allen would characterize these young men as resilient fighters. Through the course of the scrimmage — amidst the numerous momentum swings and times of doubt and uncertainty — they were somehow able to find a way to strike back.

In some instances, it came through the offense: a long run, a critical pass completion, or a devastating block. In other incidences, it was the defense that came through: stripping the ball loose for a fumble, a goal line stand, or a drive-busting sack.

The common denominator in almost every exceptional play was the influence of senior captain Pete O'Connor. He was without a doubt the heart and soul of this team. On offense, he set the tone for the entire line. And if this team had a strength — judging strictly by its performance in the scrimmage — it was the experience and the physicality of the offensive line.

On defense — once again — they were clearly stronger and more experienced up front than they were in the secondary. What made matters worse was that their best defensive back, Roger Collins, was under suspension for the first two games. Their best athlete was Mike Owens, but he was a bit tentative, and he was going to be carrying the ball a ton on offense. Tommy Schultz was a gifted athlete, but not having played football prior to this season was going to make him a liability, especially when it came to stopping the run. Jeff Nash was a two-way player and very dependable, possessing a keen football awareness. Don Jacobs got burned deep — fortunately the Rapids City receiver dropped the ball — yet a valuable lesson was learned. The next best option was bringing in David Riley. In the past, Jim had preferred to keep his quarterback on the sideline during defense, but this year the Jaguars weren't going to have that luxury... at least for the first two games.

The other possibility in the secondary was Adam Foster — also under a two game suspension — but Coach Allen had been around long enough to recognize a bad apple. If the truth were known, Jim had been hoping that this Billington transfer would see the light and quit before causing further damage to the team.

Perhaps I can help accelerate the process? thought Jim, somewhat ashamed of harboring such resentment towards one of his players.

Unfortunately, the playing status of Adam Foster had been dictated by Superintendent Dr. Paul Jones.

After Pete O'Connor was fully exonerated of all charges by the Juddville Police Department, Dr. Jones had decreed that Pete and Coach Abraham should immediately be reinstated — the latter had been forced to take a temporary leave of absence. True to form, Dr. Jones's ego was much too large to let matters rest without finding some other way to muddy the waters, and it came through the player of Adam Foster.

The unfavorable reputation of Adam reached its peak when he and his shady companion, Josh Evans, attempted to steal Pete's authentic UFL jersey from his front porch in broad daylight. As fate would have it, four of Adam's teammates showed up to pay Pete a visit at the time of the theft.

A skirmish ensued, resulting in Josh Evans pulling a knife on the quartet of Juddville players; fortunately, it was to no avail, for Steve's foot was mightier than steel. When the Juddville police arrived, they apprehended Josh Evans while Adam Foster conveniently disappeared. The Juddville coaching staff had assumed Adam Foster's dismissal from the team was a foregone conclusion.

No one had expected Angel Foster to suddenly enter the picture, and it came in the form of an emphatic phone call to Dr. Jones. Her emotionally-charged complaint to the chief of Juddville Schools alleged that the Juddville Coaching Staff had failed to inform her of any of her son's behavior/discipline issues. Furthermore, Ms. Foster claimed she had attempted several times to communicate with Coach Abraham throughout the week, but he had never returned any of her phone calls.

Dr. Jones had promised to look into her concerns. After speaking on the phone with Coach Abraham for thirty minutes, Coach Abraham and Dr. Jones had reached a compromise. Keith had been leaning towards a complete dismissal of Adam Foster whereas Dr. Jones had simply wanted to issue a reprimand, allowing the coaching staff the discretion of assigning extra conditioning as they saw fit.

"Are you kidding me, Paul? At the beginning of the week you and the media were vilifying one of the best kids to ever wear a Juddville uniform. In fact, you suspended him without due process. And now, we have a player caught red-handed stealing from a teammate; worse yet, he was an accomplice in an attempted assault on four of his teammates — and to make matters worse — involving the use of a knife. Prior to the fight, he was caught vandalizing our locker room, spitting on and urinating in a teammate's locker, and had duly earned a reputation amongst his teammates as a cheap shot artist, and now all you want to do is give him a slap on the wrist?"

"Keith, you have to look at the situation from the boy's point of view. He's got no father, and they just moved to Juddville this summer. He's got no friends except an older boy on probation who was just released from prison. His mom says that if football is taken away from him, he will slide deeper and deeper into trouble. You don't want that on your conscience do you, Coach?"

"Did you say 'conscience', Paul?" fired back Keith. "I can't believe you are lecturing me about conscience."

There was not a sound for the next 15 seconds.

Having sensed that Dr. Jones wasn't going to budge on his insistence that Adam be allowed to remain a part of the team, Coach Abraham offered a compromise.

"Well, Paul, I don't think a little extra conditioning will suffice. I think the coaching staff might concede to take Adam back if he receives a two game suspension. That way we can see if he is serious about becoming a contributing member of this team before we allow him to suit up for a game."

"Two game suspension did you say?" asked Dr. Jones.

"Yes, he can serve it along side of Roger Collins."

"Roger, yes... I'm quite familiar with him. I've spoken with his mother on several occasions this past week."

And so went the official reinstatement of Adam Foster.

Pete was absolutely, positively on top of the world. He had never dreamed that he would play so well in the scrimmage. He couldn't help but laugh as he reminisced over a few choice collisions. What really had him feeling good though was the performance of the team. They had absolutely railroaded Mapleview, and they had established themselves without a doubt as the superior football team in the scrimmage although Rapids City and Watertown were certainly impressive football teams. Sure, they had given up a few scores, but they had created several key turnovers to offset those scores. Furthermore, their offense had scored on each team.

Enough said. Next up, the Pennington Pirates. Pete couldn't wait to get started. Immediately after the scrimmage he wanted to lift in the high school weight room, but he knew his mother had been at the scrimmage and was looking forward to taking him out for lunch to celebrate. He would have to forego his workout until later in the afternoon.

David had mixed feelings over his performance in the scrimmage. A typical adolescent response would be to dwell on his bootleg touchdown pass in the red zone or to relish one of his long QB keepers. But he was deeply concerned about whether his performance was good enough to secure his position as starting quarterback. David was a realist, and he knew that once Roger Collins had served his two game suspension, his days at the quarterback position would be numbered.

Furthermore, his performance on the other side of the ball was even less impressive. His missed tackle against Mapleview resulted in their only score against Juddville.

After changing into his street clothes, he walked out to the parking lot, looking for his dad's car, hoping to escape the disgruntled eyes of his critics. His dad beeped the horn and leaned out the window, waving wildly.

"Over here, Champ! You played fantastic, son! I am so proud of you."

The color of David's face turned tomato red. He hastily occupied the front passenger seat, slouching down to dashboard level while he considered how to politely tell his dad to roll down the window and stop calling him "Champ".

"Dad, please. You're embarrassing me. Can we go, please?"

Completely taken off-guard, Mr. Riley complied. "What's wrong, son? I thought you'd be happy after a scrimmage like that. Did something happen?"

"I don't think I did that great, okay? I mean, I should have scored three touchdowns today if I had any kind of speed. And did you see my first pass? It was a duck. And then I came up empty on an open field tackle against Mapleview, the worst team on the field. How can you possibly think I had a great scrimmage?"

"David, don't you think you're being a little hard on yourself? You made some big plays out there today. I don't know much about football, but I know some. What I saw out there today was leadership. The offense scored on all three teams, and you didn't turn the ball over once. Sure you made a few mistakes, but who didn't? You've got to put the errors behind you. Learn from them, but don't dwell on them."

After about a half minute of quiet, David replied, "Yeah, I guess you're right, Dad. But I can't help but worry about losing my position to Roger when he comes back."

"Your position? It's not yours, David. It belongs to the team. And right now you have earned the privilege of filling that role. If you continue to work your tail off, perhaps that responsibility will still be yours. You've just got to trust the Lord for the rest. And let's always remember to be grateful just to have the opportunity to represent Him whether it's on the football field or somewhere else."

David's paranoia was gradually set to ease. His dad always had a way of putting things into perspective. David smiled at him approvingly. He was already feeling much better.

"So what's the plan for lunch, Dad?"

Of all the consequences of Roger's suspension — including sitting out of the scrimmage and missing the first two games — having to be a manager along side Adam Foster was the icing on the cake. After the scrimmage, the two had the privilege of putting away all the equipment, including emptying out the ice buckets and rinsing out all the water bottles. Then Coach Abraham gave each of them a garbage bag and told them to go through the bleachers — even under them — to pick up trash.

As was expected, Roger's bag was full and Adam's was half-empty. There was nothing Roger would have like better right now than to beat the living crap out of that Billington punk. He was quite sure that Coach Allen wouldn't mind either, but he knew if Coach Abraham ever found out, he would most definitely be dismissed from the team. Therefore, the best he could do right now was to visualize how hard he was going to hit Adam in practice next week.

Coach Abraham met them at the gate of Raymond Sanders Stadium.

"Thank you, boys. Make sure you behave yourselves this weekend, and we'll see you at practice on Monday."

For once, Roger was relieved to see his mother, parked in her silver BMW, engine running, her attention focused on the latest, best-selling romance novel.

"See you Monday, Coach," said Roger, intentionally opting not to offer a simple departing word or token gesture to his despicable teammate.

As he approached his mother's vehicle, there was still no acknowledgement from her. A little miffed, Roger swung open the passenger door and sat vehemently down next to her.

Suddenly, Mrs. Perkins turned on him. "I thought you said to pick you up at 11:00? Do you know what time it is? It's 11:30! I've got better things to do on a Friday than sit in this car for a half hour while you're doing heavens knows what. And how come everybody else is gone except for you and that other player?"

"It's awfully nice to see you too, Mom," responded Roger sarcastically.

"Watch your mouth, young man, unless you feel like walking home," pausing a moment before continuing, "I asked you a question. Why are you two the only ones still here? You're not in more trouble are you?"

"No, Coach Abraham had us put away a few things and then pick up the trash around the field. The other player is Adam. He's that loser from Billington. He's suspended for the first two games, too."

"I don't think it's fair to have you doing the custodian's job, especially with that Adam kid. Do you want me to talk to Coach Abraham?"

"No, I don't, Mom. That's the last thing I want you to do. Let's just get out of here."

"Mmmph... men, I will never understand them."

The rest of the drive home was in silence. Seething in anger, arms cradled firmly across his chest, Roger was desperate for an outlet. Stewing at home the rest of the day wasn't the answer, and hanging out with teammates and listening to them brag about their exploits in the scrimmage wasn't going to make him feel any better either.

Then an idea popped into his head: *call Pete.*

As soon as his mom had parked the BMW in the garage, Roger bolted for the phone in the kitchen. He had to look up Pete's name in the phonebook first. He vaguely remembered the name of his street; it had some type of fruit in it. There it was: Strawberry Lane. That was it.

He quickly dialed the number.

No answer. He'd try again later after lunch.

Since Coach Abraham and Coach Oliver lived so close to school, they had chosen to run home to shower and change before meeting Coach Allen for lunch to review film and prepare for their first game next week. Keith was hoping to find Carol and Julia at home, but when he walked into the kitchen he discovered a note saying they had gone shopping.

Once again his conscience had a confrontation with guilt. Keith fought off the urge to escape down to the basement where he could practically hear his faithful recliner beckoning to him.

He grabbed a pair of clean briefs, khaki shorts, and a plain olive green tee-shirt, and begrudgingly headed for the master bathroom to take a brief shower.

In less than twenty minutes, Keith was feeling somewhat rejuvenated and back on the road in his Honda Civic. One brief detour to Little Caesar's for a couple of medium pizzas, and he would be back on "the clock". Scrimmage day was one of the longest days of the season: a two hour scrimmage against three opponents, followed by two to three hours in a coaches meeting, and topped off with two to three more hours of scouting their first opponent.

Keith had always enjoyed scrimmage day so much in the past. Now he couldn't wait for it to be over. Maybe it had something to do with the fact that he had no one in his family to share it with anymore. Was Julia's and Carol's absence from the scrimmage some type of indictment against him and the team? How could he blame them if they wanted nothing to do with Juddville football? No, Carol would never desert him like that. She loved Juddville football, and more importantly, she loved him.

It was only last weekend at Lakeside Park when Julia had found herself amidst a heap of trouble due to her pathetic excuse for a boyfriend and her ill-advised decision to engage in underage drinking. She would have felt very awkward, indeed, sitting in the bleachers amongst the Juddville fans, enduring the muffled whispers and subtle stares. Nevertheless, Coach Abraham couldn't help but worry that he was becoming a stranger in his own house, and that his influence was becoming significantly diminished.

Chapter Five

Stooping low enough to look through the half-open window, Pete said, "Thanks for the lift, Roger. We should lift together more often."

"No problem, Pete."

"You're going to be pretty sore tomorrow. Just remember: no pain, no gain."

"I'll try to remember. Hey, what are you doing tonight anyway?"

Pete was unsure whether he wanted to be truthful or not. He would never have imagined spending a Friday afternoon with someone whose throat he had wanted to rip out only just last week. Yet when Roger had called asking if he wanted to go lift at the Body Shop, and even offering to drive? Talk about an offer he couldn't refuse. But hanging out with Roger on a Friday evening? That was an entirely different proposition.

"I'm probably just going to stay home and watch a football game. What are you doing?"

"I don't know. Maybe, catch a movie. I've got to find a girlfriend to keep me from going crazy the next two weeks."

"Well, if you're bored, you can come on over and watch the game. You'll know where to find me."

"I'll keep that in mind, Pete. Promise me one thing, though. Stay away from Lakeside Park."

"Not to worry, my man. I'll never set foot there again after dark. That's for sure."

Roger nodded and then squealed his tires as he sped down Strawberry Lane.

As Pete returned to his trailer, he recalled the scene that had taken place here in his own neighborhood only four nights ago. The memories were still vivid: the Juddville Police car; Coach Abraham, Coach Allen, and Coach Oliver; twenty-seven Jaguar teammates; and never to be forgotten, the presence of his biggest fan and most faithful supporter, his mother. It would always be for Pete one of the Top Five Moments etched on his highlight reel. The reason for this spontaneous gathering had been to celebrate the news that the Juddville Police Department had decided to drop all charges against him.

In contrast, the O'Connor home was quiet and peaceful on this Friday night. As Pete entered the front door, he noticed his mom sacked out on the couch, so he tiptoed to the kitchen. The newspaper was lying out on the table; he chose to ignore it even though his normal instincts would have directed him to open it up immediately to the sports section.

After experiencing firsthand the one-sided coverage of the Juddville Gazette on a story involving himself, Julia Abraham—the Coach's daughter—and Brian Taylor, Pete wondered how many of its pages were contaminated by lies and unsubstantiated rumors. Perhaps, he was over-reacting, but it was certainly going to take some time before he would be able to trust the media again.

He looked at the clock over the stove. It was 5:30, and he was famished. He wondered if he ought to make a few sandwiches or hold out to find out what his mom had planned for dinner.

Bored and little bit tired, Pete decided to retreat to his bedroom. On his way out of the kitchen he lifted up the newspaper and flipped it over, so he wouldn't have to see the words "Juddville Gazette".

Entering his bedroom, he walked over to the bookshelf and found last year's yearbook, pulled it off the shelf, and plopped down on his bed. First, he located his picture in the junior class section. He had to admit, he had looked pretty geeky, but he was at least 15 to 20 pounds lighter in that picture. On top of that, he must have been wearing a hat that day because he had a terrible case of "hat head".

Next, he flipped to the sports section and found Juddville Varsity Football. The team photo that had been taken immediately after the championship game was one of his absolute favorites; he was always impressed by that look of "Champions" on the faces of the players and coaches. Pete was hidden on the left side of the second row, dwarfed by the players in the two rows above him. His number had been 22.

So much had changed in the past year: last year a running back, this year a linemen; last year a scout team player, this year a starter and a captain—so much more pressure.

46

Another spectacular photo in this section was the impromptu shot of Coach Abraham hoisting the State Championship Trophy over his head, surrounded by his exuberant players. There was such happiness in his eyes, a look of contentment and pride. It seemed like such a long time ago. Coach seemed to be carrying a lot of weight on his shoulders lately. It had to be due in part to his daughter Julia, and of course, the pressure of defending a state title.

Pete had always been so impressed by Coach Abraham's composure during the heat of a game, virtually impervious to stress, or so it seemed. Pete often imagined what a formidable player Coach must have been back in the day. Nevertheless, every man has his limits. One thing Pete knew for sure was that Coach Abraham cared about people, and Pete was pretty sure that right now Coach was torn between the needs of his daughter and those of the team.

All alone in his room on a Friday night, Pete began to feel the gradual onslaught of boredom. The feelings were overpowering, so much so that he began to consider the unthinkable.

Maybe I should go on a date?

Pete methodically paged through the student pages of his yearbook, starting first with the juniors. When he saw Melanie's picture, he was transfixed for a brief moment by her alluring smile; a moment later, the sudden churning of bile in his stomach reminded him of her infidelity, and he defiantly departed from last year's juniors to the sophomores.

There was one girl in particular that he wanted to look up. Cathy... was her first name. He was quite certain of that. Her older brother's name was Ken. He had played center on last year's football team. Ken Robertson... that was it. Pete went to the page where the R's were located.

Cathy was the first picture in the second row from the top. The photo barely looked like the Cathy he had met out at the party last weekend. Evidently, she had ditched the glasses, and had obviously abandoned the book-nerd look.

Pete reminded himself that it didn't matter what she looked like last year; all that mattered was that now she was a babe. If only he could get up enough nerve to call her and ask her out...

Not feeling too confident at the moment, Pete decided to grab his UFL magazine, go outside, and plop down on a lawn chair behind their trailer.

When Roger got home from working out with Pete, his mom and Bill were dressed to the hilt. His mother was wearing an aqua blue summer dress, with her best diamond earrings; Bill was wearing a pink, long-sleeved looking looking black tie, and pin-striped pants. His mother had been applying red lipstick in the bathroom while Bill was savoring a martini at the kitchen table.

Roger's mom came out of the master bathroom to greet him. "Hello, Roger. Did you have a good workout? I hope you didn't hurt your back. The last thing you need is a hernia."

"Come on, Mom. I'm being careful." Changing the subject, Roger asked, "What are you guys all dressed up for? I hope you're not expecting to drag me along with you..."

"No, Roger. Why would we want to do that? You'd spoil the whole evening. We're celebrating. Bill earned a promotion at work. Isn't that wonderful?"

It only took a few moments for Mrs. Perkins to come to the realization that her son wasn't going to offer any words of congratulations.

Instead, he communicated to her his most urgent need. "What's for dinner, Mom? I'm starving."

"If you want I can put a pizza in the oven for you, or I can just give you some money to get a burger somewhere."

"I guess I'll go to Burger King then."

"Roger, I want you to come right home afterwards. I don't want you going out this weekend. I think I was pretty lenient not taking your car away from you. As I told you before, you're being suspended for two games is punishment enough as far as I am concerned. But I don't want you going out and getting in more trouble. Do you hear?"

"I hear. How late are you and Bill going to be?"

"I don't know. Probably not too late. By the way, Roger," suddenly becoming somber, "you got a letter from your dad today. It's right here on the counter."

"From Dad?"

"You know anyone else from California?" asked his mom as she leaned forward and kissed Roger on the cheek.

"Yuck, you got lipstick on me!"

"Oh, Roger, do you have to be so rude?" Mrs. Perkins turned her head sharply away from Roger and held her arm out for Bill who quickly accepted, and they promenaded through the kitchen towards the door to the garage.

Before the door to the garage closed, Roger heard his mother's piercing voice one more time. "We'll see you later, honey. And no drinking, you can't afford to get in anymore trouble at school."

48

"Whatever," said Roger, as he picked up Bill's empty martini glass off the counter, and loaded it in the dishwasher.

Swiping the envelope off the counter, Roger headed straight to the living room. He sunk into the comforts of his favorite over-stuffed, reclining chair. Sliding his right index finger all the way down the length of the envelope, holding his breath in anticipation, he pulled out the letter and unfolded it on his lap.

Roger cringed as he digested the opening paragraph. After reading through the letter, he crumpled it up into a ball and threw it forcefully at the large-screen television.

Only minutes ago Roger had felt fully-drained — both mentally and physically — from his workout with Pete. Now he felt like his blood was about to boil over with rage. He returned to the kitchen and grabbed the keys off the counter.

Where to? Don't know, thought Roger. *Just have to get out of this house.*

Speeding down the winding driveway of his North Shores sub-division, Roger decided his first stop was Burger King. After that, he would just have to play it by ear.

The preliminary scouting report on the Pennington Pirates was highly favorable. The Jaguar coaches were unanimous in their appraisal that Juddville was the better team. Nevertheless, the game itself presented many challenges. For one, it was going to be very difficult to fight the temptation to look past their first opponent, and start focusing upon the second game of the season which was against their rivals, the Billington Bulldogs. Concern number two was that Pennington had an outstanding junior quarterback that could throw the ball deep and accurately. He also possessed a quick release that made it nearly impossible for the defense to get to him in time to disrupt the pass. The third area of concern — especially to Coach Allen — was the stingy Pennington defense, particularly against the run.

Throughout the entire Pennington scrimmage the Pirates were formidable against the run whether it was an inside run, an off-tackle play, or a sweep around the end. In fact, against Madison Heights — one of the best wing-T offenses in the state — they held them to one score, and it was a play action pass that their cornerback had stumbled on, leaving the receiver all alone for a twenty yard touchdown reception. Their linebackers were very adept at reading guards which was the key to shutting down the wing-T. Most teams would instinctively be fooled by the deceptive faking of the quarterback and running backs. But if you train your linebackers to keep their eyes on the pulling guards, the guards will lead them to the play nearly 100% of the time.

Another successful strategy is to have your interior defensive linemen fire out low—even bear crawl—into the guards, knocking them into the back field, thereby preventing them from executing their trap blocks. Some teams have even gone so far as to instruct their defensive linemen to tackle the offensive guards, tripping them up by the ankles.

The hour drive back to Juddville had been relatively quiet. Coach Allen was somewhat assured that his long-time coaching comrade was back. Keith had proven himself by the adjustments he had made in the scrimmage against Rapids City. Furthermore, a huge bonus was the addition of Coach Oliver whose presence was already paying huge dividends with the development of the offensive and defensive linemen. By the time they had arrived back at Juddville High School, the coaches were plenty exhausted, so they said their "goodbyes" and immediately went their separate ways.

Jim's first stop was Little Caesars. Before leaving from the high school, he had called in the order from the phone in the coaches' office. By the time he reached the restaurant, his order was already up. He quickly paid for the pizza with cash and was back in his car within a couple of minutes.

Even though this would be Jim's second helping of Little Caesars, the smell of the two pizzas sitting on the front passenger seat was too much for him. He popped open the lid of the box that was on top and grabbed a slice of pepperoni pizza while steering the minivan with his left hand.

Naturally, the mozzarella cheese scalded the roof of his mouth, and he yearned for a cold one to chase down that savory bite of pizza—which was out of the question, of course. Devouring his first piece in three and a half bites, he decided to hold off on his next piece until he got home.

Friday night was Jim's favorite night of the week. It was like the tape at the end of the finish line. What greater feeling than to lean forward as you cross the finish line, knowing that your mission was accomplished and that a much-deserved rest was just waiting in the wings. Tonight, he would eat pizza with his family, have a couple beers, and most likely fall asleep on his favorite recliner.

As he pulled into his driveway, he felt relieved that one of the most challenging weeks of his coaching career had ended—and ended well. He parked in the garage and balanced both pizzas ever-so-carefully upon his right hand as he navigated through the chaos and clutter of the garage. A quick sidestep to his right, barely missing Luke's bicycle lying on its side, followed by a graceful crossover step to elude Katie's dolly stroller, and Jim could smell the end zone. All that was required now was one giant step over three sets of flip flops, and then booting the junior-sized football from its temporary residence on the steps into the house.

Opening the door knob with his left hand, Jim announced in what remained of his raspy coaching voice, "Pizza's here. Who wants pizza?"

All of a sudden, a trampling of little feet from the living room.

"Daddy, Daddy, I want pizza. I want pizza," pleaded his three year old daughter, her hair still wet and neatly combed back from her recent bath, the smell of her clean skin and the softness of her pink pajamas impossible to resist. He set the pizzas down on the counter, and picked her up for a much anticipated hug.

Kissing her on the cheek, Jim said, "Oh Katie, I missed you so much today."

The next one to enter the kitchen was Luke who went right for the pizza.

"No hug?" asked Jim, looking at his oldest son.

Luke sprinted over to his dad, gave him an uninspired hug around the waist and bolted back for the pizza. When he lifted up the cover, he exclaimed, "Hey, there's a piece missing!"

Still holding his daughter in his arms and walking over to the box to have a look, Jim responded, "What the heck? Are you kidding me? We've been ripped off. They sold us a pizza that was one piece short. I can't believe it. Give me those pizzas. I'm going to go get our money back."

Mary and Kevin came into the kitchen next.

"Hey Mary, check this out. They sold us a pizza that was one piece short."

Unable to resist, she responded, "Kind of like your brain, Jim. One piece short."

Luke was the only one who got Mom's joke, and he started laughing uncontrollably. "Ha ha ha. Dad's brain is one piece short," he repeated.

Now Katie and Kevin joined in on the laughter, and Mary stepped towards her husband to make peace. Kissing him affectionately, "Is that pizza sauce I taste on your lips, Jim?"

"Uh oh… busted," confessed Jim. "Is there anything around here a guy can drink?"

"Sure is, Jim. I'll get us both one."

Mary was back with a cold Budweiser immediately. As he pulled back the tab and heard the pressure escape from inside the can, he felt his own stress level begin to dissipate. This had been one rollercoaster of a week. Now he wanted to take a 24 hour break from anything that had to do with football. No meetings, no film, no phone calls, no planning… no football, period!

Sitting down at the kitchen table with Budweiser in hand, he noticed the Juddville Gazette that Mary had left out for him. He tossed aside the front page, followed by the national, state and local news, and turned immediately to the sports.

Aah, Week Two of the UFL exhibition season. Who's on this weekend I wonder?

Chapter Six

"Hey, Keith," said Carol, as her husband entered the living room. "You look exhausted. Did you get something to eat?"

"No, honey, and I am famished."

"There's some leftover shrimp salad in the refrigerator if you'd like," said Carol, semi-reluctant to offer any assistance.

Looking down at his watch, he noticed that it was only 8:15. Julia and Carol were sitting together on the couch paging through old photo albums. There was a peace about them that made Keith envious. He wanted to join them, but he felt like his presence might upset the harmony that existed between the two. Not wanting to intrude, Keith asked, "You two up for a movie later or maybe a noncompetitive game of Aggravation or Yahtzee?"

"Did Dad just use the word *noncompetitive*, Mom?"

"I thought that's what I heard him say, Julia. But he mispronounced the word didn't he? Poor guy. Can't blame him. Probably doesn't even know how to spell the word much less define it."

"What do you think, Mom? Should we let him win this time?" joked Julia. "Last time I think he went through a half a box of tissues."

"Yeah, maybe we'll have to take it easy on him this time around." After pausing a few seconds, "Nah, I say we kick his bootie."

Happy to see a return to normalcy in the Abraham home, Keith asked, "While I am trying to find something to eat in this house, can I get you two anything? Maybe I could make a snack or something?"

Julia started to laugh. Then her mom joined in, making her youngest daughter laugh even louder. Keith stood in the middle of the living room, clueless as to what could possibly be so funny. Carol was laughing so hard she tipped over onto her side. Julia was holding her side as tears began to stream down her face.

"Is anyone going to tell me what is so funny?" asked Keith, whose senses seemed a bit dull at the moment.

Mrs. Abrahams was unable to articulate a response, so Julia attempted to offer an explanation. "I'm not really sure I can speak for Mom," struggling to continue, "but I was cracking up just trying to imagine what kind of snack you could possibly…"

Giggle fits resumed. Looking in vain to her mother for relief, Julia couldn't help but laugh even more hysterically than before.

"I get it now. Ha Ha. You think I'm incapable of making something to eat, don't you? Well, I am just going to have to prove you two wrong. Give me thirty minutes and I will have you two eating your own words."

Carol couldn't resist, "Which I'm sure will taste a lot better than whatever you are planning on making."

Opting to bow out before incurring further abuse, Keith headed to the kitchen having no idea whatsoever as to what he was going to prepare. As he entered the kitchen, he noticed a handwritten note on the counter right next to the phone. It was written in Carol's handwriting:

Call Mr. Owens
729-1001

Funny, Carol didn't mention it. Did she forget or deliberately choose to not say anything.

Coach Abraham lifted the note off the counter, started to reach for the phone, and froze for ten seconds.

Is this something I need to do at this moment? It's already putting me in a bad mood, and it's Friday night for crying out loud. This will have to wait.

Folding the note in half, he walked over to the chair where he had set his briefcase and placed the note next to his clipboard where he could easily find it.

I'll get a hold of Mr. Owens tomorrow, or better yet, Sunday evening. That'll give him some time to cool off… or get run over by a semi.

Walking to the pantry he searched from shelf to shelf for something easy to make. On the top shelf he found the perfect snack: Pillsbury Brownies. He once made them for Carol's birthday. Any simpleton could make brownies.

He grabbed the box and set it down on the kitchen counter. Then he checked the freezer for vanilla ice cream. An unopened carton. Sweet! Now all he needed was one more ingredient. He searched throughout the refrigerator and could not find it. He looked one more time. Hidden behind a large bottle of ketchup he found it: Hershey's chocolate syrup.

First, he grabbed a large stainless steel mixing bowl from the bottom drawer and placed it quietly on the countertop. Then he opened the box, forcefully ripping open the waxed paper bag containing the brownie mix before dumping it into the bowl. Next, he grabbed an egg from the refrigerator, cracked it on the counter, and added its gooey contents into the mix. Then he found a measuring cup and added the exact amounts of water and oil. Lastly, he grabbed a serving spoon and stirred the brownie mix in large circular motions for about two minutes until all the lumps were gone.

Shoot, I forgot to preheat the oven, remembered Keith.

Suddenly, a voice spoke quietly to him. It wasn't audible, yet it was as if his mind had a voice of its own.

Slow down. Enjoy this moment.

"One more 45 pound plate on each side," said Pete, proudly sticking out his chest. "I feel strong today."

"Go for it, kid," said all-pro UFL linebacker, Kent Karchinski. "How many reps?"

"Three," answered Pete, chalking his hands up as he stared at the bar now loaded to 315 pounds.

"You want a lift off, Pete?" offered the all-Pro linebacker.

"Yeah, on the count of three, please."

"This is you now, O'Connor. All you! Come on, you can get this."

After dropping the block of chalk into the square wooden box, Pete began to pace back and forth, growling like a rabid dog, just short of foaming at the mouth. Making fists with both hands, he pounded them into his forehead, attempting to propel himself into a deeper frenzy.

Growling one last time, Pete approached the bench with extreme urgency. He slid back under the bar, grabbing the knurling equidistantly with his right and left hands. Planting his feet underneath him, eyes flashing with rage, he grunted, "Ready."

His all-time hero slowly and purposefully began the count, "One... two... three..."

The bar felt light in Pete's hands as he lowered the bar to his chest. He felt an enormous amount of power proliferate in his upper body as he prepared for maximum exertion. Suddenly, an incessantly-annoying pounding forced its way to the forefront of his consciousness.

What is that noise? Who is making that racket? Who would dare interrupt me when I am about to...?

Like an overheating radiator unable to contain itself a moment longer, Pete launched himself from the couch. As he dashed for the front door, he promptly regained his wits. He checked the time on his watch; it was 9:11 p.m.

Who could be knocking on my door at this hour...and just as I was about to go for a new max in the bench press?

As he turned the knob of the front door, he took a deep breath. When he saw who was standing on his front step, his heart plummeted in disappointment. It was Melanie—one of the last persons he ever wanted to see again.

—

54

She was standing all alone wearing a white, tight-fitting spaghetti-strap top complemented by denim cut-offs that covered very little of her bronze thighs. Her silky, blond hair rested gently on her shoulders, and the effect upon Pete was immediate.

Before Pete could articulate an appropriate response, Melanie made the first move.

"Mind if I come in?" her coy smile and brown, enchanting eyes providing reinforcement. "I *really* need to talk to you, Pete."

Unable to come up with an excuse quickly enough, Pete found himself opening the door all the way, stepping out of the way, thereby allowing his ex-girlfriend free access to the privacy of his home.

He looked over to the couch where he had been sleeping so soundly only moments ago.

"Have a seat, Melanie," pointing to the couch.

Do I sit across from her on the recliner or right next to her? Don't want to be rude.

"Pete, you were so awesome in the scrimmage this morning. You were by far the best player on the field. I am so proud of you.

"At the beginning of the week I was afraid you might never get the chance to wear a Juddville jersey again. I couldn't believe what was happening to you. Even though the paper and the TV weren't identifying you by name, word travels. And when I heard how Brian Taylor had manhandled Julia and how he was trying to force himself on her before you came to the rescue…"

Melanie paused, hoping to read Pete's eyes.

His mind jolted back to the previous Saturday evening out on the beach at Lakeside Park; it was a memory that he was so desperately trying to put behind him. Yet to be honest, he didn't mind hearing the story from Melanie's perspective. She made him sound so heroic. At least, she could recognize that Brian Taylor was in no shape or form a *victim*.

Suddenly, he found himself speaking. "Yeah, for awhile there I was feeling about as low as can be… I don't regret what I did, but when I saw Brian's ugly mug on the front page of the newspaper… I don't know. Maybe I could have backed off sooner. But he just kept begging for more."

"Well, I'm glad the *true* story came out. Nobody deserves to play this year more than you, Pete. I know how hard you've worked."

"Thanks, Melanie."

Pete's living room grew uncomfortably quiet. He could hear the clock ticking in his mother's bedroom. Melanie leaned back on the couch, turning to Pete, and gazing at him with inviting eyes. In super slow motion, her hands inched their way down to the bottom of her shirt, grabbing the hem with her fingers.

Leaning forward on the edge of the couch, eyes staring down at the coffee table, Pete was frozen in place like an ice sculpture. It was becoming increasingly obvious that Melanie had ulterior motives for coming to see him.

Ever so slowly, she began to roll up her shirt, exposing her bronze colored midsection. He was trying to block her out from his line of vision, but her shirt was already up to her bra. It was painfully obvious to Pete that he could do anything he wanted with Melanie right now.

He could take her into his bedroom where they would rip off each other's clothes and roll between the sheets. His mother was out with her friends at Ernie's Pub and wouldn't get home until 1:00 a.m. at the earliest. But what about afterwards? Pete had no desire whatsoever to reenter a relationship with Melanie. So what would it be? Collect his dues for the two times she had cheated on him and then sayonara?

No, he could never use a person like that, especially after the kind words she had just said to him. So he sat motionless, staring at the table like a middle linebacker zoning in on a quarterback under center.

Having intuitively read Pete's rejection, Melanie sat back up, pulling her shirt back down, her complexion turning a few shades of red. Combing her hair back behind her ears with her fingertips, she took a deep breath and opened up her heart.

"I understand why you can't forgive me, Pete. I do. And I don't blame you a bit. Not a day passes when I don't regret what I did. We had a good thing going, and I had to go and ruin it."

Tears began to drip, one-by-one, down the contours of her face, their flow unimpeded as she plowed ahead.

"I'll be honest with you, Pete. The first time I cheated on you, I didn't really feel that bad when I apologized. I knew you'd forgive me. But the second time... I could see how I hurt you, and I knew I had severely blown it... Then when this whole Brian Taylor nightmare hit the newspaper and TV, I knew how much you were hurting, and I was hurting too. I wanted to find someway to come beside you, but I knew if I tried to get involved, I might hurt you even more..."

Afraid that she was going too far, Melanie stopped abruptly. She had reached a dead end. Her words had evaporated into thin air.

Pete felt like he had to get on his feet and move around. It was getting far too steamy in here. He felt like he was chin deep in manure, desperately wanting some air before he suffocated.

"Let's go for a walk. I need some fresh air."

Roger burned nearly two gallons of gas driving through the streets of Juddville trying to get his head straight. He felt like he was approaching his breaking point. Part of him was screaming out for a party, somewhere he could go hang out with other kids, kids who could relate to the pressure and disappointment he was feeling.

Obviously, he realized that he was already suspended from participating in the first two games of the football season. Wasn't that enough trouble already? He could hardly afford to take the risk of getting caught breaking training rules a second time… the consequences being suspended the entire season.

If Roger went home, he would be all alone — no Mom, no Bill — nothing to do but sit around and think about how disappointed his dad was going to be.

Nevertheless, it was almost 9:30 — decision time. Roger opted for home. He would be all by himself until at least 10:30.

As he turned into his driveway, just the appearance of their two-story Victorian style home induced a splitting headache. He hated this place. It was over-stuffed with all the "things" he had ever wanted, yet it was lacking that which he needed most. Right now he was at a crossroads, and he had no clue which way to turn.

He retreated to his favorite place: the basement. Maybe a little music would make him feel better. How about a little Ozzie? He plugged in the headphones, turned the volume way up, and stretched out on his couch. Roger's thoughts were screaming to be set free:

I hate my mom; she's always manipulating me. I'm too old to be treated like a baby. Why is she always trying to control me? No wonder Dad left.

Only a spineless wimp like Bill could put up with her. Dad, Dad, how could you force me to live with these two? Let me out of this cell! I am burning up.

There's an idea. What if I burned down this stinking house? That would show them. All their exotic furniture, the extravagant furnishings, and all the designer clothes torched up in flames. All their valuables up in flames, the least of all me.

Don't worry, Mother. You are fully-insured — I'm sure Bill would be quick to remind you. All your things will be quickly replaced. You just won't have me around anymore to be the wet blanket. You just won't have me to boss around, but you'll still have Bill.

Dad won't miss me. I'm not a part of his life anyways.

———

The plan began to slowly unfold in Roger's mind. First, he would go scrounge up a handful of his mom's strongest prescription drugs. A couple belts from Bill's favorite bottle of Crown Royal to wash them down. Grab the gasoline can from the garage and empty it throughout the first floor. Drop a lit match in the kitchen, and retire to the basement for the grand finale of all naps. A one-way ticket to Never Neverland.

Goodbye, cruel world. Good bye, family. Goodbye, Jaguars. Goodbye, Pete?

As Roger thought about his plan, however, he kept thinking about Pete. Yeah, he could be a bit of hard-ass at times, but he had a definite cool side to him. At least, you knew exactly where you stood with him. He cared... about the team, anyways.

At the moment, Roger didn't feel like he was a member of the team, but in two long weeks, his suspension would be lifted.

If only I would have kept quiet, thought Roger. *I'd still be eligible to play this week, and Dad would get to see me play on Friday night.*

Roger made up his mind that he needed to go see that bad boy, Pete, and he was going to go see him now. But before he left, he decided to complete just one small part of his diabolical plan; he would mix a couple shots of Bill's Crown Royal with a splash of Coke on ice for the road.

After walking with Melanie for nearly an hour, Pete was anxious to return to his trailer. Although he would never admit it, he had actually enjoyed her company. For the duration of the walk they had kept a minimum of a foot's distance between them. At no point had he felt the urge to hold her hand or even brush shoulders. Instead, it was just friend-to-friend, nothing remotely close to being intimate.

It seemed like old times, without all the physical attraction. When they said their goodbyes, it felt a bit awkward for Pete not to kiss her, but those days were gone. In his mind, he had resolved to never forgive her, yet in truth, he probably had forgiven her, but he would never ever forget. Melanie would have to be the last female on the planet before he would change his mind. But they could still be friends. Perhaps, she deserved that much anyways. She was quite convincing when she told him how much it had bothered her when he had been wrongly accused by the Juddville Police and the media.

When Pete turned to walk up the front steps to his trailer, he fumbled with his keys. He hoped she hadn't read this as a sign that his resolve was weakening. But as he looked back, he was relieved to see that Melanie had already started up the engine of her dad's cherry red Mustang. He was glad he could finally have some time alone.

As he entered his trailer, Pete immediately headed for the kitchen. All that meaningful conversation had made him extremely hungry. He decided to check the freezer for any frozen pizzas.

Bingo! One Tombstone pepperoni and sausage pizza coming up. He preheated the oven to 425° and unwrapped the pizza. He reopened the fridge to check to see if there was any extra mozzarella cheese.

He found a half a bag of grated mozzarella, so he spread its contents on top of the pizza to make it cheesier. Then he carefully placed the pizza on the second-from-the-bottom rack and set the timer for 15 minutes. He checked the time on the clock oven.

10:15 p.m.

I bet the second half of tonight's exhibition game is about to begin.

A violent banging at the front door put his plans back on hold.

Now who could it be? Not Melanie again? Hadn't he made it abundantly clear he wasn't interested?

Or maybe... Adam Foster and his loser friend Josh?

Pete hesitated to move from the security of the kitchen to the potential threat of danger awaiting him at the front door. If he entered the living room, whoever was at the door would see through the window that he was home. If he stayed put in the kitchen, maybe they would just go away.

Bang, bang, bang.

Bang, bang, bang.

That was the last straw; it went against all his beliefs to hide away in the kitchen.

As Pete entered the living room, it didn't take him very long to recognize the source of the banging. Through the front window, he could see his teammate Roger waving like a lunatic. Startled, and then relieved, Pete opened the door for his teammate.

"Come on in, Roger. What's going on?"

Roger stayed put on the top step.

"Oh, Pete... my main man. I just had to come by and visit my hero. I just had to see what my hero was doing..."

Pete could smell the liquor on Roger's breath. His first instinct was to slam the door in his face. Then he thought about drop kicking him off his porch. Instead, he opted for an entirely different response, for he could sense something was bothering his teammate, something hidden behind his drunken stupor.

Grabbing hold of his left arm, Pete yanked him into his trailer and shoved him onto the couch where he would be in a perfect position for Pete to rip him a new one.

"You moron! You're already suspended. What are you thinking? Two games on the bench not enough for you?"

Answering calmly, "I got a letter from my old man today, Pete."

Reaching into his pocket, he pulled out a folded envelope. He opened the flap and pulled out the letter.

Handing it to Pete, he said, "I don't know what I am going to do."

Roger sat silently while Pete read the letter. When Pete was finished, he hadn't a clue how to respond.

His teammate broke the ice, "Pete, have you ever had something that you wanted... something you wished for every single night when you went to bed... night after night... day after day... year after year...

"And then that moment finally comes... that moment you've wanted so desperately. Only now it can't happen the way you wanted because you screwed up... because you messed it up so badly that the chances of it ever happening are next to impossible."

Pete looked at the pain in his teammate's eyes. He understood that pain. It was hauntingly familiar.

"I am sorry, Roger. I really am. Believe it or not, I used to have a similar dream. But now that's all changed. I made a choice to delete my father from my life forever. Actually, my situation with my dad was worse. At least your dad's not locked up behind bars. At least your dad took the time to write you a letter. There's still hope for you and your father. You've got a phone number where you can reach him. And who knows, maybe your dad can postpone his trip until later in the season when you're eligible to play again."

Roger's eyes began to brighten.

"What did your dad do to get locked up in prison?"

"He got behind the wheel when he was way too loaded and plowed over two teenage brothers."

"How long ago did it happen?"

"Seven long years. Apparently, he's up for parole soon, but I could care less if he ever gets out."

"He never writes you?"

"Nope, I've got a stack of Return-to-Sender letters in my bedroom. He won't even let us visit him. We're as good as dead to him."

"That's pretty rough going, Pete. I heard rumors that your dad was in prison, but I never imagined the pain he was putting you through."

"I've tried to put it behind me. Yeah, I still hate his guts, but I try not to think about him anymore. It's my mom who really got the short end of the stick."

Roger interrupted, "Oh yeah? Well, I'm quite sure that my mom is the reason my dad left. She is colder than the White Witch of Narnia. But I'll never forgive my dad for leaving me behind to live with her and Bill. My step-dad is such a dweeb."

60

"Look, Roger. You've got to remember one thing. It doesn't matter how badly we screw up, there is no way we can possibly outdo what our fathers did to us. They flat out deserted us. What kind of man does that to his own son? If I ever get to be a dad, I know I will **never** desert my kid."

"Yeah, maybe you're right, Pete. But I am so ashamed about letting the team down, and I feel even worse about how I deserted you when you needed a teammate to watch your back."

"Hey, it happened. It's over. You've got to let it go. Sometimes I wish I would have bolted, too. It would have kept me out of all that trouble."

Hearing the timer go off in the kitchen, Pete asked his teammate, "Want some pizza?"

Chapter Seven

Julia Abraham slept like a baby Friday night. It was the first morning in over a week that she felt refreshed when she rolled out of bed. It was 9:00 a.m. Her mom and dad were already awake, of course.

They had already finished off their pot of coffee. The Coach was sitting in his recliner reading the sports page. Carol was poring through the remainder of the Juddville Gazette.

"Good morning, Julia," said Carol. "Would you like some breakfast? Maybe some bacon and eggs?"

"No, thanks, Mom. I'll just have cereal."

"Oh, honey, we're all out of milk. You wouldn't mind running to DJ's would you?"

"Sure, whose car should I take?"

"You can take mine," offered Coach Abraham. "Did you have a good sleep last night?"

"Fantastic. It must have been the brownie sundaes you made, Dad."

"My purse is in the kitchen, Julia. Take enough money to buy two gallons of milk."

"Sure, Mom. You need anything else?"

"No, that should do it."

"Thanks, Julia," said Keith.

After pausing a brief moment to check her appearance in the mirror in the entryway, Julia strolled out of the Abraham front door where she was nearly blinded by the bright, Saturday morning sun.

As she inserted the key into the ignition, she reflected upon how her life plans had been so drastically altered over the course of one week. Today would have been her first weekend as a freshman at Tyler College. Now those plans were on hold. Her revised plan was to attend Lakeland Community College and hopefully find a part-time job.

After spending an entire week cooped up inside, Julia was beginning to suffer from cabin fever—even though it was way out of season. The first few days of her captivity were by necessity, but now that she was feeling somewhat safe and secure, she recognized a need in her life for some excitement, something more than an evening of Yahtzee with her parents. It wasn't that she wasn't appreciative of her parents' efforts to make her feel loved and supported; it was just that she needed to be around people her own age, people who shared the same perspective. Furthermore, her parents were so old-fashioned and conservative; they could easily model for a Norman Rockwell painting.

Backing out of the driveway, she made sure there were no little kids riding their bikes on the street. At this hour of the morning, there wasn't much activity in the neighborhood. She proceeded slowly to the end of their street and turned right onto Henry Street.

Coming up on her right was Maple Village, followed by the high school. Another half-mile and she was pulling into the parking lot of DJ's. She parked her dad's car as close as possible to the entrance and hopped out of the car, placing the keys in her purse. The store was empty with the exception of a rotund clerk sitting at the counter pressing one powdered donut hole after another into her mouth. She seemed impervious to the amount of white powder clinging to her lips and fingers.

Julia found the dairy products without much difficulty, so she was standing at the counter with two gallons of ½ percent milk in less than a minute. The clerk finished off her last donut hole, wiping her mouth with her forearm. She considered licking the powder off her forearm, but decided it would be best to wait until the customer had left.

"That'll be $4.00, please."

Julia handed her a five dollar bill. In vain, she tried not to look at the bottles of liquor on display behind the clerk. One particular bottle of Peach Schnapps seemed to be staring her down.

"Would you like a bag?"

Snapping out of her trance, Julia answered, "No... no thanks."

Julia quickly grabbed a gallon of milk with each hand—her purse slung over her right shoulder—and backed out the door, letting the door close by itself. When she saw who was parked next to her dad's Honda, she nearly dropped the gallon of milk from her left hand. It was a navy blue Chevy Nova, the vehicle in which she had been a frequent passenger the better part of the summer.

Double-clutching both gallons of milk, Julia stepped up her pace and walked briskly past his car. She set the milk on the roof of her dad's car and nervously retrieved the keys from her purse. After opening the door and setting the two gallons on the floor on the passenger side, she stole a stealthy look at her ex-boyfriend's car.

Even though his face was hidden behind dark-tinted sunglasses, she was positive of his identity. Suddenly, he removed his glasses and looked right through her. The expression on his face was one that she had never seen. Gone was the look of kindness and infatuation; in its place, fury and vengeance.

She frantically started the engine. As she pulled away from Brian's car, she was unable to avoid seeing those dark, sinister eyes in her passenger-side mirror. Her heart began to beat faster as she pulled out onto Henry Street. She increased her speed to 40 mph — 15 miles over the speed limit.

Approaching Juddville High School, she spotted the blue Chevy Nova in her rearview mirror. Julia held her breath, fully aware that her dad's Honda Civic could not outrun Brian.

He was swerving back and forth inching himself ever-so-close. His front bumper had to be within two feet of her rear bumper.

Julia could see his despicable face in the mirror, and it was quite obvious that he was thoroughly enjoying himself. All of a sudden, she heard a car horn beeping in front of her.

With not a moment to spare, she swerved to her right, just missing a gold SUV that was approaching on her left.

"Damn it, Brian," she screamed aloud, realizing she had inadvertently crossed the center line.

She slowed down to the speed limit and took a deep breath. Beads of perspiration were now forming on her forehead.

She could see her street up ahead. She pushed down on the turn signal and slowed to 10 mph. There was no oncoming traffic, and she made the left turn with ease. She heard Brian's horn blaring behind her, followed by the roar of his souped up engine as he continued down Henry Street. When Julia pulled into her driveway, she was breathless and her arms were beginning to glisten with perspiration.

As she entered her home she set the two gallons of milk down on the kitchen counter and sprinted to her room. Carol jumped to her feet and quickly followed while Keith remained seated at the kitchen table feeling as useless as a door without hinges.

Pete emerged from his bedroom at 10:00 a.m. on Saturday morning. His plans were to eat a very light breakfast, head to Raymond Sanders Stadium by 11:30, complete his running workout, and then kick back and enjoy the last Saturday of summer vacation before reporting to work that evening at 11:00 p.m.

Realizing that a shower would be pointless, he hurriedly brushed his teeth and walked extra-quietly past his mother's bedroom into the kitchen. He opened the refrigerator to grab the milk, but noticed that there was no milk to be found. Instead there was a pitcher of apple juice.

Today he would have to improvise and have something besides Cheerios for breakfast. He saw a half loaf of bread and decided to go with a few pieces of toast smothered with melted butter and strawberry jam. A glass of OJ and toast should provide him with enough energy to complete his running workout without giving him a bloated feeling. The last thing that he wanted was to leave his breakfast out on the field like he had last weekend.

He had made plans to run with David, and he was certain that his teammate would never forget last Saturday's performance.

What was it David has said? "Now I know what the 'O' in your last name stands for, O'Connor… Cheerios."

No, he would not give David that pleasure. This week it was David's turn. As a result, Pete opted for only two pieces of toast instead of four.

After eating his light breakfast, Pete grabbed his cleats and headed for the door. The Juddville Gazette was waiting for him on the porch. On second thought, he decided to take the paper in the backyard and stretch out on the lawn chair for a few minutes. Turning immediately to the sports section, he was curious about the outcome of last evening's UFL game. Between the late night stroll through the trailer park with Melanie and the unforeseen visit from Roger, he had missed the entire game.

Fortunately, his favorite team, the New Jersey Dragons, didn't play until Monday night. He couldn't wait to see Kent Karchinski play on national television. They were playing the Chicago Thunder. The Thunder had drafted Caleb Jones, a power running back, in the first round of this year's draft. He weighed 235 and ran a 4.4 forty. Pete couldn't wait to see Karchinski's first collision with the unproven rookie.

Pete decided that he would have to put a "No visitors" sign up on his front door Monday night. The best part about Monday night's game was that Juddville didn't start school until Thursday, so Pete could stay up and watch the entire game and not have to worry about getting up in time for morning practice on Tuesday. Monday was the last morning practice; starting on Tuesday, practices would begin at 3:00 p.m.

After reading through the brief write-ups of last night's UFL games, Pete reassembled the paper for his mom, placing it on the semi-organized coffee table in the living room.

He checked his watch. Time to go. In another hour, he would be done with his workout and would have the rest of the day to relax.

I hope David didn't forget about running today.

Naw, he'll be there. He gave me his word.

It was highly unusual to be afforded the luxury of sleeping in past 10:00 a.m. on a Saturday. When Jim squinted at the clock through his blurry eyes, he immediately became suspicious.

"Mary? Mary?" he called out down the hallway as he stumbled for the bathroom.

After emptying his bladder and brushing his teeth, he continued his investigation downstairs. When he got to the kitchen, he discovered his family waiting around the kitchen table, sitting with their hands folded, hardly making a peep. His wife had a mischievous smirk on her face.

"Good morning, honey."

"Good morning. Why are we all sitting around the table so well-behaved? Am I missing something?" asked Jim.

"Don't you remember what today is, Jim?"

"I'm quite sure it is Saturday."

"That's right, Daddy," answered Luke. "Don't you remember where we're going today?"

"I honestly don't remember. McDonalds?"

"Come on, Dad," said Kevin. "You know where we're going. We're going to look for a doggy!"

All of a sudden, Jim put two and two together. He had been the victim of every form of persuasion and harassment for the past three months. The objective: talk Dad into getting a dog.

Mary had wanted a dog for a long time—most of the twelve years of their marriage—and she had strategically put her three children to work. She knew that eventually, he would cave into the extreme pressure of their three adorable kids, particularly their daughter Katie.

So when Katie said, "I've wanted a doggy my whole life, Daddy. Can we get one today? Can we get one?"

Jim glared at Mary and responded, "That's dirty pool, Mary. You ought to go into politics someday, you know that? You know how to get whatever you want, using whatever tools necessary. How many times did you have to rehearse this little skit?"

65

"Five," responded Luke, staring down at the table after his mom shot him a look of warning; her amazingly-powerful eyes were legendary, second only to Medusa. One look into her eyes, and you immediately turned to stone.

"All right. All right. You win. "

The Allens—minus one—shouted exuberantly as if celebrating a game-winning field goal.

Waiting for the hoopla to subside, Jim asked, "Can I at least get some breakfast?"

"Of course," responded Mary, rising from her seat, flamboyantly opening the door of the oven and then casually pulling out a warm plate containing a three-egg, ham and cheddar omelet with a hefty portion of hash browns on the side.

Luke hopped off his seat and sprinted to the kitchen counter; he grabbed the glass of orange juice and brought it ever-so carefully to his dad. Next, Kevin hopped off his chair and retrieved the silverware from the counter top that Mary had rolled up tightly inside of a napkin. With great pride and formality, he delivered the utensils to his appreciative father.

"What about you, Katie? Don't you have anything for me?"

Mary helped her down from her booster seat. In slow motion, she tiptoed over to her daddy's chair.

"Just this, Daddy." And she gave him a big wet, sloppy kiss on the cheek.

Hook, line, and sinker.

Chapter Eight

Roger didn't answer the phone all day Saturday, and for a very good reason: he had promised Pete that he wouldn't go out and party.

After showing up at Pete's semi-drunk on the previous night, Roger had been extremely grateful that Pete hadn't turned him into Coach Abraham — or worse yet — taken the responsibility for disciplining him into his own hands. He was well aware of the amount of damage Pete's fists could inflict on the human body. Roger had witnessed firsthand his pummeling of Brian Taylor.

As a result, he had vowed to stay in his basement Saturday night, barricaded from all the peer pressure to go out and drink. He knew a couple teammates like Dan Hardings might try to get a hold of him to find a party, but not on this night. There was too much at stake. He had already forfeited two games of the season, and he still had no idea what he was going to tell his father when he arrived at Juddville on Friday, just in time for the home opener.

At the moment, he was bored out of his mind. He wished there was some yard work or other form of manual labor he could do to take his mind off his problems, but his mom hired out all the yard work. Bill just wasn't that kind of a guy, and his mom had never seemed to have much success motivating Roger to do any type of chores around the house.

Suddenly, an incredible idea popped into his head. He could grab his clubs and go hit a bucket of balls at the driving range where chances were slim to none that he would bump into any of his friends.

Roger darted up the stairs and found his mom sitting in the sun room reading a romance novel.

"What's the hurry, Roger? Are you going somewhere?"

Ignoring his mother he sprinted through the kitchen to the living room. He continued up the winding stairs to his bedroom where he grabbed a pair of clean socks from the top drawer of his dresser. Sitting down at the foot of his bed, he pulled on his socks and quickly tied his shoes.

In less than two minutes he was jogging back down the stairs into the kitchen. His mother was glaring at him with angry eyebrows.

"I asked you a question, and you completely ignored me."

Going directly for the refrigerator, he opened the door and grabbed a 16 ounce bottle of Coke.

His back to his mother, he unscrewed the cap and took a giant swig of soda. Without looking at her, he asked, "So what did you want?"

"I want to know your plans for today."

"Nothing much," he answered as he headed for the garage.

Mrs. Perkins's mouth hung open for nearly a minute as she watched her only son walk out of her house in his customarily rude and disrespectful way.

Meanwhile, Roger found his bag of clubs in the corner of the garage, tossed them in the trunk, and was off to the driving range in no time at all. The drive was less than five minutes away. He pulled into the dusty, gravel lot and parked in a partially-shaded spot under a newly-planted maple tree. Before going into pay, he removed his clubs from his trunk and set them by the bench in front of a vacant tee. A minute later he came out with a $5 bucket of balls.

Roger decided to begin his workout with his driver. He looked up at the 300 foot marker and wondered if he could hit a ball that far. As angry as he felt right now, he thought he might just reach 450 feet.

As Keith finished the last remnants of lunch, he decided he could not procrastinate much longer. He swallowed the last flavorful bite of his roast beef and provolone sandwich on fresh Vienna bread. He licked the mustard, mayo, and tomato off his fingers and stared at the phone lying in the middle of the table.

Carol and Julia were on a walk. Something was clearly bothering Julia this morning. Last night she had seemed to be her old self, but she had been on edge ever since she had returned from the store.

Keith wanted to ask Julia what was troubling her, but the last thing he wanted to do was further upset her. So Carol had offered to make him lunch before they left, and he politely accepted the offer—even though he would have preferred eating the fabulous sandwich in their company instead of all alone.

He looked at the phone message that Carol had scribbled down last night. Finally, he lifted up his glass to empty the last swallow of cold milk. Just as he was reaching out to grab the phone, it started ringing.

Maybe this is Owens now.

"Hello," said Keith, in an emotionless monotone.

"Coach Abraham?"

"Yes, this Keith."

"This is Paul Jones. I hate to bother you on a Saturday, Keith, but I received a phone call of great urgency this morning from a football parent. He told me he had left a message last night and was still waiting for you to respond."

A number of hostile replies were spinning through Keith's mind, and he was in no hurry to speak as he waited for each thought to run its course through his brain's filter. He was not one bit bothered by the silence coming from both ends of the conversation; in fact, he was kind of enjoying it.

"Keith... Are you still there?" a hint of irritation beginning to develop in the superintendent's voice.

"Yes, sir. I'm sorry, but I don't remember you asking me a question."

"Coach, I know it's been a rough week for you and your family, but I think it would be in your best interests to promptly return a concerned parent's phone call."

"Hmm... did I just hear you say 'concerned parent'? Surely, Paul, you can't possibly be referring to the parent who had to be asked to leave from Raymond Sanders Stadium yesterday."

"Yes, I heard all about it, but don't you think Mr. Owens is entitled to a prompt, professional response — at least for the boy's sake?"

"Excuse me, Dr. Jones, but I'm quite sure I'm not interested in hearing any more of your professional advice. Earlier this week I was forced to take a leave of absence, and I am quite certain, the school board acted according to your professional advisement.

"Once the truth came to light, however, you were compelled to reverse your decision, allowing me to return to the enormous task of preparing a football team for its first game. Naturally, your wounded ego would be compelled to insist on one ill-advised condition. And without consulting a single member of the Juddville Coaching Staff, you decreed a certain player should be allowed back on the team, a player who in just one week's time had committed acts of vandalism, misconduct, theft and assault. All this in light of your knee-jerk mishandling of Pete O'Connor who was found innocent by the Juddville Police Department of the charges that you were so quick to assume were justified."

"Keith, Keith, Keith... don't get all worked up. I'm just trying to pass on some friendly advice."

"Maybe you didn't hear me, Dr. Jones, so I'll repeat myself. I am not interested in hearing any of your advice. And your casual use of the word 'friendly' is a bit much, I think, given the circumstances. Furthermore, last time I checked, today is Saturday. Most people consider Saturday a non-work day, so unless you have anything to say that is important, I suggest we continue this conversation on Monday. And I would appreciate it immensely if you would stop meddling in the football team's affairs. It would seem you might have more important concerns with a new school year upon us."

After about 15 seconds of silence, Dr. Jones replied with a slight edge to his voice, "Monday, you say? Suit yourself, Keith. But I might want to point out one significant detail, however: Mr. Owens's connection to the school board. Perhaps, you were not aware that he is the brother of our school board president, Valerie Snow."

"No kidding. I might have guessed. No wonder she has tried to keep her relation to Mike under wraps for so many years. Can't say that I blame her. But that sure explains a lot."

"Coach, I would like to suggest that you get some much needed R and R the rest of this weekend. I'll tell Mrs. Snow that you and your family are out of town. I'm sure she'll pass the information on to her brother. In the meantime, you better get your head straight."

"Touché, Dr. Jones. Touché."

Hanging up the phone, Keith was bombarded by mixed emotions. He could not believe what he had just said. First, he felt guilty about some of his comments. To be sure, his boss deserved to be called out, to some degree, for his mishandling of recent affairs. Nevertheless, Keith couldn't help but bemoan a few of his vindictive comments. As a man who professed to be a Christian and who had always tried to act in an honorable, respectful manner, he was worried that he had just irreparably tarnished his reputation and character. The scary thing was that it had all transpired over the course of a mere five minutes.

What am I doing? What is my problem? Am I starting to crack? I've got to do something before my career and my life are in ruins.

Word of God

Coach Abraham tried to remember the last time he had read his Bible. Was it two days ago or three? He wasn't even sure where he had left it. After looking on his bed-side table and then in the basement, he finally found it in the living room on the coffee table under a couple of football magazines.

Before sitting down for a long overdue appointment with God, Keith poured himself a large glass of sun tea before returning to his favorite chair in the comforts of his living room.

He lifted his Bible off the table, and opened it up on his lap, hopeful that God might have a special word for him. Previously, he had been studying 2 Corinthians, having left off at the end of Chapter 3.

The next chapter began with the words, "Therefore, since through God's mercy we have this ministry, we do not lose heart…"

Lose heart? Anyone seen mine in a while?

Keith continued to read, trying to decipher the language of the Apostle Paul, desperate to find some type of application in his precariously unstable condition. When he got to verse 7, all at once his senses became fully alert.

"But we have this treasure in jars of clay to show that this all-surpassing power is from God and not from us."

The next verse provided the essential CPR that his soul desperately craved.

"We are hard pressed on every side, but not crushed; perplexed, but not in despair; persecuted, but not abandoned; struck down, but not destroyed…"

That's me, Lord.

I'm feeling that intense pressure… trying to be perfect, but failing dreadfully.

*Why? I am just clay. Nothing more. The only good that I've ever done is because of the all-surpassing power of God at work in me. It's **never** been me. Never!*

Lose the pride, Coach.

I've made such a fool of myself. And I have been such a failure as a father.

But you're clay. That's why you need me.

I get it, Lord. Now help me to be humble enough to accept it.

"Five minutes, Mary, and the brats will be ready," Jim called out.

He placed the lid back down over the grill and grabbed his cold Budweiser off the deck rail. Katie was splashing around in the shallow end of the pool, wearing her swimmies, of course. Freckles — the newest member of the Allen family — was running around in circles in the middle of the backyard. She was chained to a cork-screw stake.

The dog was pure mutt. Part terrier, part Schnauzer, and part who knows what. The Humane Society estimated that she was about two years old.

Potty-trained? Yes.

A barker? At times.

Temperament? Gentle with children, but sometimes snipped at men.

The point of no return was Katie standing outside her cage, talking to the dog in her adorable, miniature voice. There had been no need for the court to recess. The case was closed. The verdict was in, and the boys concurred the first time they saw her jump.

"Maybe we can teach her tricks with a Frisbee?" said Luke.

"Who cares if she barks a little?" said Mary. "We could use a good watch dog."

"Does she have a name?" Jim had inquired.

"Freckles," said the volunteer from the Humane Society.

How appropriate, Jim had thought, noting the chocolate brown specks scattered across her dingy white coat.

At the moment, Jim's back was turned to Freckles. He lifted the hood, and took a giant step back as he was engulfed by a cloud of steam pouring out from the grill. After the smoke cleared, he stepped back up to the grill to turn each brownish grey brat one last time.

When he glanced over towards the pool, his blood immediately began to boil.

"Freckles! Freckles! You stop that right now," shouted Jim as he sprinted down from the deck, pouncing upon the dog in no time at all. His first instinct was to grab it by the collar and shove its snout down into the 10 inch hole she had just dug in his meticulously-manicured lawn.

But then he heard Katie interceding, "Daddy, Daddy, don't hurt her. She thinks it's her sandbox."

Jim released the dog from his grasp as Katie ran to Freckle's rescue as quickly as her little legs could move. His attitude went into complete reversal as he felt the urge to stick his own head into the freshly-dug hole to conceal his shame.

"I'm sorry, Katie. I wasn't going to hurt her," lied Jim. "I just needed to show her that digging holes in the yard is wrong."

He wasn't sure how much of his explanation Katie had heard, for her face was buried in Freckles's fur as she tried to hug away her fear.

Suddenly, Jim remembered the bratwurst on the grill, and he made a quick sprint to the deck, arriving just in the nick of time. With expert precision he removed the brats one at a time. Mary had finished setting the picnic table for dinner.

Luke and Kevin had been playing catch with the football and had heard all the commotion from over the fence that separated the pool from the "playing field".

With great apprehension, Luke inquired, "Dad, what happened to Freckles?"

"Oh nothing, I caught her digging a hole that's all. Katie thought I was going to light her up. I just had her by the collar. I would never do anything to hurt her. You boys know that... don't you?"

"Sure, Dad," said Luke, unable to conceal the distinct tone of doubt in his voice.

Meanwhile, Katie hoisted Freckles up off the ground, carrying her into the house where she would be safe.

On the one week anniversary of the Night of Infamy, Pete opted to stay home before reporting to work for his Saturday night graveyard shift at the Pancake House. After a fairly rigorous running workout with David Riley earlier in the day, his body ached, yet his energy level was surprisingly high.

It was the lingering memory of the harrowing events of the previous Saturday night that was causing him to feel slightly "wired". In the process of saving a helpless victim from an attempted rape, Pete had pummeled Brian Taylor's face into a bloody pulp, only to end up in the backseat of a Juddville police officer's car.

So on this Saturday evening, he opted not to return the phone calls of his good buddies, Dave and Nick. Hopefully, they would understand, yet the fact that neither one of them had come to visit him amidst all the turmoil the previous week had not gone unnoticed. When Pete's life couldn't have become much worse, his true friends stood by his side, and they were his Juddville teammates, not a couple of clowns who appreciated the convenience of having a fearless football player around to be their personal body guard and designated driver.

For those of his peers foolhardy enough to return to Lakeside Park for another kegger, they actually had another option this week. The latest rumor was that Roxanne Myers was hosting the weekly bash, and her home just so happened to be along the beach.

Saturday evening started extraordinarily well for Pete; his mom made her legendary lasagna with buttery garlic bread. After dinner they watched the end of the New Haven Express baseball game on TV.

When Pete was younger he played Little League Baseball, but he gave it up after the seventh grade. The game was too slow, and there wasn't enough physical contact. If it would be legal to run over the first baseman instead running over the base, the game would be a lot more appealing.

Nevertheless, when Pete was bored in the summer, he would often turn to an Express game on TV; the extraordinary skill of the pitchers and hitters and the complex strategies of the game intrigued him. Watching baseball was not an all-consuming activity either; you could easily have the game on in the background while your mind was engaged on something else. His mom liked to sit in the recliner and read a New York Times Best Seller novel while Pete preferred to read his UFL magazine or something football-related.

On any given night, there were many questions that Cindy wanted to ask her son, but tonight she was content to just enjoy his company; there was nothing more peaceful for her than an evening with Pete. He was so easily amused. Furthermore, she was painfully aware that this was the last year she would have him at home, for she was certain that Pete would be in college somewhere next fall. Although she would miss him terribly, she knew that he had to get out of Juddville; it was imperative that he discover that there was an entirely different world out there from the one in which he had been raised.

At 9:30, Cindy woke abruptly, somewhat embarrassed by having fallen asleep. The book she had been reading had fallen from her lap, and there was a drool mark the size of a grapefruit on her olive green pillow.

"What's the score?" asked Cindy nonchalantly, as if she hadn't been sound asleep for the last 45 minutes.

"Oh, the Express are up by 1, top of the ninth. But Garcia is on the mound. He just walked the lead off batter. Next guy up is going to hit a homer… guarantee it."

"Don't be so negative, Pete. How can you be so sure?"

"Just wait and see, Mom. If he blows the lead, you're scooping ice cream. If he gets the save, I will make *you* a hot fudge sundae. Deal?"

"Deal," agreed Cindy.

Much to Pete's dismay, Garcia proceeded to strike out the next batter. He secured the win for the Express by getting the next batter to ground into a double play, thus earning a hot fudge sundae for Mrs. O'Connor.

The fact of the matter was that Pete didn't mind making his mom a sundae. It seemed like such a small, insignificant gesture. His mom had endured so much and had made so many sacrifices; he could never repay her. Her eyes were beaming with joy as he set down the tasty treat on the coffee table in front of her.

"This looks positively scrumptious, Pete," digging into her ice cream treat. "Where's yours?"

"I'm going to eat when I get to work…the usual…a cheeseburger and chocolate malt. Then when I take my break in the middle of the night, I'll have some eggs and pancakes."

"I don't know where you put all that food, Pete."

At 10:30, Pete said goodbye to his mom and headed off to work for a night of bussing tables, washing dishes, and mopping floors. The next time Cindy would see him would be at lunch on Sunday, served at approximately 1:30 p.m. at the O'Connor household.

Chapter Nine

As if Jim needed any other thoughts whirling around in his mind, now he had to reevaluate his Sunday morning routine.

On Friday morning, after taking the last bite of his Denver omelet prior to the 3-way scrimmage, Jimmy Harrison had gone out on a limb and invited Jim to attend his church on Sunday. There were not too many times in Jim's adult life where he recalled being coerced into doing something he was so dead-set against. The fact that the UFL football player was staring directly into Jim's eyes from the opposite side of a booth in a public restaurant while waiting for his answer, did not make his decision any easier. Furthermore, Jim had surmised that his super-sized friend had minimal experience in taking "No" for an answer.

Consequently, Jim caved in and said, "Sure, why not?" Though he could have made up at least a dozen excuses, he had realized they all would have sounded pretty shallow.

In a way, he felt indebted to Jimmy. After all, the former UFL great had went out of his way to contact a former teammate—current New Jersey Dragon linebacker Keith Karchinski—making a rather bold request to have him UPS one of his game jerseys to a young fan that neither Karchinski nor Jimmy Harrison had ever met.

Coach Allen rarely asked favors of anyone; he preferred to do things himself; he was a self-made man. But the idea seemed to be Heaven-inspired. When he had called Jimmy to ask the favor, he wasted no time complying, and the outcome was nothing short of amazing.

One simple-yet-extraordinary gesture produced a healing effect upon Pete O'Connor. Jim was convinced that the mere gift of a genuine UFL jersey had helped wash away a world of hurt, and it may have helped restore some of the faith Pete had in the people and the world that surrounded him.

Nevertheless, Jim accepted the invitation to attend Jimmy's church. Mary, of course, was shocked yet absolutely ecstatic about the opportunity to go to church together as a family.

The service was very much like Jimmy had described. The atmosphere was very casual: people actually wore shorts, adults drank coffee from travel mugs, and there was a praise band instead of an organ — composed of electric guitars, a keyboard, and a drum set that would make Neil Peart proud. The kids had their own program, so there were no distractions. It was just one-on-one with a passionate, seemingly-sincere pastor. The message was positive, focusing on God's mercy rather than His judgment. Any mention of sin was in the context of "Us" rather than "Them", acknowledging that every single person in attendance was indeed a sinner saved by God's grace.

Consequently, the Allen family truly enjoyed their first experience at Haven Community Church. When they loaded into the van to begin their excursion home, there were many stories and first impressions shared. But Jim heard very few of them, for he was deep in his own thoughts.

All of a sudden, the Allen family broke out into hysterics — that is with the exception of Jim. Even Mary was laughing uncontrollably. If she hadn't been wearing her seatbelt, she looked like she would have fallen right out of her seat.

"What is so funny? Did I miss something?" asked Jim, clueless to the source of amusement while trying to pay attention to the traffic around him.

Mary attempted to speak, but started laughing even harder. She reached for a Kleenex to wipe the steady stream of tears flowing down her face.

"Don't tell him," pleaded Luke, from the middle seat of the mini-van.

"Tell me what?" asked Jim, a hint of annoyance developing in his voice.

A chorus of giggles and nervous laughter continued. Jim was beginning to entertain the prospect of pulling off the road to investigate this mystery.

"Will someone *please* tell me what the heck is so stinking funny?"

Mary who was enjoying herself immensely, managed to sputter out a few words, "I'm not sure, honey. I just... I just can't put my *finger* on it."

An even louder roar from the back of the van.

Then Luke chimed in, "Daddy, can I *pick* where we're going to eat?"

Much to Jim's dismay, the outpouring of laughter refused to subside.

Finally, Katie — always looking out for her daddy — provided the intelligence he was so desperately seeking.

"Daddy... Daddy... Luke flicked a booger at you, and it's stuck on your cheek."

"What?" reaching up with his right hand while controlling the steering wheel with his left. "Sick! Luke, how could you do such a thing?"

Before Jim could carry the lecture any further, Mary interjected, "Because he has the world's best teacher, and the apple doesn't fall very far from the tree, Jim... or the booger, in this case."

"Very funny, Mary. Very funny. Would someone give me a Kleenex," retorted Jim, fully aware that he was undeniably guilty as charged.

It was early Sunday evening, and Coach Abraham felt completely out of his element. Instead of spending the evening in his basement watching film on their first opponent and making final practice preparations for the week, he was driving back to school for their staff meeting. For a long time, Jim and Keith had been discussing moving their meeting time from Saturday mornings to Sunday evenings. Last year in the playoffs, several of their games had been on Saturday, so they had to meet on Sunday evenings out of necessity. When Jim had suggested a change on the drive back from the Pennington scrimmage Friday evening, Keith was reluctant, yet he felt obligated to concede to Jim's wishes after all of his loyalty and support the past two weeks.

Consequently, he agreed to the change, and he had hoped to take advantage of the change in schedule by spending more time with Julia and Carol on Saturday. Unfortunately, Julia spent most of the day with Carol. In the evening, she retired to her bedroom early, barricading herself from her parents and her peers on the one week anniversary of the worst night of her life.

As a result, Keith felt disappointed that all of his best intentions for Saturday had never materialized. How was he supposed to fix things at home when his daughter rarely left her room? Sometimes it was a lot easier to talk to his players or even to parents than it was to his own family.

In fact, earlier in the afternoon he had finally gotten around to returning Mr. Owens's phone call. It was amazing sometimes how a little bit of time healed all wounds. Naturally, Mr. Owens was singing a much different tune than he was at the scrimmage on Friday, for the possibility of being banned from attending all Juddville athletic contests for one calendar year was a consequence that any parent would find particularly devastating. Yet would Dr. Jones and the Juddville School Board actually have the guts to carry out such a severe disciplinary measure? Certainly not Board President Valerie Snow —sister to Mike, Sr.

Overall, however, Coach Abraham was pleased with how well the phone call went. Mr. Owens gave his word that he would refrain from disrupting all football practices and games. Likewise, Coach Abraham assured Mike, Sr. that his son would receive the very best coaching and would never be mistreated by any member of the Juddville Coaching Staff.

As a result, Coach Abraham was feeling somewhat energized on his drive to the scouting meeting on Sunday evening. He was relieved to be able to provide a positive report about his phone call with Mr. Owens, and he was looking forward to preparing a game plan for their first opponent, the Pennington Pirates.

Even so, to a slight degree, his conscience had been whispering to him that he should be at home, providing a strong defense for his family. Though the Abraham name was out of the spotlight — at least, for the time being — he had an eerie premonition that Julia was still in danger. Brian Taylor, her former boyfriend who had attempted to force himself on her when she was intoxicated to the point of passing out, was out of the picture, yet her troubles were far from over.

The question was how had she become mixed up with such a loser in the first place? Coach Abraham didn't have to look too far to find the answer, though. It appeared to him each morning in the mirror: the grief-stricken eyes of an aging father who had failed his family and failed his daughters while he reached the very pinnacle of success in his coaching career.

The words of Julia played over and over in his mind: "We have always been second string."

Coach Abraham felt powerless to turn things around with his family. What was he supposed to do? It wasn't like he could just resign in the middle of the season. Think of all the boys he would let down, all the parents, all the faithful Juddville fans. And what would it accomplish if his daughter continued to shut him out of her life, anyways?

Football... Family... Football... Family... A tug-of-war, constant tension. Keith truly felt like he was coming apart at the seams.

Yet, maybe he was just overreacting. Hadn't they had a brief moment of family time on Friday night eating brownie sundaes and playing Yahtzee?

If only he had been paying more attention, he could have seen that his daughter was starting to slip. There had been signs that Julia might have been hanging out with the wrong crowd: the late nights, the baggy eyes and frequent headaches in the morning.

The "plan" had been to allow Julia to overcome these growing pains on her own—wasn't that a natural part of the maturation process? After graduating from high school and surviving one last summer in Juddville, she was supposed to have been on her way to Tyler Bible College, where all would be made right, where a flighty teenage girl might be transformed into a poised, confident young woman ready to meet the challenges of a complicated, seductive world.

Unfortunately, the plan had been abruptly derailed out at Lakeside Park, and it had occurred on the eve of Julia's intended departure. As Coach Abraham parked his car in the high school lot, he realized that preparing for their first opponent was a responsibility that he could not forego for the time being. Surely, at the end of the season, he would reevaluate how much more of his life he wanted to devote to this game called football. In the mean time, he would just have to try to find more opportunities to earn back the affection of his daughter.

Chapter Ten

Back and forth, Pete rolled his head across the pillow, peering periodically at the alarm clock on the top of his dresser. The alarm was set to go off at exactly 6:45. He had been awake since 6:00, and he couldn't wait to start practicing for their first opponent, the Pennington Pirates. Finally, at 6:40, he rose out of bed five minutes early, shut off the alarm, and headed to the bathroom to officially begin his Monday.

After an extra-long hot shower he fixed himself a large bowl of Cheerios with a cutup banana. He emptied the bowl in 60 seconds or less, placed the bowl and spoon in the sink, and poured a small glass of orange juice. Before the juice barely had time to settle, he lifted the glass up and drained its contents. He refilled the glass and drank another glass, this time a bit slower.

At 7:15, Pete was out the door, walking briskly to practice, feeling especially grateful for the opportunity to practice on this first day of the week. He remembered quite vividly how one week ago this very day he was sitting at home, holed up inside his trailer, suspended from all practices until the pending assault charges had been dropped.

Over the course of the 17 years of Pete's life, the Monday previous had surely made his Top 5 Worst Day's List. It was right up there with the day his dad turned his back on Pete and his mom seven years ago.

79

Paul O'Connor was currently serving his 10 to 15 year sentence at the Carson City State Penitentiary. He was convicted for two counts of manslaughter and operating a motor vehicle while intoxicated. His irresponsible actions had resulted in the tragic deaths of two teenage brothers. How unfathomable was the pain and suffering inflicted on the family of the deceased and on the small town of Billington.

Not content to wound just one family, however, Paul made the decision to completely cut himself off from his own wife and son, refusing to meet with them during visiting hours or to respond to any of their mail or phone calls. All subsequent letters from Pete had been sent back unopened and marked "Return to Sender". That was surely the Number One Worst Day in Pete's life, but last Monday was probably number two.

That was the day he was at home suspended from practice, unable to play the game that he loved more than anything else, unable to be a part of the great Juddville Football Tradition, unable to fulfill his duties as team captain, and unable to think of one convincing reason why he should even go on living. Many would say that the captain of the Juddville football team had simply been guilty of being at the wrong place at the wrong time—though Coach Abraham's family might think otherwise. Once a third witness (Roger Collins) had come forward to corroborate Pete's story, however, he was officially cleared by the Juddville Police of all charges of assault—but only after sitting out from two days of practice.

By 7:30, Pete had arrived at the high school and was relieved to see that his padlock and the contents of his locker had not been vandalized. He was pleasantly surprised to see that more than a dozen teammates were already in the locker room, putting on their gear. Pete couldn't help but sense a bit of anxiety—or was it apprehension—in the air. Nevertheless, he couldn't wait for the official 8:00 meeting to begin. For as soon as the meeting was over, the Jaguars would be out on the field, ready to go to work.

After 45 minutes of presenting the offensive and defensive game plan, Coach Abraham dismissed the eager varsity football squad onto the practice field. Overall, the meeting was rather uneventful other than Adam Foster's unsuccessful attempt to sneak into the meeting room 25 seconds late. Coach Abraham had opted to deal with Foster individually after practice—if the Billington boy lasted that long. The vast majority of the team would have preferred that Adam never set foot on the Juddville practice field again.

On the way out to the field a few of his teammates couldn't resist the temptation to share a piece of their mind.

"Hey Adam, couldn't get here early enough to pee in Pete's locker again?" asked Steve Wilcox. "I ever catch you pimping someone's locker again, and I'll introduce you to my size 12 Reeboks. Just ask that friend of yours what my right foot feels like. I bet he is probably back in prison by now, singing soprano in the Prison Choir."

"I heard they like to rehearse while they're in the showers," added Roger Collins. "That'll give Evans some background music while he is picking bars of soap off the floor for all his boyfriends."

Adam shrugged off the comments, his head hanging downward, eyes hidden behind his droopy, brown bangs. Privately, he wished Josh Evans was back in prison, too. Unfortunately, due to prison over-crowding, his punishment was only an extension on his probation with a tether.

"You know we're playing at your old town next week, Adam. After the game, why don't you just stay in Billington?" said junior tight end Dan Hardings. "Lord knows you're a complete waste of space here in Juddville."

"Hold on there, Dan. We're not done with Adam yet, are we boys?" snickered Wilcox.

"I get first dibs on him today," said Roger. "Just wait till our first hitting drill, Adam."

In no time at all, Coach Abraham was blowing his whistle for the official warm up lap. Calisthenics and offensive individual drills went smoothly, and there was a noticeable increase in intensity, particularly with the linemen. As expected, Pete brought his exemplary effort to the 5-man sled, but there was a huge spike in the aggressiveness and enthusiasm of his fellow linemen, particularly Wilcox, Daniels, and Osborne. Coach Abraham had to hang onto the T-bar with both hands to keep from getting knocked off the sled.

During play review, the line walked through their blocking assignments versus a 4-4 defense. The Inside Trap was an easy scheme — most even front defensives were — but the Halfback Power and QB Keep presented some challenges to the offensive linemen and the halfbacks. For one, the Pennington defense liked to do a lot of stunting and angling. Consequently, the key blocking scheme for Juddville this week was "down blocking". For each play, they would be assigned a gap or area to block rather than a particular man. The scheme was relatively simple, but required lots of reps to master. Quickness off the ball and proper technique were key. Evidently, the runningbacks' individual time went satisfactorily, or perhaps the linemen were so focused that they never heard Coach Allen's voice from the other side of the field.

81

During the water break, Coach Allen handed Coach Abraham and Coach Oliver copies of the offensive play script. It contained a large proportion of inside traps and halfback powers, a handful of QB keeps and play action passes, and one counter. If team offense went smoothly, on Tuesday they might add a few new plays and even a trick play or two.

The offense performed remarkably, and with just ten minutes remaining of team offense, the 1st offense was on the last play of the script.

David Riley kneeled down on one knee in the middle of the huddle. "19 Bootleg on two... 19 Bootleg on two... Ready... Break!"

The Jaguars hustled to the line, anxious to execute one of David's favorite plays. He had mentally rehearsed his footwork, and prayed that Pete would remember to pull to his left rather than to the right. If the defense bit on the fake to the left halfback, he expected to see a lot of green in front of him. Nothing could have prepared him for what happened, however.

As Riley sunk his hips and extended his hands under center, he felt a tremor of immense proportion reverberate from the hindquarters of Craig Daniels. David was jolted backwards like he was shot out of a cannon.

"Nasty," shouted the senior signal caller, "Nasty..." frantically wiping the back of his hands on his pants. "Coach, Coach, can I go wash my hands? Daniels just..."

The rest of his words were drowned out by a thunderstorm of laughter. Coach Allen dropped to a knee, cradling his ribs as if his intestines were about to fall out. Coach Abraham's eyes were watering, and it had nothing to do with the 80 degree temperature either.

The youthful Coach Oliver was slapping his center a high five while shouting, "That's my boy, Craig. Linemen power. That's what I'm talking about..."

The Juddville offense re-huddled while Coach Allen regained his composure. Finally he said, "Let's have one more crack at that play, David."

The offense broke into hysterics again as David crossed his arms and wondered if they would be laughing so hard if they had to put their hands next to Daniels's buttocks.

About a minute later, the Jaguar offensive field general called the play and the offense broke from the huddle. Riley put his hands apprehensively under center and barked out the cadence. "Red 38... Red 38... Set... Go... Go...!"

David received the ball firmly into his hands, reverse-pivoted with his left foot as fullback Owens sprinted by on a fake smashing into the defensive tackle. Riley stretched out the ball to left halfback Bast, riding the fake handoff an extra count. Then he pulled the ball out and put it on his hip as he bootlegged to the left.

"Pass, pass," shouted Roger Collin's voice from the secondary. "Watch for the tight end on a drag."

Left guard O'Connor hit the rushing outside backer in the mid-section and then swung his hips around, executing a perfect hook block. David sprinted out to the open passing lane and waited for the tight end dragging across the formation.

The coverage on the drag route was tight, so David looked to the deep corner. Cox had a step on the corner but he was already too deep for his arm, so David took the third option and secured the ball under his left arm pit, running for a modest 7 yard gain. The inside linebacker caught David from behind.

"Water break," commanded Coach Abraham from his position on the defensive side of the ball. "You've got exactly two minutes. I want everybody to water up. Hubba... hubba..."

Roger jogged along side David on the way to the water trough.

"Can I give you a little advice on the bootleg, David?" asked Roger, an uncharacteristic tone of sincerity in his voice.

"Sure, Roger, I'll take all the help I can get."

Stopping about ten yards before the water, Roger simulated his hands being under center and crouched into a quarterback stance.

"When you make your fake to the halfback — in order to really sell the fake — turn your head back all the way around in the same direction the halfback is running. Then put the ball on your hip and sprint the opposite way... like there is no tomorrow. You should gain more time and space to throw, and the receiver dragging across the field should be wide open."

Then Roger demonstrated the head turn one more time saying, "Turn your head like this... and then run for your life."

A light bulb in David's head turned on as he comprehended Roger's coaching tip. Side by side they continued their conversation on the way to the water.

"Thank you, Roger. I really appreciate it. I'm a little nervous about our first game. I've never started before, and I am so paranoid about letting the team down."

After hearing David's admission, Roger dunked his head under the water spray, wishing he could go back and rewrite the past. If only he could replay his first week of practice where he had worked his way out of a starting quarterback position with his egocentric attitude. Moreover, he wished he could permanently blot out his decision to get so drunk out at Lakeside Park. He had become so intoxicated that he was unable to backup his teammate in a scuffle, opting to run for cover instead, leaving Pete all alone to respond to Julia Abraham's cry for help.

After taking a few gulps of water, Roger turned to David and said, "No matter how well you play, David, you'll be making a much greater contribution than me."

Coach Abraham blew his whistle, "White offense..."

"I'd give anything to be in that huddle right now," admitted Roger as they hustled back for the next segment of practice.

"Don't worry, Roger. Your time is coming. In two weeks, you'll have my job, and I'll be the one fighting for second string quarterback."

"What are you talking about? You're a natural leader, David. Just do what you do and take command in that huddle. All you need is more game experience, and Friday night, you're going to get it.

"And listen to me: don't worry if you throw an incompletion or bobble a snap. No one expects perfection. Even future Hall of Famer Denny Maxwell of the Los Angeles Bulldogs makes mistakes. It's part of the game. You've just got to shrug them off and go on to the next play. You're the leader out there, and you've got to remember that this team respects everything you do, David, and don't you forget it."

"Collins and Riley, stop your chit chatting and get your rear ends in the huddle," commanded Coach Abraham. "What do you think this is anyways, a Monday Morning Book Club?"

After running a total of six offensive plays with the White offense, Red offense was called back into their huddle for punt team. The coaches made a few substitutions. For the time being, Bryan Cox inherited the punting job. Roger's two week suspension probably hurt more in the punting department than at any other position. Bryan's form was inconsistent, but if he got a hold of it, he could kick the ball 30 yards downfield. Daniels, fortunately, was an excellent long snapper, so at least there shouldn't be any worries in that department. Hardings and O'Connor were still struggling to snap spirals, but they were getting better each week should something happen to Daniels.

Following a fairly uneventful team punting session, Coach Abraham lined up his players on the goal line. Today's conditioning consisted of ten 30 yard sprints, ten 20 yarders, and finally ten 10 yards sprints. The Jaguars were quite disciplined on this day, fortunately, and they had to only run two extra sprints. One was for Adam Foster jumping, and the other was for Mike Owens not having his mouth guard in place.

Because it was already 12:15, Coach Abraham brought his team together for post-practice comments.

"Men, it's all business now. We've got a game in four days and only three more days of practice. Pennington is a worthy opponent with an intelligent, hard working new coach. But we get to play them at our place. Today's practice was a pretty good one for a Monday, but we have to pick up the intensity, particularly in the hitting game. We have to get more physical on both sides of the ball. Many of you are fairly inexperienced, I know, but you have to take advantage of every single drill as an opportunity to get better. We have to be more aggressive blocking, we have to be more violent when fending off blocks on defense, and we have to be willing to come up and crush the running back when we tackle."

Coach Allen concurred with Coach Abraham, and also reminded his players to make sure they paid attention to all the details of their assignments.

Finally, the Juddville Head Coach called for all the players' hands in the middle of the huddle. His voice began to tremor as he barked out his closing remarks.

"Listen up, Jaguars. The battle approaches. It's either hit or be hit. The name of the game is HIT. On three. One... two... three..."

"Hit," shouted the 29 strong Juddville Jaguar team in unison.

Before leaving the field, Coach Abraham personally administered the mandatory bonus conditioning for the two suspended Jaguars. The workout included lunges, bear crawls, pushups, sit-ups, and last but not least, gassers. Both Adam and Roger gave great effort and wisely chose to keep their thoughts and opinions about their punishment to themselves.

Chapter Eleven

After Monday's grueling practice, Coach Allen was anxious to head home and take a refreshing plunge into his swimming pool. But at high noon, he was well-aware that his business at Juddville was far from over. The coaching staff would be meeting for at least an hour and half to go over game plan and personnel. Then Jim would have to check into his classroom to begin preparations for the coming school year. Tuesday morning was the official day for all teachers to report back to school. Many teachers had already started setting up their classrooms the previous week. Jim generally put off this task until the very last moment.

There was usually very little time for teachers to organize and to prepare their rooms on Tuesday and Wednesday, however. Tuesday's agenda would include an official welcome back meeting in the auditorium for all staff, including bus drivers, cooks, custodians, secretaries and paraprofessionals. Jim was curious as to how well the superintendent's opening remarks would be received. Dr. Jones was making quite a few enemies and not just amongst the football staff.

After his 20 minute speech, there would be the traditional state-mandated blood-borne pathogen video, followed by the annual teacher union meeting—it was a negotiation year again. Next, teachers would report to their specific building meetings. Lunch was a semi-jovial picnic at Farnsworth Elementary School. In the afternoon there might be an hour left for Jim to report to his middle school classroom to prepare his first week of lessons. Then it would be out to the practice field for the first afternoon practice of the season.

Wednesday would be meetings in the morning with about two hours of preparation time for teachers in the afternoon. On Thursday morning, the busses would be dropping off this year's new crop of students. At this point in the school year, life would become an intense balancing act. But this wasn't Jim's first time around the block, and who was going to feel sorry for him anyways? He just had the last three months off, after all.

The Juddville players had their own plans for Monday afternoon. At the insistence of Larry Moore and Gary Osborne, the first stop was Burger King. After a thorough sampling of all the major fat groups, the team was heading over to the beach for some swimming and obligatory sightseeing.

Pete had been planning on working out, but he knew that as one of the team captains, his attendance at the beach was mandatory. If he wolfed down a Whopper with Cheese or two and drank plenty of fluids this afternoon, he could always head over to the Body Shoppe after dinner for his upper body workout. After all, the cool Lake Michigan water sounded pretty good to him right now.

"Honey, I'm home," announced Keith as he walked into the living room, shutting the front door securely so as to prevent any of the broiling August temperature to infiltrate into their air-conditioned home.

He kept walking through the living room and into the kitchen. The lights were all off, not a single sign that anyone was home.

"Carol? Julia? Anyone home?"

Still no answer.

Now what am I supposed to do? thought Keith. He was planning on surprising Carol and Julia by taking them out to lunch. It would be his last opportunity of the summer. He had assumed that when he got home at 1:30, they would both still be home.

Why would they be home, you idiot? Do you really think they were expecting to see you before 6:00 during football season?

Keith decided to just grab a quick bite to eat, watch a little film on Pennington, and then maybe go for a 2 to 3 mile run. By then the women should be home. He was disappointed that they were not going to be able to go out for lunch, though.

Holding his breath and making a wish as he opened the refrigerator, he counted to three and slowly opened his eyes, praying that there were some leftovers that he could just pop into the microwave to satisfy his gnawing hunger. He was pleasantly surprised to see some leftover pot roast from Sunday sitting in a blue microwavable container. Perfect! He placed the container in the microwave and set the timer for a minute and a half. While his lunch was heating up, he poured a large glass of 1/2% milk.

In no time at all, his instant-ready feast was all set for takeoff. When he removed the lid, the savory beef and red skin potatoes were steaming. The smell was absolutely heavenly.

I wonder if the paper is here yet, thought Coach Abraham.

Keith decided to trot out to the mailbox — perhaps he could just count that as his run — and grab the paper while he allowed his lunch to cool off a bit. As he opened the front door, he noticed a car that he hadn't seen around the house in the last two weeks. A rusty, navy blue Chevy Nova. It was traveling at a snail's pace on the near side of the road. The driver was clearly staring at the Abraham residence.

Keith picked up his pace, heading directly towards the unwelcomed vehicle.

"F… you, Abraham," shouted the former Jaguar and ex-boyfriend of Julia.

Coach Abraham was almost to a full sprint, but he wasn't quite quick enough.

The loud, squealing tires were succeeded by a dense cloud of burnt rubber, and that was all that remained of the Abrahams' worst enemy by the time Keith reached the curb. He lifted his hands up to the sky and screamed out in frustration.

"Come back here, you worthless piece of crap," shouted Keith. As soon as the words had left his mouth, it dawned upon him how foolish he appeared right now to any of his neighbors who might be looking out their windows. Moreover, he became terrified to the bone as he imagined a number of scenarios that might have developed had Brian opted to turn around and accept his challenge:

Would I actually have taken a swing at Brian?
Would I have backed off and been the responsible adult?
What would the reaction have been of Carol… and Julia?
Would a physical confrontation have been worth the possibility of getting arrested, fingerprinted, and hung out to dry once again by the media?

Keith concluded that what he really needed right now was a 3 to 4 mile run to burn off some aggression and to get right with God. This conflict was way too big for him to handle alone. There was far too much at stake: his daughter's physical and emotional well-being, the defense of his family's reputation and honor, as well as Keith's prospects for continued employment as a teacher and head football coach for Juddville Public Schools.

The 4 mile run was torturous, as usual, and it didn't provide him with any quick, easy solutions to his current troubles. Nonetheless, Keith did feel a significant measure of peace in his heart, mind, and soul. Throughout the run, as he continued to plead to God for a quick and decisive intervention, God's singular reply was very quiet and very simple:

Trust me, Keith. Just trust me.

After a quick shower that failed to adequately cool him off—so much so that he had to walk around with a towel wrapped around his neck to continuously wipe off the perspiration that would reappear on his forehead every 5 to 10 seconds—Keith found the plate of leftovers and reheated them a second time in the microwave.

Feeling alone and bored, he opted for what came naturally to him at this time of the year whenever he had a half hour or more of free time: watching film. Grabbing the scrimmage tape from his briefcase, Keith descended to the lonely confines of his basement to study the Pennington Pirates.

The Pirate offense clearly revolved around their talented junior quarterback, Seth Howell. He had height, 6'3"; speed, rumor had it 4.5 in the 40; and a gun, he could throw the ball 50 yards on a rope. His favorite receiver was #83, Alex Matthews, who had decent speed, ran great routes, and wasn't afraid to go up for the ball in traffic.

Their favorite offensive set was the off-set I with a flanker and a split end. They liked to throw short passes from a 3-step drop. Howell would take the snap, quick step with his right, cross-over step with his left, plant with his right and throw — making it next to impossible for a defensive line to get to the QB in time to affect his throw.

Matthews's favorite route was a simple yet precise 5 yard hitch. He would plant with his outside foot, turn sharply to the inside, coming back to meet the ball already in flight. His hands would extend out in front of his body to welcome the ball into his possession; then he would spin towards the sideline and accelerate like a deer running for its life.

Once the defense started to cheat up and try to take away the hitch, the Pirates would go for the jugular and throw the deep fade. Matthews would stutter step like he was going to pull up for the hitch and then open up his hips and break towards the sidelines on a deep banana route. Howell would pump fake and throw the ball to a spot about 30 to 35 yards upfield.

In Coach Abraham's 25 years of coaching, he hadn't seen too many quarterbacks with as much pin-point accuracy and poise as the Pennington quarterback. Keith was quite certain that the Jaguars did not have a defensive back who could match up with their favorite receiver. They might have to consider doubling up on Matthews as a result — at least on definite passing downs.

Looking at the diminutive size of Pennington's offensive line, Keith wasn't too concerned about their running game. It looked like their center couldn't weigh more than 170 pounds soaking wet. Nose tackle Greg MacDonald ought to have a hay day steamrolling him. A couple of monstrous hits on the snapper early in the game might be enough to disrupt the quarterback's timing and confidence the rest of the night. MacDonald was a stud wrestler who knew all about leverage and leg drive. If he could get under the center's pads, Coach Abraham was certain that the center would be backpedaling or falling straight back into the quarterback's lap. Their running backs were extremely average, at best, but they did have a player who didn't dress for the scrimmage, and he looked like he could be "seriously-athletic".

On his legal pad, Coach Abraham jotted down the following notes:
- Double up on Matthews in obvious passing situations.
- Pressure the quarterback by giving the center the beating of his life.

Coach Abraham would assign Coach Oliver the responsibility of making sure their nose tackle was primed for demolition duty on Friday night. He was quite sure Gary would be ecstatic about this coaching responsibility, and he was equally confident that MacDonald would be licking his chops over his assignment for game one. As for the Pennington Pirate center, best of luck Friday night.

The final challenge was stopping the running game. Their favorite running plays were the toss sweep, the fullback trap, and the halfback power. None of their rushing plays had much success in the scrimmage. Their most successful running play had been a 30 yard sprint draw that caught their opponent off-guard while they were backed off in pass coverage. The linebackers had read pass and began dropping back to their hook zones, and a gaping hole emerged. The receivers ran off the defensive backs and then became blockers once the defense read run. The strong safety had the best angle to bring down the halfback, but he couldn't shed the tight end's block.

As far as the rest of the defensive game plan, Keith was leaning toward playing a lot "vanilla" or base defense. A lot of stunting would probably not be very effective because they still wouldn't be able to get to the quarterback in time, and the linebackers would be needed to shut down the passing attack by filling hook zones and by impeding crossing patterns.

For the next two hours, Keith studied his opponent, rewinding and playing, rewinding and playing, rewinding and playing, analyzing, memorizing, digesting, hypothesizing, what-if-ing until his eyelids became so heavy that he fell asleep with the remote still in his hand.

At 5:30, Carol found him still asleep, the TV on, the screen nothing but snow. She decided to let him sleep a little longer, for he had endured many sleepless nights over the last two weeks.

Chapter Twelve

Tuesday was a grueling day for Coach Allen and Coach Abraham. Sitting in teacher meetings all day from 8:00 until 2:45, and then heading out to the sun-scorched practice field for three hours was the equivalent of holding two jobs. The coaches talked shop while they changed into their coaching attire.

"Let's spend a little more time on punt team today," said Coach Abraham. "We need to make sure we give them plenty of reps this week. Bryan will do fine if we give him enough opportunities to gain confidence."

Coach Allen responded, "Normally, we wouldn't worry so much about our punt team before the Pennington game, but I think we need to assume they'll be out on the field once or twice. Field position will be critical in defending against their passing attack. If we can keep them backed up in their own end, they might be more hesitant to throw the ball."

"I agree, Jim. If we can take care of the ball and not give up any costly turnovers, we can dictate the flow of the game. It all comes down to the trenches. I am pretty confident in our line. I am going to work them pretty hard today. That's for sure."

"You ready, Coach Oliver?" asked Coach Allen.

"You bet, Coach."

"How did your first official day of student teaching go?" asked Keith.

"Pretty good. I am looking forward to working with Mr. Peterson. He's hilarious."

"Yeah, maybe you can teach him a few new jokes. His jokes are older than Pi," quipped Jim.

"Ha... That must be some of that math humor," commented Keith. "Enough of this school talk, let's get ready to kick Pennington's butt."

Individual offensive time was brief but intense. The offensive line spent most of the time in the chute, firing out low against shields while keeping a wide base as they progressed down the eight-foot long rubber boards.

"Go again, Wilcox. You're too slow. You can't expect to move anyone when you are going half-speed," exclaimed Coach Abraham.

Steve sighed and got back into his stance as three fresh linemen joined him.

"Right shoulder block on two," shouted Coach Oliver who was positioned behind the drill in order to make sure each player's footwork was correct.

"Set Hit... Hit!"

"Short, choppy steps," shouted Coach Abraham, "wide feet, wide feet... hands inside, hands inside."

Finally, as they progressed to the end of the boards, Coach Oliver yelled, "Finish."

And the four blockers lifted the shield upwards and rolled their hips forward, attempting to pancake their teammate holding the blocking shield.

"That's the way to get pancakes, men," shouted Coach Abraham. "And you've got to be violent!"

"Next group, face to the right. Bucket step with your left. 36 Trap. What shoulder?" asked Coach Oliver.

"Left shoulder," responded the linemen in unison.

"On one. Fire out now. Explode into the shield," commanded Coach Oliver.

Fifteen minutes in the chute, and the line was exhausted. After a 30 second water break, they reviewed their basic blocking schemes versus a 4-4 defense and any basic adjustments should they see any 5-2.

At 4:00, the tight ends split from the line and joined the backs for passing. Coach Abraham went with the tight ends while Coach Oliver stayed with the interior linemen who were engaged in fierce one-on-one battles in a pass blocking drill.

A half hour later, the team joined together for 40 minutes of team offense. Coach Abraham coached the scout defense. He had one inside linebacker stunting every play, and on occasion brought the corners inside and stacked them behind the outside LBs in 5-4 look.

For the most part, the offensive line picked up the stunts. On more than one occasion, the backfield was reprimanded for not carrying out their fakes.

"Riley, you have to sprint as fast as you can for the sideline every single play. Just like you would if you had the ball."

"Owens, keep those legs of yours pumping and get to that end zone. If you don't draw at least one defender, we will never be able to run the ball outside."

Overall, the running game looked pretty sharp. The play action passing game, however, was abysmal. Riley, could not throw the football. His best passes were wobbly, and he was not confident in his decision making. Coach Allen fervently prayed that they would not have to throw the football against Pennington, but if the Pirates brought nine in the box, they might not have a choice.

After team offense, Coach Allen coached the scout offense against the starting defense. Coach Abraham had all of Pennington's plays drawn out on 8 by 10 ½ manila cards. The reserves just had to locate their position on the card and then carry out the assignment as illustrated. Most of the players were playing their normal position, but sometimes a player was asked to play out of position.

A good scout team is a key component in the success of a football program. An effective scout team requires a minimum of eleven capable players who are mentally and physically tough. Of even greater importance, however, is humility, for scout team players seldom receive any credit for their labor as they sacrifice their bodies to simulate the opponent's offense and defense. Through their unselfish contributions, the starters are in a much better position to succeed during crunch time. If a scout team is physically weak and fails to adequately execute the upcoming foe's best offensive and defensive plays, the starters will invariably find themselves "shell-shocked" by the strength, speed, and execution of their opponent come Friday night.

Since Riley would be rotating in on defense and his backup quarterback, junior Don Jacobs, was the starting strong safety, Roger Collins inherited the role of scout team quarterback. Fortunately, it was a role for which Roger was well-suited; in fact, he was the only quarterback on the team with enough arm to even come close to simulating the Pennington Pirate Top Gun.

While Roger Collins assumed the role of the Pennington Pirate quarterback, Adam Foster — also under a two-game suspension — inherited the role of playing their top receiver, Alex Matthews.

What Adam could provide was decent speed and agility, with hands that were a bit shaky. The first time the scout team ran a 5 yard hitch, as soon as he planted his outside foot to turn back towards the quarterback, the ball nearly knocked his helmet off.

Normally, the quarterback would be slightly irritated by a receiver who was not prepared to catch a perfectly thrown ball. Roger, however, was snickering. The non-reaction of the Juddville Offensive Coordinator was completely out of character.

"You might want to get your hands ready a little sooner next time, Adam," said Coach Allen with a look of disdain on his face. "Good thing you were wearing a helmet or that ball might have drilled a hole through your face."

The Billington transfer glared at Coach Allen, choosing to remain silent rather than incur further verbal abuse.

The next two plays were running plays, and then Coach Allen called a hitch-and-go. Mike Owens was covering Adam in man coverage with help over the top from free safety Tommy Schulz.

As Adam lowered his hips as if to plant and turn back towards the QB, Roger pump-faked. Owens bit badly on the fake, going for the pick, and Schulz was slow to slide over. Meanwhile, Foster had quickly spun to the outside, opening up to full throttle, with no defensive back within 10 yards. Roger threw a perfect spiral, hitting Foster right on his fingertips.

Much to the surprise of his entire team—and to the dismay of the defense—Adam miraculously brought the ball in and sprinted the remaining 10 yards to the end zone. When he got back to the huddle, Coach Allen thought for a moment that he recognized a smile on Foster's face.

That's a first, thought Jim.

Roger Collins gave a nod of approval to his receiver. There was no denying that the boy from Billington had just run a great route and had made an even greater catch.

And the best part of it all was that the defense just got better. The scout team had shown them exactly what would happen on Friday night if both the corner and free safety bit on a double move.

Coach Allen was silent as the scout offensive huddle reconvened. The wheels were turning as he thought about some options he might have for putting points on the board two weeks down the road. Perhaps, the Juddville Jaguar offensive playbook might have to expand in the near future. Defensive coordinators were becoming pretty adept at shutting down their Wing-T offense. Perhaps, it was time to supplement their running game with a new package of passing plays.

After team defense and a much-deserved water break, the Jaguars broke into special teams. Bryan Cox's punts were inconsistent. The majority were end-over-end, traveling 20 to 25 yards in the air. About one-in-five would come off his foot with a perfect spiral, sailing 35 to 40 yards with excellent hang time. The bright spot on the punt team was that Craig Daniels was an all-pro snapper. He could snap the ball on a line with enough mustard on the ball to jam a finger. It would be next to impossible for a team to block a punt without the punter bobbling the snap.

Special teams was followed by conditioning. Players were divided into defensive groups to run gassers— two times across the field and back equaled one gasser. The defensive line ran with Coach Oliver, the linebackers with Coach Abraham, and the defensive backs with Coach Allen. If all the players ran their gassers in the assigned times, they only had to run four. The defensive line had to run under 50 seconds. The linebackers had to run under 40 seconds. The secondary had to break 35 seconds.

The defensive line was led by MacDonald and Smith, but severely handicapped by Moore and Osborne. The entire group would have to run an extra gasser because of their slow times. The linebackers were led, of course, by Pete O'Connor. None of the linebackers dared to miss their time for obvious reasons.

The biggest excitement came in the defensive back group, and it had nothing to do with who was last or who didn't make their required times. The first gasser was won by Adam Foster which prompted Coach Allen to call out a few of his starters, particularly Owens, Jacobs, and Schulz. Making matters worse, Roger Collins finished second for the DBs. Not one of his starting defensive backs finished in the top two.

After a minute rest, the second gasser ensued, and again the winner was Adam Foster. This time the one who was ticked off wasn't Coach Allen; it was Roger Collins. On the plus side, however, all of the DBs made their time.

On the third gasser, Roger earned his revenge, beating Adam by two steps. For the fourth and final gasser, Coach Allen issued a challenge:

"Whoever doesn't finish in the top two, does twenty bonus pushups. Just for fun, of course."

Coach Allen was baffled by the sudden display of extreme competitiveness in Collins and Foster; at the same time, he was annoyed by the inability of his starting defensive back unit to finish in the top two.

Mike Owens and David Riley were neck-and-neck with about 20 yards to the finish line. In the last 5 yards, Mike pulled ahead of David. Unfortunately for both, they were nearly five yards behind Roger and Adam who crossed the sideline simultaneously.

"All right DBs, up position. Count 'em out, you've got 20," announced Coach Allen with great pleasure.

Mike Owens, David Riley, Jeff Nash, Don Jacobs, and Tommy Schulz were wise not to complain.

As the rest of the Jaguars completed their last gasser, the enthusiasm grew contagious. As usual, the linemen finished last, so the defensive backs and linebackers were congregated around the finish line to cheer on Osborne and Moore.

"Come on Ox," shouted Pete. "You're almost there. Don't let the Beast beat you."

"Here comes the Ox. You'd better pick it up, Big Larry. As they reached down and touched the far sideline, they both looked like they could collapse at any second. Larry took an extra few seconds to get started again. Osborne was quicker in transition. He quickly jumped five yards ahead of Larry.

But Big Larry had a little more left in the tank. When he reached the final hashmark, he kicked it into a gear no one had seen before and just flat out sprinted by the Ox for the victory. Both players were congratulated for their efforts by their teammates — even by the other defensive linemen who had to run an extra gasser on their behalf.

"Bring it in, men," commanded Coach Abraham. "Excellent finish. Excellent finish. That kind of effort in the fourth quarter will win us a lot of ball games this year."

"Beat Pennington, on three..." shouted the head coach. "One, two, three..."

"BEAT PENNINGTON!"

On the drive home from practice, Coach Allen's mind was racing fast forward. From an offensive standpoint, today's practice was adequate. The line was firing out with strength and purpose. Mike was hitting the hole with authority and speed. The two halfbacks, Bast and Nash, were playing with confidence.

Everything was just rosy, except...the most important position on the field. Without question, Friday night's starting quarterback was clearly outplayed by a player under suspension for the first two weeks. The biggest weakness of David Riley was his arm. Second was his lack of speed, and it was pretty clear to everyone on the team that he wasn't going to outrun too many players this year.

It was at times like this that Coach Allen had to literally force his mind to think positively. With the exception of Pete O'Connor, who else had leadership potential on this team? David. Who was smart enough to understand the big picture of their offense? David. Who was least likely to have any on-or-off-the-field character breakdowns? David.

When it came to the intangibles of the quarterback position, David scored exceedingly well. But when it came to playmaking skills, he was woefully deficient.

Tomorrow's practice was defensive emphasis. At the end of the practice, the offense would have about 30 minutes to polish.

On Friday night, Coach Allen figured the offense would need to put 14 points on the board in order to win. He expected the defense to hold Pennington to one or two scores.

By the time Coach Allen had reached home, he was semi-relaxed and breathing normally, and he was looking forward to one of Mary's home cooked meals. Perhaps, she had whipped up a turkey casserole or a pot of steaming, spaghetti seasoned with just the right amount of basil and fresh garlic. After a gut-busting meal, he could soak in the pool and reconnect with his kids while his eyelids fought the inevitable gravitational pull.

Unfortunately, he was in no way prepared for the chaos that awaited him. Luke was the first to bare bad news, greeting him in the garage as soon as he opened the door to the minivan.

"Daddy, Daddy, guess what Freckles did. Guess what Freckles did."

Jim was reluctant to make a guess. He feared that whatever he would say would quadruple the drama, and he was absolutely petrified of how he might respond once the pet crisis was divulged.

"She peed in the house, didn't she?"

"Nope, she dug a huge hole in the yard," confessed Luke, "but Mom says that you can't be mad... she says it's just part of having a pet."

"Did anyone fill in the hole?"

"Mom says you might want to take a look at the sprinkler head first."

"What? Are you kidding me?" screamed Jim. "She'd better not have touched a sprinkler head."

Setting down his Juddville duffle bag, he headed straight through the garage to the backyard. The hole wasn't difficult to locate. Picking up his pace to a brisk jog, he was hovering above the crime scene in a matter of seconds.

Jim sank to his knees and brushed away the dirt surrounding the sprinkler head. He could see that the cap was removed and its shape was so contorted that it would never be able to snap back onto its rightful place. The tubular chamber was also ruined. Four of Freckles teeth were sharp enough to puncture the head. When he grabbed the head to see if it was still securely attached, he felt it wiggle.

After attempting to tighten the head by turning it clockwise, it became immediately apparent that not only was the head ruined, but it would spring such a leak—more like a fountain—that he would have to shut off the entire sprinkling system until he could replace the head. And he was quite sure the hardware store would not still be open at the current time of 7:30 p.m.

"Damn it," shouted Jim, forgetting to look behind him to see if Luke had followed him out to the backyard.

"Oops," muttered Jim, as he saw the backside of Luke sprinting towards the house.

"Mommy, Mommy... Daddy said a bad word. Daddy said a bad word, Mommy."

Great, thought Jim, *so much for a peaceful night at home. Keep away from me, stinking dog... if you want to live to see your next birthday.*

Pete was absolutely giddy after their second day of preparation for the Pennington Pirates. Instead of rushing off the practice field to workout in the school weight room, he chose to hangout in the locker room and chew the fat with his teammates. After a half hour of listening to all the boasting and bantering, he strolled home from practice, deep in thought over the state of his team.

Offense had gone exceptionally well, and the defense was coming together. He was a little bit nervous about how well their secondary would hold up against the Pirates' passing attack. He would feel a lot more confident if Roger Collins was eligible to play.

Normally, to be mentally prepared to start at one position was a lot to expect from a sophomore. Mike Owens was not only being expected to carry the brunt of the load in the offensive backfield, he was now going to be asked to play strong corner on defense—and against a team that liked to throw the ball around.

This week's opponent was going to be Juddville's first test, but the real test would come the following week on the road against their rivals, the Billington Bulldogs.

Nevertheless, Pete was well-aware of the age-old adage "You gotta play 'em one game at a time." And this week's game against Pennington was case in point. As a matter of fact, it didn't really matter who they were playing this week. He just couldn't wait to crush someone of a different color jersey.

Speaking of crushing someone, thought Pete, *isn't that Adam Foster up ahead?*

As Pete turned into the trailer park, he saw Adam turn left onto Strawberry Lane. He decided to follow him to find out where he lived. Foster was becoming an enigma of sorts on the Jaguar football team. Just when he had become so despicable that nearly every player on the team wanted to strangle him, he shocks everyone by having an amazing practice by displaying extraordinary hustle and playmaking ability.

Suddenly, Adam turned his head sharply around and stared back at Pete. The thought of catching up to his teammate crossed his mind, but then he remembered the urine soaked practice pants at the bottom of his locker, and the nasty loogie Adam had left on his padlock the first week of practice. Moreover, Pete could never forget how irate he had become when he found out that Adam had attempted to steal his brand new Keith Karchinski UFL jersey.

Forgive? That would take some time. Forget? That was an impossibility. Yet, the two boys shared one thing in common: they both had lived in Billington. For Adam, the connection was of grave significance. Pete, however, was surprisingly oblivious to any connection to Adam. For some mysterious reason, he was unable to connect the dots between their pasts.

As Pete approached his trailer at the corner of Apple and Strawberry Lane, he slowly turned up the driveway, taking his time so he could observe what direction his teammate was taking next. Adam continued to the next road, which was Pear Lane, and turned left.

Once he was out of sight, Pete walked up the steps of his porch. Fully aware that his mother was at work, as she always was during the evenings on Sunday through Thursday, Pete hoped that dinner would be waiting for him in the oven. As he opened the front door, he could smell one of his favorite meals coming from the kitchen.

He threw open the oven door and his suspicions were confirmed.

Chicken enchiladas. Ah... the intoxicating scent of rich tomato sauce and melted cheddar cheese smothering tortillas stuffed with spicy chicken.

Pete couldn't wait to take his first bite. He grabbed a large glass from the cupboard and poured a large glass of milk. Next, was a knife and fork from the silverware drawer, and in no time at all he was in heaven.

On Coach Abraham's way home from practice, he had one important stop to make.

In a way, it was an appointment... proactive ... premeditated. Keith Abraham had resolved to no longer sit back and let fate have its way. Not when it affected someone so dear to him... someone so vulnerable. No longer would his evil adversary be given free rein to torment his family.

The rules were about to change. From now on, to get to Julia, Brian Taylor would have to go through Coach Abraham. Consequently, this "defensive" coordinator was going to change his strategy and go on the "offensive".

The Sub Shoppe was located on the outskirts of Juddville. As Keith pulled into the parking lot, he immediately spotted a navy blue Chevy Nova, the same vehicle he had briefly encountered in his neighborhood the day before. He pulled up next to it and parked.

Picking up the typed message from the passenger seat, his body temperature began to rise, and he had to wipe the sweat from his brow with his forearm. It was Do-or-Die time. Throughout the course of the day, he had doubted whether he would actually have the guts to go ahead with it. But now here he was. The moment of truth.

Keith grabbed the 8 ½ by 11 paper. After proofreading it one more time, he folded it into quarters. Then he opened his car door and stealthily walked over to Brian's car, slipping the note underneath his windshield wiper. Next, he turned and headed for the store's entrance.

When he opened the door, a gush of cool air brought a welcomed relief to his perspiring body. Three people were in line to place orders. As a result, Brian didn't see Keith right away.

He didn't bother to look at a menu. He wasn't here for dinner — he had a higher purpose in mind — but he was thirsty. To the left of the counter was a cooler six feet tall filled with an assortment of Pepsi beverages.

He felt the urge.

Why not, thought Coach Abraham, *a Mountain Dew would taste great right now. Haven't had one of those in over a decade.*

Without a moment's hesitation, Keith strolled over to the cooler and grabbed a bottle of liquid gold before returning to his spot in the back of the line.

Five minutes of waiting patiently and he was face-to-face with his enemy. His rehearsed sneer was ready for show time.

"May I help you," asked Brian in a raspy voice, a noticeable bluish-yellow tint beneath both eyes, the lingering after-effects of a couple of Pete O'Connor roundhouses.

Keith leaned forward, allowing his laser-like eyes to sear directly into the skull of his daughter Julia's former boyfriend.

"No, as a matter of fact, young man… I'm just here to offer you a little friendly advice…"

Followed by an awkward stillness… After several seconds had transpired, the Coach delivered his short but poignant message:

"Stay away from Julia or the worst is yet to come. If you think Pete gave you a beating…"

Before Keith had the opportunity to finish his sentence, a pair of customers entered the store.

Without turning to see whom it might be, Coach Abraham wisely altered his dialogue with Brian Taylor.

"I'll just have this Mountain Dew."

"That'll be 78 cents," responded the distressed assistant manager.

As Keith collected his 22 cents in change, he turned and literally bumped into a close friend who was accompanied by his wife.

"Pastor Jenkins," said Coach Abraham, "Your turn to cook tonight?"

"How could you tell?" laughed Larry.

"I guess it's better than the alternative. Isn't that right, Marilyn?" responded Keith.

"Oh, you'd be surprised, Keith. Larry is actually a magician on the grill. It's just a little muggy for a barbecue tonight," coming to her husband's defense.

"On a liquid diet tonight?" asked Pastor Jenkins. "Hitting the caffeine pretty early this season, aren't we?"

"Oh, every once in awhile I've got to breakdown and have a Dew."

Lowering his voice, Pastor Jenkins whispered, "How are Carol… and Julia?"

Keith's face turned crimson. He turned 180 degrees towards Brian who was still positioned by the cash register.

At the same moment, the reverend made a quick recognition—after all, his face had been prominently displayed on the front page of the Juddville Gazette. With a puzzled look, Larry inquired nonchalantly, "That's him, isn't it?"

Coach nodded. "We'll talk later, Pastor. Carol will throw me out if I hold up dinner much longer."

"I understand, Keith. I completely understand. Give me a call when you've got a spare minute. You hear?"

"I will, Larry. As soon as I get the chance."

As soon as Keith was outside of the Sub Shoppe he gasped for air. *What am I doing? Is this anyway for a grown man to act?*

Without a moment of hesitation, Coach Abraham retrieved the note from Brian's windshield, crumpling it into a ball and shoving it into his front pocket. The note would have been redundant and foolhardy. Even still, he had looked his enemy in the eye and had spoken his peace. And if Brian refused to go away? Things could get messy. Things could get messy, indeed.

Chapter Thirteen

Wednesday morning came awfully quick. Coach Abraham had slept horribly. Every time he awakened, it would take 15 minutes for him to fall back asleep, and the cycle seemed to repeat itself on the hour, every hour, throughout the entire night. When his alarm clock went off at 5:30, it seemed he had barely slept at all. He was tempted to hit the snooze button a few times and sleep until 6:30, but he knew he had an appointment that he could not afford to miss.

Tuesday had been disastrous. As a result, Keith's conscience was taking a severe beating: accusations about his conduct at the Sub Shoppe, accusations about his motives as a coach and as a father, accusations about his enormous ego, and accusations questioning his sanity.

What was I thinking? Sure, Brian Taylor is a good-for-nothing, low life. And yes, he had tried to force himself on Julia two weeks ago when she was in a drunken stupor. But what kind of grown man goes out into the public looking for trouble?

Nevertheless, Keith couldn't help but derive a certain amount of pleasure just fantasizing about taking a few swings at his daughter's worst nightmare.

His team… now that was a thought that seemed to have eluded him this morning—approximately 60 hours from game time. Normally during a game week, he would be obsessed with the task of making sure that every possible detail was taken care of and every possible scenario that could arise during the football game would be covered and covered thoroughly. This was certainly not the year for him to become lax in his duties, not with this team's lack of experience.

Before focusing his attention on Wednesday's practice plans, Keith filled up his trustworthy chestnut brown mug with a cup of Maxwell House coffee. Then he opened his Bible to the place he had bookmarked: the 2nd book of Corinthians, Chapter 4.

Keith remembered underlining the passage with his blue ballpoint pen. After rereading it again, he closed his eyes and tried to think deeply about the words that were written so long ago by the Apostle Paul.

I am definitely hard pressed right now. My family… my coaching… my relationships… even my sanity. But it says right here that I've got a treasure. The gift of the Holy Spirit. This old body of mine is just a broken-down vessel made out of clay. What's truly important is what's inside.

The more Coach Abraham meditated on this promise, the more solace he received. As he went back to this passage, he latched onto the encouragement of verse 16:

"Therefore we do not lose heart. Though outwardly we are wasting away, yet inwardly we are being renewed day by day."

Lord, I feel like I am truly wasting away. This clay vessel is literally crumbling to pieces. I am desperate, God. I am so desperate for you to renew me this day, by your power that lives in me. Without you, I am hopelessly lost.

As Coach Allen began to back out of his driveway in his navy blue minivan, he put his foot on the break abruptly, and shifted into park. He opened the driver's door and sprinted through the garage and into the house. Sitting by the Mr. Coffee maker was a nearly-forgotten travel mug filled with piping-hot Seattle's Best coffee.

Back on the road again, Jim was beginning to feel the pressure. Starting the day with teacher/staff meetings, followed by a couple of hours of classroom preparation, and finishing with the last major practice before the season opener.

Wednesday was primarily a defensive day. Hopefully, the individual time would be brief, intense, and without any unexpected surprises out of his defensive backs. After a defensive pass skeleton session with the inside linebackers, they would run a brief team defensive session against the scout offense. Normally, they would spend most of this time versus the run, but since Pennington was more of a passing team they would probably mix up the plays about 50/50.

The last major segment of practice would be team offense. Normally, it is a quick run through to make sure the line and backs were all on the same page with their blocking assignments and blitz pickups.

The big question was the game-readiness of Juddville's offense. Would the line and backfield execute as one? Would David Riley be able to lead the offense in the heat of battle? What about runningback Mike Owens? How would the sophomore hold up as a starter on both sides of the ball?

As Jim got closer to school, his focus zoomed in on teaching preparations—his real job. On Tuesday, he had accomplished next to nothing in his classroom. Today, he would have to hang up posters and bulletin board decorations, and he would have to make sure that all his lesson plans and instructional materials were good to go for Thursday and Friday.

After a middle school staff meeting at 10:00, the rest of the day he was free to work in his room. Naturally, some of the time would be spent getting caught up with the rest of the staff, enjoying a few good laughs, and etc. He would probably have to do lunch on his own which would provide him a half hour to make a few last minute adjustments to the practice plan.

Overall, Jim was feeling pretty optimistic about the new school year, as well as the young football season. They had performed well in the scrimmage, and he was certain they would be able to compete with every opponent on their schedule. But if he was to be completely honest with himself, with so many of last year's state championship players graduated, there wasn't going to be as much pressure for this team to get back to the state finals—not external pressure anyway.

Yet the question that always haunted Coach Allen going into a new season was this: would he be able to keep his composure during times of adversity, during times when everything seemed to be going wrong, during times when he wanted to strangle someone? If so, then everything should turnout just fine.

Who am I kidding? thought Jim. *As soon as Owens fumbles the ball or Riley throws up a duck, I am going to go ballistic. It's inevitable. The only thing that's changed is that Luke, Kevin, and Katie are getting to the age where they're studying everything I do. And that could only spell trouble.*

On Pete's last day of freedom, he lounged around the trailer, bored out of his mind, extremely antsy for the beginning of Wednesday's football practice. It was a pleasant August summer day; the thermometer reading 75 degrees at noon.

If his single-minded devotion to the sport of football wasn't so strong, he would have opted for one last trip to the beach. But there was no way he could take the chance of sapping his energy prior to the last workday of game week. Last year it wouldn't have been such a big deal as a scout team player. Now things were different. Not only was he a starter, he was a starter on both sides of the ball. In fact, he might not even see the sideline at all.

In two days, Pete would find out whether his conditioning this summer had been sufficient. In the mean time, he was going to make sure that he did all the right things. He was going to adequately hydrate himself, drinking so much water, in fact, that he would have to visit the bathroom every other hour. This morning he had consumed his usual portion of Cheerios with a sliced banana. Now as he prepared lunch, he was about to consume two peanut butter sandwiches, two nectarines, and a large glass of milk.

His emotions were so overcharged he thought he was going to start sweating Jaguar blue out of his pores. All morning long he was strutting around in his #54 New Jersey Dragon jersey, the jersey that was sent to him by his all-time favorite football player Keith Karchinski.

Once the temperature in the trailer had escalated to 80 degrees, he had to strip off the jersey and exchange it for a cut-off tee shirt. Another reason Pete was particularly excited was that today after practice they would be receiving their brand new home jerseys. Furthermore, Coach Abraham had assured him that he would have first dibs on #54 if he wanted it.

Last season, when Pete had been playing backup linebacker and scout team runningback, his number was 22. Having the honor of wearing the number of the UFL's greatest linebacker was fair compensation for having to move from the backfield to the line.

After inhaling his lunch, he went out on the porch to check if the mail and/or newspaper had arrived yet. At the very least, he had to get outside, or he was going to go nuts. A short stroll around the park might be just what he needed to release some of his pent-up anxiety.

Pete opted to walk to the end of Strawberry Lane and then take Lemon over to Blueberry and then circle back home on Apple. It was about a half a mile; fortunately, there was enough shade to keep from getting scorched.

For the most part, life in the trailer park was relatively peaceful at this time of day. Most of the adults were either at work or sleeping. The majority of the kids were probably gorging themselves upon one last marathon of cartoons and videogames or by swimming in the pool.

As Pete strolled through the neighborhood, he was amazed by how quickly the last seven years had passed. He remembered how he had once thought the trailer park was so gigantic — almost like a small town. Now that he was a senior in high school, everything seemed so pathetically small and compact.

He really couldn't complain much about the neighborhood, though. It was all his mom could afford. It had been relatively safe and had provided a few friends over the years to play pickup games of football, basketball, and baseball. But now he felt a compelling need to stretch out his wings and find out how the rest of the world lived. This season, he hoped, would provide him with a one-way ticket out of Juddville.

When he reached the corner of Blueberry and Peach, he was nearly run over by teammate Adam Foster on his bicycle. In every single one of Pete's experiences with Adam, he never had been able to make even a semblance of eye contact with him.

On this occasion, there was no exception as Pete's teammate continued to ride past him albeit at a slower pace.

"Hey Adam, where are you off to in such a hurry? Wait up."

His teammate slowed down and turned to look back at Pete.

A thick blanket of silence occupied the space between them. Pete deemed the latest actions of his teammate as par for the course; he had never met anyone so antisocial.

Not sure how to go about starting up a conversation with a brick wall, Pete said, "Did you know I used to live in Billington?"

Adam's reaction was strange, to say the least. He turned his head in the opposite direction of Pete and pedaled his bike as if he were being chased by a pack of ravenous wolves.

Am I missing something? Pete thought to himself. *You'd think he'd be happy to find someone who…*

Two-thirty could not have come sooner. Coach Abraham looked around his classroom. He had certainly accomplished more than he did yesterday. All of his favorite posters were hanging up.

Over in the corner where his desk was located, he hung his "My Way or No Way" poster; the message was beneath a daunting close-up of a grim-faced, silver back gorilla. His other main-stay posters were his bright, neon-pink "Success Comes in Cans, Not in Can Nots"; his "What is right is not always popular; what is popular is not always right"; and his classic "Never ever quit".

His desktop was remarkably clean and organized. His handout for the first day—student expectations and objectives for the semester—were printed and ready to go. His class roster was in chronological order and stapled together in one packet. Prominently displayed by his desk was his state championship team photo from last season. Less conspicuous were the photo of Keith and his wife and the individual shots of his two daughters. He wished he had a recent photo of all four of them together. They would have to rectify this and have a family photo taken this Christmas or whenever Mary was able to come home for a visit from New York.

He leaned back in his chair and looked around the room, reflecting for a moment on the number of hours he had invested in this classroom. How many times had he had prepared this room for the first day of school? Twenty-six. Not surprisingly, he put less energy and less change into the room's appearance each year. He hadn't ordered a new poster in a decade. Why waste the tax payers' money?

Nevertheless, the room did have a positive atmosphere. That was what mattered most. It certainly was patriotic enough. As a U.S. History teacher, he had the privilege and duty of adorning his walls with the faces of favorite American heroes. It was inspirational, to say the least, to have the faces of President Washington and Lincoln staring back at you on a daily basis. One of his absolute favorites was his poster of Martin Luther King, Jr. Washington, Lincoln, King... all men with a dream for their country, a dream inspired by God, a dream viewed as revolutionary at the time, and a dream requiring extraordinary courage and divine favor to bring to completion. Such men did not blink an eye in the face of adversity nor were they intimidated by criticism.

Keith couldn't help but smile as he recalled the many enthusiastic faces that had occupied this classroom over the last 25 years—more than two thousand, no doubt. And what a privilege to be granted the responsibility of teaching a subject so crucial to the future of democracy. Surely, he had made a difference in some of those lives.

Over the past two and a half decades, Keith had tried to live by two commandments from the Bible: love God with all your heart, mind, and soul; and love your neighbor as yourself.

He would be the first to admit—especially, in the past month—that he had come up short more often than not. Nevertheless, each day was a new beginning, and up to this point, God's grace had been sufficient to sustain him through the good times as well as the bad.

It was time to gear up for the next challenge of the day, which was a tall order to be sure. This year's Jaguars had improved so much in two weeks—like gold, that had been refined by fire. It was vital that today's practice move them one step closer to their goal of earning their first victory at Raymond Sanders Stadium on Friday evening.

Not in a big hurry to bake in the mid-afternoon sun, Keith reviewed the practice plan for the day in the comfort of his classroom. Traditionally, Wednesday was his day, a day to focus on defense.

After warm-ups and kickoff drill, the next segment would be a tackling circuit. Each of the three coaches would be in charge of a different aspect of tackling, and the players would cycle around to each station in their position groups: defensive line, linebackers, and defensive backs.

Tackling circuit was followed by individual defense. Usually a portion of this time was spent combining the defensive backs with the inside linebackers for 7-on-7 pass skeleton. A scout offense—minus the line—would run the Pennington Pirates pass routes and outside running plays.

During this time period, the defensive line would have their fun working on their pass rushing in a live drill like Kiss the Maiden. Bull rushes, ferocious forearm ripping and clubbing were a few of the means to achieve the end of sacking the quarterback. More often than not, the exchanges would become so heated that the two combatants would have to be separated by Coach Oliver. If the truth were told, most of the DBs and LBs would give their right arm to be a defensive lineman during this segment of practice.

Finally, the defense would come together for team defense against a scout offense. The scout team would attempt to simulate the opponent's offense though severely outmanned. Usually, the defense by this point in the week was out for blood. The scout team runningback was certainly not a position of envy on Wednesdays. As a matter of fact, Pete O'Connor was one of the previous year's "Hamburger Squad" runningbacks, and he had the scars to prove it. To make matters worse, on the rare occasion that the starting defense would get burned for a touchdown, all hell would break loose.

Needless to say, it was the favorite practice day of Coach Abraham's. There was less standing around, less explaining, more movement, more hitting, and more enthusiasm. The tempo would be brisk and the intensity white hot.

After the defense had concluded its business, the remainder of practice would be turned over to Coach Allen and the offense. Jim had the freedom to take as much time as needed to polish the offense's arsenal of rushing and passing plays—even if practice had to be extended past 7:00 p.m. Furthermore, the degree of effort and focus sustained by the players would determine the amount of conditioning required at the end of practice.

It was time. Coach Abraham turned off the lights and locked his classroom door. As he walked down the hallway towards the locker room, he had a definitive bounce to his step. Suddenly, a voice came from behind.

"Coach Abraham, you are a tough man to track down this time of year."

With a slight annoyance, Coach Abraham turned to face his building principal who had been his boss the past three years though Keith was more than 10 years his senior. A typically fancy dresser, he was wearing kelly green slacks, a neatly pressed white dress shirt, and a screaming green tie.

"Oh... hi, Matt," said Keith.

"I hate to disturb you before practice," said Matt Ingalls, "but can I have a minute of your time?"

"Sure, I've got a minute," sighed Keith.

True to form, his boss began with a joke.

"An English teacher was conducting a lesson to his last class of the day. A student raised her hand, interrupting him with the all-too-familiar question, 'Are we going to get graded on this?' You know what the teacher's response was? 'Why are you so worried? Are you a block of cheese?'"

It took a couple seconds before it registered. Coach Abraham erupted in heartfelt laughter, "Ha ha, that's a good one."

Looking both ways down the corridor, Mr. Ingalls cleared his throat and then proceeded, "Just one more thing, Coach... I want you to know how bad I felt when you were getting the shaft by Dr. Jones and the board. That just wasn't right, hanging you out to dry like that. It makes me wonder just how safe any of our jobs are around here. That's why I wanted to give you a little heads up.

"I happened to see Mike Owens, Sr. and his sister, Valerie Snow, heading into Dr. Jones's office as I was leaving our administration meeting. I heard about the incident at the scrimmage. I just want you to know, you've got my complete support, Keith. Just thought I'd give you a little heads up."

Coach Abraham patted his principal on the shoulder, looked him straight in the eye, and said, "Thanks, Matt. I'm grateful. And you know you can always expect the same from me. To be honest with you, I think we've got the incident with Mr. Owens handled now. I'm not sure why he would still be meeting with Dr. Jones, and I don't really care. I've got a football team to coach. If the superintendent wants to meddle some more in our program, he can go ahead and try. I've got to believe that the Juddville faithful won't tolerate much more of his idiocy. One more bone-headed move on his part, and he'll only be cutting his own throat."

In a carefully muffled voice, Matt responded, "Just watch yourself. The man's only got one principle: look out for number one."

As the team broke for water at the conclusion of individual defense, the coaches huddled together to make last minute adjustments to their plans for team defense. Coach Abraham handed the scout team play cards to Coach Oliver.

"Gary, let's run passing plays at about a 3 to 1 ratio. Jim, I want to make sure we get plenty of reps in our Cover 3 and Cover 1. Yesterday, Collins and Foster gave us a great look on offense. If we can get that kind of effort out of them again today, I will put you up for a raise."

"I didn't know I was getting paid," replied Gary.

"In addition to the weekly payment on the scoreboard on Friday nights? Yes, you are also going to receive some monetary compensation. Don't you think you've earned it?"

"I guess," smiled the rookie coach.

"Don't get too excited, Coach," said Jim. "By the end of the season, it'll amount to a few cents per hour. Just ask my wife if you don't believe me."

The players returned from their water break and immediately broke into their huddles. The defense congregated around their leader. No one had ever instructed Pete to lead; it was purely instinctive, both on his part and upon those destined to follow.

"Alright boys, go hard every play. Pay attention to the strength and coverage calls and most importantly, fly to the ball.

"What's the name of the game?"

"Hit," exclaimed his teammates.

"Can't hear you. What's the name of the game?"

"HIT!"

On the first play, the scout offense ran a sweep out of the I-formation. Pete was the near backer. As soon as the ball was pitched he was pursuing like a lion tracking its prey. The scout team fullback, Rob Bast, had the assignment of blocking the first opposite color jersey to show.

The two bodies collided at the line of scrimmage. Pete struck the would-be blocker with his hands and then ripped underneath with his inside arm, freeing him from the fullback's block.

The scout tailback, a junior back with good speed but a high degree of tentativeness, saw Pete coming. He started to go down before any contact was made. The defensive captain pounced on him and drove him into the August grass.

"Come on, Billy," griped the captain. "You've got to give us a better look than that... Pennington's tailback isn't going to go down without a fight."

Billy Johnson returned to the huddle embarrassed about having his cowardice exposed. Fortunately, Pete's comment had only been heard by one maybe two teammates.

The remainder of team defense was rather uneventful. The scout team's offensive line tried their best to block the physically superior defensive line and linebackers, but even their best efforts were in vain. The runningbacks ran hard until the hole closed up two steps prior to their arrival. Roger had less success throwing the ball than the previous day. The secondary blanketed Adam, allowing him very little room to maneuver. With less than five minutes remaining of team defense, the Jaguars encountered another setback.

It was just a simple five-yard hitch from Roger Collins to his favorite receiver—by default—Adam Foster. As soon as he planted his foot, the ball was already in the air.

Mike Owens was in tight coverage. Adam extended his arms and snagged the ball effortlessly with both hands. Just as Owens was about to close in on the tackle, Adam made an abrupt spin move to the outside. The sophomore corner clearly had not anticipated this move, and his left leg crumpled underneath him. He dove for the receiver's foot but came up empty.

Safety Don Jacobs caught up to Foster about 15 yards later, shoving him out of bounds, his hands punching up through his shoulder pads, and finishing with a right elbow under the Billington boy's chin.

Glaring down at the scout team receiver, Jacobs deliberately neglected to help his teammate up from the ground. As soon as Adam was on his feet the strong safety sneered, "Next time you catch a pass in this zip code, you won't be getting back up."

Adam kept his mouth closed, shoved the ball harmlessly into Don's chest, and jogged back to the offensive huddle. There was one player, however, who wasn't so quick to rejoin the huddle.

Mike Owens was rolling back and forth, holding his left ankle.

His teammates held back, in complete denial of the possibility that their teammate might be hurt. Finally, Pete jogged over to investigate.

"Come on, sophomore. On your feet… next play."

"I think I hurt my ankle, Pete," responded Mike, grimacing in pain.

Coach Abraham and Coach Allen hurried over to the wounded player. Jim was just about to lay into his sophomore corner, but bit his tongue.

"Relax, son, and let me have a look at it," said Coach Abraham, rolling down the sock and immediately noticing some swelling.

"Doesn't look too bad," said Keith. "but just to be on the safe side, let's get some ice on it right away. Jim, can you take care of that, please."

"Right on it, Coach. Do you think you can walk on it, Mike?"

"I'll try."

Jim reached down with his right hand and lifted Mike up on his feet.

"Give me your arm, Mike."

With Coach Allen's arm stabilizing his two-way starter, they hobbled off the field to the sideline where the med kit and ice cooler awaited them. Mike ripped off his helmet and lay on his back while Jim removed his left cleat and sock. Grabbing a bag of ice and an Ace bandage, he wrapped the ankle tightly and then used the football helmet to elevate it.

"You're going to have to ice this ankle several times tonight and tomorrow. Ever have any ankle trouble before, Mike?"

"Not really, Coach. You think it'll be okay?"

"That's up to you. It will probably require you to play through a little pain Friday night. I don't have to tell you how important you are to this team."

"I'm sorry, Coach."

"Sorry? You can't help getting hurt sometimes, Mike. I've got to get back out there. You'll be fine. Don't worry. When you're young, the body heals quickly from this type of injury… if you do the right things."

As Coach Allen returned to the field, he felt a strong urge to vomit.

Are you kidding me, thought Jim, *our number one offensive weapon and our only shut-down corner goes down 48 hours before game time. He'd better heal quickly, or we're in big time trouble.*

Reality quickly settled in during the last two plays of team defense. Mike's backup at corner was David Riley. This was a temporary assignment; one that would be rectified in two weeks upon the return of Roger and Adam.

Riley did not have the speed or aggressiveness to play defense. He had decent ball skills, but Coach Allen had little or no confidence in his ability to make a tackle. Plain and simple, they were going to be forced to make a position change.

Adjustment number one was to move Jeff Nash from weak to strong corner. Adjustment number two wasn't going to be as simple. They could move Jacobs to weak corner, but then they would lose their strong safety, and Tommy Schulz wasn't physical enough to move over to the strong side from weak safety. Or they could move Schulz to weak corner and try to hide Riley at weak safety, but then they would have two players having to learn new positions in the next 48 hours. Assuming Owens would be healthy enough to suit up to play Friday night, they could move Mike to free safety where he would face less pressure, and if they were lucky, less cutting.

After an extra long water break, necessitated by the injury to their number weapon in the offensive backfield, the coaches had decided upon a temporary solution.

First year player, senior Tommy Schultz would replace Owens at fullback. Though clearly undersized and inexperienced, Tommy was the next best athlete on the board. He would fill in at fullback today for he knew the position, and if they moved too many players around in the backfield it would result in mass confusion. The status of Mike was uncertain; if it was a sprain, with a lot of ice and a little luck, he would be good to go on Friday night. They would know by tomorrow's pregame practice if his condition was worse, and then they would be forced to make more substantial personnel adjustments.

Tommy performed admirably on his first two plays. As the beneficiary of a humongous hole on his first play, he scampered 40 yards untouched on a 34 trap. On the next play, a 36 trap he made an impressive cut, put his shoulder down and gained 7 yards before being wrapped up by the scout team safety, Adam Foster. Because Tommy had learned all his plays at the fullback position, the offense was able to run the entire offense without much difficulty. The only problem, however, was that the defense they would be facing on Friday night was coached by one of the finest defensive minds in the state.

It was no coincidence that the intensity of their hitting sharply declined. The coaches were becoming agitated, for the offense seemed to be just going through the motions. Perhaps, they were fatigued or just afraid to have another player go down to injury.

After receiving the next play from Coach Allen, David nervously wiped off his sweaty hands on his practice pants. His mind went through the obligatory mental checklist as he approached the line of scrimmage.

Crouching under center, David barked out the commands, "White 33... white 33... Set... Go!"

Center Craig Daniels snapped the ball crisply into David's hands. The signal caller turned counter-clockwise as Tommy charged by his hip, taking the fake and filling for the pulling left guard. David extended the ball outwards to left halfback Rob Bast who carried out his fake with expertise.

Riley placed the ball firmly on his hip and bootlegged to the left behind the pulling guard. The defensive end was upended by Pete O'Connor, and there was nothing but green in front of the scrambling quarterback.

Looking upfield, David noticed the cornerback had abandoned his man—the playside tight end Bryan Cox. Unfortunately, Cox was already 15 yards away and at a full sprint. David checked down to his second option—the backside end, Dan Hardings—who was running a drag route across the field. Dan had a step on the linebacker, and David thought he could lead him and make the easier completion since he was actually coming towards him rather than away from him.

The moment the ball released from David's hand he knew it was a duck. The ball fluttered behind Hardings. Fortunately, the linebacker played it safe and batted the ball down rather than go for the pick. The receiver reached back for it, but was unable to even make contact with the ball. Both the end and linebacker fell roughly to the ground as the ball rolled to a stop.

Coach Allen counted to himself, *one one-thousand, two one-thousand, three one-thousand, four one-thousand...*

"Are you kidding me, David?" cried Coach Allen to his quarterback who was seeking sanctuary in the offensive huddle. "Why would you force the ball to Hardings when Cox was wide open? I could have completed that throw with my left hand."

Not wanting to inflict further injury upon his backfield already in much disrepair, Coach Allen chose to curtail his criticism of his starting quarterback. Since it was no secret that this year's Jaguar passing game was sorely deficient, it might be better to spend the majority of the time salvaging what was left of the running game. If a victory on Friday night was contingent on Juddville's ability to throw the ball, they were in severe trouble.

Therefore, Jim chose to direct his attention towards the offensive line, challenging them to get off the ball as quickly and aggressively as possible.

"Come on, Osborne. You've got to be quicker or you'll never get to the linebacker."

"Hardings, is that all the longer you can sustain your block?"

"Joey, you've got the easiest block of them all. Just step down to your inside gap and make sure there's no backside penetration. Cut him for crying out loud!"

Finally, at the tail end of team offense, "O'Connor, I thought you were supposed to be so tough. Have you knocked down one person today? We've got a game in 48 hours, men."

When David looked at Pete's face in the huddle, he expected to see humiliation. Instead, he was amazed to see an odd sense of joy in the captain's eyes.

How could he possibly be enjoying this? wondered David.

As he called the next play, he wondered if Pete would mess up.

"Red 18... Red 18... Set... Go... Go..."

David received the snap and handed off the ball just as a humongous hole opened up. Pete drove his shoulder pad into the thighs of the scout team defensive tackle, plowing him back three steps before taking his feet out from under him. Tommy Schultz sprinted 25 yards untouched all the way to the end zone. As soon as he turned around to head back to the huddle, he was tackled by Dan Hardings, followed by Bast, Nash, and Cox. The linemen, always sticking together, were a few steps behind. Last but not least was Riley who had carried out his fake to the opposite sideline, drawing not one, but two defenders with him.

"Now that's how we execute a play around here!" exclaimed Coach Allen.

He looked over to Coach Abraham and nodded. After all of the years they had spent coaching together, they had an uncanny ability to read one another's minds. The message of the moment was clear: that was as good as good was going to get, signaling the end of Wednesday's offensive session.

The reality of their situation was dire, however. To lose their top skill player just two days before their first game was disastrous. No surprise, Coach Allen was beginning to develop a headache, and it wasn't due to dehydration.

This unanticipated challenge was the last thing the Juddville Jaguars needed. By the time team offense had ended, the ice pack had been removed from Mike's ankle, and he was up on two feet, hobbling on the sideline.

After 10 minutes of specialty, the cardiovascular treat-of-the-day was circuits. The team was divided into three groups. Coach Allen, Coach Abraham, and Coach Oliver each had their own drill.

Coach Abraham had the 5 agile bags setup in a parallel line with about 2 feet of separation between each bag. He would be having his group run through the bags using a variety of movements: two steps between the bags, one step between the bags, a side shuffle, a kangaroo hop, and finally, a "W" drill with the agile bags arranged in a zigzag pattern—the perfect course for transitioning between backpedaling and sprinting.

Coach Oliver preferred drills that encouraged more intimacy with the turf. He chose bear crawling 10 yards and back for warm-ups. His drill de jour was also from a crawl position, three players at a time. On command the players would start buzzing their feet; then he would point left, right, backward or forward. Each time he pointed left or right, they had to roll over and return to all fours. As soon as one trio of players reached the point of exhaustion, the next group of three in line would have at it.

Coach Allen preferred to stick with one drill. Simplicity was the key. In football, you get knocked down and you have to get back up. Down ups was one of the least favorite football drills of all time. Back in Coach Allen's day, he hated the drill with a passion. The group that started with Coach Allen would feel lucky, for they would get the worst station out of the way first.

Keeping track of the time was Coach Abraham. Each station was two and a half minutes long. Number one rule was no walking to a station. If you didn't hustle from station to station, you would be putting the lives of your teammates at great risk.

By the time each group of players had rotated through each station, there was little or no conversation between them. Concentration was directed fully towards capturing their next breath.

At the conclusion of conditioning, Coach Abraham brought them into a tight circle. He had given some thought to what he would say to them while he was running them through the agile bags.

"Listen up, men. There are things in life that you can control and there are things in life that are beyond our control. What we can control is our physical and mental preparation. This week you have done an excellent job pushing your bodies to the maximum. I have been so impressed with your all-out effort during drills and scrimmage. For those of you that are new to football, tomorrow is our first pre-game practice where we actually scale back the physical intensity. But that doesn't mean we can relax mentally. Pregame is a dress rehearsal for Friday night's game... one last practice to make sure that everyone knows their assignments and everyone's mind is focused on accomplishing our first goal. You have to understand that this game of football is mostly mental..."

Steve Wilcox couldn't resist, "So that's why MacDonald's so good at it!"

The team responded with muffled laughter, but the coaches didn't find the comment all that amusing.

"That's exactly what I'm talking about, Steve. Look at Greg. Is he our strongest player in the weight room? Nope. You can barely bench 200 pounds, can you, Greg? Is he the fastest sprinter? I'm sure the track coach hasn't been trying to hound you into running on the 4 by 100 relay next year is he? What about size? Is Greg the biggest on our team? Again, not even close. You're about 185 pounds on a good day, aren't you, Greg? Then why do you think you're so difficult to block?"

"I've got a good d-line coach," answered MacDonald, a matter-of-factly.

"Aw, how sweet," responded Larry Osborn. "I'm getting all teary-eyed."

"Seriously, Greg. Be honest. When you get in your stance and line up over center, what is going through your mind?"

"Watch the ball...don't jump offsides...watch the ball... don't jump offsides," responded the embarrassed junior. "And then I am thinking about what direction I will pursue once I smoke by the center."

"Yes! That's what I'm talking about. You don't believe for a minute that the center can block you, do you? That's confidence, and that's the kind of positive attitude that we need to see more of around here. When you think you can... you will. But you got to believe... in yourself...in your teammates... and in your coaches.

"And when we all channel that same attitude and same energy into one purpose, we have TEAM. And when we have TEAM, together everyone achieves more.

"We had a player go down today. I think he's going to be fine, but you have to realize that those types of setbacks happen. Injuries are part of the game. Great teams rally around their fallen teammate; they do so by raising their own level of performance. I expect nothing less from you.

"Bring it in. TEAM on three. One... two... three..."

"TEAM."

Chapter Fourteen

"Houston, we have a problem," uttered Jim to his rearview mirror as he pulled out of the Juddville High School parking lot.

How could things have gone so suddenly from bad to worse? Yesterday, Jim's thoughts were consumed by the ineffectiveness of their number one quarterback. Today, his number one offensive weapon goes down with a sprained ankle.

By the time Jim had reached home, he still hadn't come up with any solutions. The key questions were exactly how serious was Mike's injury and how much pain was he willing to play through? Jim remembered that Mike had played through his entire JV season without incurring a single major injury. If they lost Mike for the first two games, they would have to make significant changes on offense, changes that would force them to take two steps backwards.

The offensive line would inevitably lose their best trapping linemen, and the backfield would inherit a player who hadn't carried a football in two weeks. Yet, Jim knew if there was anyone he could depend on to do whatever the team needed, it would be Pete O'Connor. He had played offensive back last season as a junior, and both years on the jayvee, as well.

The problem would be the gap left in the o-line. He only had to go back a week and a half to be reminded of the regression in blocking that occurred when Pete had been out of commission for two practices due to an unwarranted suspension. Nevertheless, the prospect of this week and potentially next week—against their rivals, the Billington Bulldogs—without a decent runner in the backfield was the definition of the word *nightmare*.

The success of Juddville's offense was contingent on the inside running game. Without an effective inside trap, there would be no off-tackle play, and certainly no quarterback keep—not to mention any play action passing game. Unfortunately, moving Pete back to runningback was a move that would have to be considered. It was a move that Jim would hold off suggesting to Keith for the time being although Jim was quite certain that Keith would already be pondering the move himself. With any luck, however, Mike's injury would only be a minor one, and he would at least be able to help them on offense on Friday night.

As Jim pulled into his driveway, he took a deep breath and tried to relax. Tomorrow was the first day with students. It was also the first pre-game practice. Thus, it would be his first taste of trying to juggle the challenges of coaching football with his full-time job of teaching middle school students.

Last year, he remembered the personnel decisions they were facing at this point in the season: who was going to be the *backup* at safety or at tight end? All of the number ones had already established themselves. But last year's team was state champions, which was now ancient history.

Jim entered a quiet house. He heard a snicker coming from the living room closet. An invigorating scent of garlic and tomato was emanating from the kitchen... was it spaghetti night at the Allen's?

Tiptoeing into the kitchen, he saw a pint-size foot protruding from underneath the table. He bent down slowly and gently tickled the bottom of the mystery foot.

A giggle escaped.

He tickled it again, only this time grabbing the foot with his left hand, so the foot could not be pulled back. A tug of war ensued.

"Got you," proclaimed Jim.

"Oh no, you don't," countered his youngest boy Kevin, kicking back at the invasive hands. Finally breaking free, he crawled out from the opposite end of the table and sprinted by his dad.

"Help, help. Troll on the loose."

"Who you calling Troll?" answered Jim, rededicating himself to the pursuit of his prey. "I'm going to get you."

He chased Kevin into the living room. The boy unwisely chose to circle around the coffee table. Jim reached over the table and grabbed the nearest limb, drawing him into his body like a gigantic octopus. Then he lifted the 4 and half year old boy above his head and then slammed him onto the comforts of the couch.

The next move was compulsory: up came Kevin's shirt for one relentless raspberry. Suddenly, as if transformed into the Tasmanian Devil, his dad started blowing air farts on his exposed belly; his ears seemingly deaf to the cries of desperation for his dad to stop.

Mary was the next on the scene.

"Jim, let the poor boy breathe."

"He called me a Troll."

"You are a Troll."

"But Trolls are known for their extreme stupidity."

"And your point is?"

Just then Jim felt not one, but two sets of arms ensnared around his ankles. He looked down to see that his oldest boy Luke had joined the fray.

"Help me, Mary. I'm outnumbered, two to one."

"Glad to hear you can count that high, honey."

The conversation at the Abraham household was of a far different nature. Julia and Carol were seated on the living room couch while Keith sat all alone, dejected, on the love seat.

"What do you mean 'you just happened to bump into him'?" asked Carol. "It sounds like you went looking for him, Keith."

"I told you he came by the house on Monday. And I told you what he shouted at me."

"So that meant you had to go to his place of work to antagonize him?" asked Carol.

Keith's face was flush as he tried to explain his actions. He saw the blank expression on his daughter's face. As usual, he was completely unable to read Julia, her thoughts and feelings so alien to him.

"I had intended to just buy…" began Keith, but then realized his cover story to buy a Mountain Dew was just not going to fly with either of them.

"Julia, what do expect me to do? Just sit idly by while that boy continues to harass you. When I saw that blue Nova sitting outside of our house, I just went berserk. I wanted to grab hold of his face and rip off the skin. Then when he pulled away and shouted at me to F-off—in the middle of my own neighborhood—I vowed right then and there that I would go on the offensive."

"Keith, don't you realize you're just going to set him off? I wasn't going to tell you this, but this wasn't the first time he has stalked her. Now you've made matters worse. And how can we go to the police after you went into the Sub Shoppe and threatened him."

"The police? The Juddville Police?" laughed Keith hysterically. "You think they're going to be of any help? Those incompetent fools? They didn't give a rip about Julia the first time. What makes you think they'd act any differently now?"

Coach Abraham's youngest daughter sat in a trance. Her mother's hand was on top of her hand, but she was becoming increasingly unresponsive. Carol started to cry softly at first, gradually escalating to uncontrollable sobbing. Her daughter remained unaffected. Keith felt the rage boiling inside of him.

"Julia, I am truly sorry. I know I acted rashly. I know I shouldn't have ever gone to see Brian, but I just couldn't bear the thought of him hurting you again."

Finally, Keith's daughter spoke. And it wasn't the words he wanted to hear.

"Dad, it's really quite pathetic to hear you talking about not being able to bare the thought of someone hurting your poor Julia…"

The room grew silent. Mary and Keith were completely clueless as to where she was going with her last comment.

"Can't you just stay out of my life? Don't you think it's a little late to be concerned about your poor Julia? In case, you haven't noticed, Dad, I'm not a child anymore. While you were coaching your football teams, I grew up. And as soon as I get the opportunity, I'll be out on my own. Some place where I don't have to be embarrassed anymore… some place where I won't have to try to live up to your impossible expectations."

"Julia, you're going too far," interrupted her mother. "You know your dad loves you very much."

"Do I, Mom? Really? How much? Enough to make a fool out of me in public?"

"I'm sorry, Julia. But I just can't sit and listen to you berating your father like this. He's a good man. He's a..."

"No, she's right, Carol," interrupted Keith. "I deserve this."

"Don't even start it, Dad. This isn't about you for once. I will handle this myself. I don't need 'The Coach' to come to the rescue. Just leave me alone, would you? You were pretty good at doing that for majority of my life. Let me go back to being second string."

Keith slumped back in his seat, his eyes awash with tears, and his heart broken into a thousand pellet-size pieces.

There was nothing more that Keith could say. He had no more voice... he had lost all authority. For the moment, Julia seemed content with the amount of pain she had spilled onto him.

Breaking the silence, "I still think we need to see about getting some type of restraining order," Carol tearfully insisted.

"On what basis?" asked Keith, in a quiet, broken voice. "We have no evidence. None from the beach. None from her encounter with Brian outside of DJ's."

"Let's at least make a report with the police. We can't just pretend that nothing happened," pleaded Carol, the frustration in her voice becoming more and more apparent.

"I've got an idea," suggested Julia, in a voice barely audible. "I could go stay with Mary in New York."

The Abraham living room was engulfed in a blanket of silence. Julia couldn't discern whether her parents were actually taking her idea into consideration or trying to formulate a convincing response.

Carol was the first to break the silence.

"Honey, you are an adult now. And you are capable of making adult decisions. But right now I think you are in an emotionally-fragile state. I think you need to be around your Dad and me for awhile until you've had time to heal."

"What are you talking about, Mom? That's hilarious. Around Dad? If you haven't noticed, Mom, it's football season. In fact, there's a football game this Friday night, and you know what that means for Dad. See you in December, family."

Unwilling to let her daughter continue on with her latest tangent, Carol interrupted, "Have you even talked to your sister about this?"

"As a matter of fact, Mom, I have. And she said that I have an open invitation."

"But for how long, dear? Have you thought about how long you want to live in big city like New York?"

"I don't know, Mom. A couple of weeks... a month... two months... maybe until January when the second semester starts at Tyler College. That is if I decide to re-enroll."

Right now the state of the Juddville Jaguar football team was the furthest thing from Keith's mind. All he could think about was what a failure he was as a father. The prospect of seeing his last child move out of state under circumstances such as these was unbearable. Yet whatever he might say would be received with even more resentment.

Oh God, what a mess!

Keith, you are clay. Let me take this burden. Trust me. You need to let go.

Keith cleared his throat before speaking. Lifting his head and trying to sound as sincere as possible, "Julia, no matter what you think, I do love you. I know I haven't been much of a father ... I'm sorry. I truly am.

"Carol, I suggest we give this idea some thought. After dinner we can call Mary, and get more information. The thought of you right now in a huge city like New York is pretty frightening right now, Julia. But if that is God's will for you, honey, who am I to stand in the way? As much as Mom and I would miss you dearly, I am sure your sister would absolutely love to have your company."

Carol couldn't believe what her ears were hearing. "You aren't actually..."

Cutting in before his wife could finish, Keith interjected, "There is someone that we haven't allowed to participate in this discussion. If it's okay with you, Julia, would it be alright if we take a moment to pray?"

A part of Julia wanted to regurgitate on the spot if she had to listen to one more of the "The Coach's" legendary prayers right now; another part was taken completely off guard by his tacit approval, and she was curious to hear what else her dad might have to say on the subject of New York.

Keith moved over next to Julia and Carol on the couch and affectionately reached for his daughter's hand. Bowing his head, Keith began to pray as Carol started shaking convulsively.

"Father, there is no one who can possibly love us and understand us as much as You. Please guide Julia as she considers her next move. We trust You, and we ask that You would make Your plan clear, and that You would always keep us all under the safety of Your Almighty wings. We love you, Lord. And we especially love, Julia. I know that I have hurt her in the past. And I ask your forgiveness, Lord. Help me to find a way to make amends. In the name of Jesus, we pray. Amen."

As Julia released herself from her dad's grip, she wiped her sweaty palms on her favorite pair of Calvin Klein blue jeans. His prayer had made her feel uncomfortable; it seemed like her dad in some roundabout way was trying to guilt her into staying. She sprung from the couch and darted to her room.

Carol looked to her husband. Keith hugged her as they shed many more tears of hurt and frustration.

"Any phone messages from Dad," asked Roger as he meandered into the kitchen.

"Hi ya, kiddo," said Bill, at the kitchen table with a Caesar salad in front of him.

Ignoring his step-dad, who insisted on calling him a name that made him want to punch him, Roger rephrased his question.

"Mom, did my father leave any messages for me by chance?"

"Were you expecting one?"

"Yeah, kind of I guess. He said he was going to be in town for the game this week, and that he would get in touch before he arrived on Friday."

"Doesn't he know you won't be playing?" asked Bill, unable to conceal the smirk on his face.

"Something funny, Bill? I am not sure I understand the joke," said Roger, his posture combative.

"Don't get so defensive, son. It is a bit ironic, wouldn't you agree, Kate? His dad finally comes to see him play, only he'll have to see him standing on the sideline."

Roger snapped. He took three quick steps toward the kitchen table and bench pressed the table into his step-father's sternum. Bill rocked back in his chair, banging his head into the wall.

Shreds of Romaine lettuce and croutons fell onto his lap. At first he seemed to be in a daze. Then he became furious when he noticed the creamy dressing spattered all over his tie.

Mrs. Perkins was horrified to the point of rendering herself speechless.

Her husband's outrage was uncontainable. "Kate, are you going to do something? He just ruined my silk tie."

Holding his chest as if applying pressure to a bullet wound, "And I am quite sure he did damage to my ribs..." His last words trembled as if he were about to break out in tears.

Finally, Kate blurted out, "Look what you've done, Roger! Why would you do such a thing? Go to your room... now!"

"Gladly," he snapped back, showing neither remorse nor the slightest bit of concern for Bill's well-being.

Alone in his bedroom, Roger sprawled out on his queen-size bed, wallowing in the supreme comfort of his navy blue comforter and firm, over-stuffed pillows.

Guess I showed that moron who's boss around here. Is Mom for real? No wonder Dad left her. Only to be replaced by Bill... Dollar Bill.

Ha... That's a good one. I think I'll call him that from now on.

Roger's eyes began to water as he imagined what could have been. Closing his eyes, he pictured himself at Raymond Sanders Field, barking out the cadence as he scanned the Pennington Pirate defense from left to right.

The center snapped the ball crisply into his confident hands, the laces of the ball communing with his fingertips as he rolled out to his right. He planted his right foot and threw a magnificent spiral towards Jeff Nash who was wide open on a Go-route. The ball sailed 35 yards, dropping perfectly into his outstretched hands as he ran full speed into the end zone.

The Juddville fans were on their feet, expressing their admiration with a thunderous ovation. Roger looked up on the top row of the bleachers. He saw his dad clapping emphatically, broadcasting his approval for the whole world to see.

An abrupt knock on the door, and Roger was jolted from his reverie.

"May I come in?" asked Mrs. Perkins.

Pretending not to have heard anything, Roger rolled over onto his side, facing the wall.

Another knock on the door, this time louder.

"Roger, it's me, honey. Open up, please."

Her persistency continued to earn no response. Leaving no other option, she grabbed hold of the door knob and opened the door an inch. Roger feigned possum.

Balancing a tray in her right hand, she pushed the door open slowly with her left.

Poor boy is so tired, she thought. *I'll just set this down on his desk. He must be starving.*

Gently, she set down the tray toting one of Roger's favorite meals: Chicken Alfredo. The sauce was made from scratch with real cream, ricotta cheese, and freshly-grated parmesan cheese. The fettuccine was purchased fresh, none of that cheap out-of-the-box pasta for Roger.

Along with the main dish was a fruit salad, containing juicy-red watermelon, marble-sized blueberries, and sumptuous strawberries. A large glass of chocolate milk completed Roger's meal.

Mrs. Perkins turned to leave, pausing a moment to take in one more maternal look at her son. She was amazed by how quickly he had transformed from a little boy into a full-grown man—a point that even Bill would sorely admit to now.

As soon as Roger heard the door close, he rolled over to investigate his dinner, and he was not dissatisfied.

After all, Max only got a hot bowl of soup in *Where the Wild Things Are.*

Pete was a bit antsy. With no football to watch on TV and his mom at work, he was feeling a bit on the lonely side. He wished there was someone he could hang out with… like a teammate or, God forbid, a girl.

He had eaten alone tonight. His mom had prepared one of his least favorite meals: macaroni and cheese mixed with cut up hot dog pieces. It satisfied his appetite, but failed to bring much pleasure to his taste buds. By the time he had polished off the green beans and two large glasses of milk, he was quite stuffed.

Since there was at least an hour of daylight left, he decided to ride his bike to the Pancake House and pick up his paycheck. He was a little low on cash; he could stop at the ATM on the way back. If all went well Friday night, he might be in the mood to go on a date. The only question was with whom.

Pete would have his radar set at full-strength at school the next day — the official beginning of his senior year. Football season at Juddville was the time of year when dates were easy to come by for most players, except for the extremely shy ones, that is.

As he walked out of the front door of their trailer, he noticed right away that the neighborhood was a great deal quieter this evening. Walking over to his bike, he wondered if he would ever be able to save enough money to buy his own car. A lot of kids his age had their own wheels, but there was no way Pete could afford the car payments and the cost of insurance.

For the most part, his mom was generous enough with the use of her truck. He was usually able to borrow it on the weekends whenever he needed it. Furthermore, she never bugged him about putting gas in the tank, nor did she ask him to pay for the increase in her insurance for having to add him to her policy.

Nevertheless, Pete thought it would sure be nice to be able to drive his own car to and from school or to pick up a girl on a date. It was getting kind of embarrassing to always have to ask his mom to use the car.

Feeling a bit bloated from hot dogs and Mac cheese and quite fatigued from their most intense football practice to date, Pete opted to pedal his bike at a slow to moderate pace. With school starting the next day, there were no kids playing at the clubhouse playground and only a handful in the pool. Summer was surely coming to an end.

Pete slowed his bike to a complete stop as he prepared to turn left onto Henry Street. A thunderous noise was swiftly approaching from behind. As he turned to look behind him, he was somewhat astonished to see Josh Evans on his Yamaha with a backseat rider, Adam Foster, holding on for dear life.

He must have an amazing lawyer, thought Pete, remembering that the last time he had seen Evans was when he was being carted off by the Juddville Police after attempting to assault four of his teammates with a knife.

Pete couldn't help but notice a tether attached to his ankle, as they pulled up along side him at the busy intersection. They stared each other down, neither desiring to blink or to show any sign of being intimidated.

Josh scowled at Pete, revving his motorcycle to full throttle before giving him the finger. As usual, Adam Foster seemed lost in his cold, distant world.

Turning left onto Henry Street, Pete was grateful to be heading in the opposite direction. His eyes were relieved to not have to look at two of Juddville's finest scum bags.

The bike ride to the Pancake House took 20 minutes, for there was no reason to hurry. The last thing he wanted to do right now was work up a sweat, and the relaxed pace allowed his thoughts to return to football.

He visualized his favorite offensive plays: the 34 Trap and 22 Power. He had grown to love the challenge of pulling behind the center and the anticipation of a violent collision with an opposing defensive linemen or linebacker.

Pete parked his bike in the back of the restaurant and walked all the way around to the front, so he could come in through the main entrance. As he walked into the restaurant he tried to appear as casual as possible.

When he saw who was waitressing, he was glad that he hadn't tried to set any speed records on his bike, and he congratulated himself for remembering to spread on a thick application of Speed Stick before leaving the house. Amber Dorr was taking an order, and her back was turned to him. He forced his eyes not to wander though one her most distinguishing features was prominently on display.

After she had finished taking the order, she turned in Pete's direction. *Was that a smile on her face,* thought Pete.

"Hi, Amber. Are the checks in?"

"You still work here, Pete?"

"Of course I do. Just graveyard on the weekends during football."

"I love football," her eyes beaming with excitement, "I can't wait until Friday night."

"You're coming to the game?"

"What else is there to do in this town on Friday nights in the fall?"

"Did you start classes at JCC yet?"

"Oh yeah... last week, but I am only taking 9 credits this semester. I've actually got one of my textbooks in the break room."

"I don't even want to think about textbooks."

"Well, you better start thinking about them, Pete, unless you want to work here all your life."

Pete couldn't believe how natural it felt speaking with Amber. He had met her four months ago during Spring Break when one of the regular busboys took a week of vacation, and he had the good fortune of working the same shift as her. She was without a doubt the most attractive girl who had ever spoken to him. She had graduated the previous year from Juddville Christian and was enrolled in Juddville Community College. He was surprised that she hadn't gone off to a four-year college—somewhere far away from this small town.

"I better put this order in, Pete. Can I get you anything to eat?"

Without a moment's hesitation, he responded, "Yeah, that would be great, but I'd better get my check first... I'll be right back."

The familiar smell of the kitchen greeted him as he walked through the Employees Only door. The smell of uneaten French fries soaked in ketchup and maple syrup and sausage links sharply contrasted the pungent odor of industrial strength dishwasher detergent. He walked past the dishwashing station, beyond the cooler and freezer to the manager's office.

The door was open, and Assistant Manager Alex Swanson was sitting at the desk, his fingers tapping away on the keys of an adding machine. He was an ambitious man in his mid-twenties who had worked himself up the ladder from busboy, to cook, to management.

"Here for your check, Pete?" inquired Alex, his mind still preoccupied with numbers.

"Yes, sir."

Alex finally looked up at Pete with a grin on his face.

"Ready for the opener on Friday night, Pete?"

"You know it."

"How we looking so far? Got a chance of repeating this year?"

"Oh, you know how it goes, sir. One game at a time."

"That's the attitude. Everything going all right... with the authorities and all?"

Pete felt his eyes begin to burn, involuntarily shedding a miniscule amount of forbidden water. Clearing his throat and nonchalantly rubbing his eye before attempting to speak, Pete choked out, "Yeah, that's all history now. Everything finally got straightened out."

"I'm glad. We were all pretty worried for awhile. I never figured you were the type to go looking for trouble. You sure got the best of that moron, though."

Pete chose to remain silent.

"I tell you the honest-to-God truth, Pete. I'd never want to mess with you," joked Alex. "Well, I'm just finishing up. Let me grab your check."

Reaching over to the safe, he pulled the door open and grabbed a thin stack of envelopes. He thumbed half way through the stack and pulled out Pete's.

"Here you go, Pete. Why don't you sit in the back, and we'll make you a sundae. Just tell Amber it's on the house."

"Thanks, Alex."

"You bet. Just make sure you take it to those Pirates on Friday night. And don't be thinking ahead to the next game either. One game at a time, remember?"

"I'll do my best, you can be sure of that, sir."

"I know you will, Pete. You always do."

Pete folded the envelope in half and put it safely in his front left pocket. He casually walked to a booth in the back, slid all the way to the end of the vinyl, chestnut brown bench seat, and waited in anticipation for the re-emergence of Amber.

As he waited patiently, he couldn't help but study her every move as she conversed with customers. She had such an authentic smile and bubbly personality. Her hair was golden brown and tied back in a simple ponytail. Her eyes were dark chocolate and mysterious. Her nose was skinny and gently sloped. The contour of her face was angular, converging sharply to a perfectly-molded chin. Her lips were thin and precise. Her teeth sparkled brightly like the stadium lights on a cool Friday night in October.

His stomach was a butterfly sanctuary as she turned to walk in his direction. It required nearly all of his self-control to redirect his eyes from following their natural instincts. Instead, his eyes were treated to the abundant energy of her radiant smile. All of a sudden, Pete found himself taken captive, unable to breathe or even to blink. He returned an awkward smile, petrified of how silly he must look at the moment, yet not really caring, all the same.

"Alright Pete, what would you like tonight?"

"Actually, Amber, it's my lucky night. Mr. Swanson said I could have a sundae on the house. How could I possible turn that down?"

"Really? If I were you, I'd order a banana split."

"That does sound pretty good, but I'm thinking hot fudge sundae instead."

"Coming right up, Pete. Would you like anything to drink with that?"

"Just some ice water, please."

"Okay, Pete. Give me a couple minutes, and I'll make you the best dessert you've ever tasted."

A few minutes later, Amber was setting before him a heaping dish of vanilla ice cream, smothered in dripping hot fudge sauce, covered with fluffy whipped cream, and crowned with a succulent maraschino cherry.

"Enjoy!"

"Thank you, Amber."

Pete endeavored to spend as much time as possible, savoring his hot fudge sundae, picking away at it, pleading with the vanilla ice cream not to succumb to melting.

When the sundae bowl was finally empty, he reached for his glass and took a long sip of ice water. As he set the glass down, he was ecstatic to see Amber approaching.

"I hope you don't mind, but I only have one table right now and I could sure use a minute off my feet."

Pete felt his heart doing somersaults as she sat down, scooting all the way down the bench until she was directly across from him. His breath took a leave of absence when her knees gently brushed against his knees.

"So how many nights are you working?" relieved to have been able to articulate enough words to complete a sentence.

"They've got me working three nights a week and the day shift on Saturdays and Sundays. You know I make more tips on Sundays than the rest of the week put together? You would not believe how jam-packed this place gets between 10:00 and 2:00. How about you? When are you working?"

"I'm just working graveyard on Saturday nights. It's enough to give me a little spending money during football season."

The conversation grew quiet. Pete could hear plates being stacked back in the kitchen.

"Well, you've got to tell me your number."

Number? Did she say 'number'?

"Uh... it's... 335-4872."

His response sent Amber into hysterics, and Pete was at a complete loss as to what could possibly be so funny. Amber made several honest attempts to suppress her laughter, but it was hopeless. Pete laughed along with her because he found her even more alluring while she was laughing — even if it was at his own expense.

Finally, after no less than two minutes, she began to ever-so-tenderly explain the reason for her outburst.

"I am so sorry, Pete. What I meant by my question was what is your football number, not your phone number."

"Oh," he responded awkwardly. "Of course, how could I be so stupid?"

"Don't say that, Pete. It was just a simple misunderstanding. It's alright, really. How could you know what I meant?"

Already feeling thoroughly embarrassed and having nothing to lose by pressing onward, Pete inquired. "Speaking of numbers... could I have your number — phone number, that is?"

Pete held his breath as he waited for her reply.

"I would love to give you my number, Pete, but I would have to make sure it's okay with Joey first."

"Oh... I see," unsure why he had been so ignorant as to actually believe that a girl as beautiful as Amber could possibly be unattached. He felt the sudden rush of blood to his head as his hopes shattered into tiny shards of glass.

"I am sorry, Amber. I didn't mean to..."

"No, don't apologize, Pete. How could you have known? I better check on my other table. Hey, good luck Friday night. I'll be watching for number...?"

"Fifty-four."

"I enjoyed talking with you, Pete. You're so sweet," said Amber as she scooted out of the booth. "I'll be cheering for you on Friday night."

"Thanks, Amber."

As Pete slid out of the booth, he snagged a dollar bill out of his wallet and set it in the middle of the table.

What just happened? thought Pete. *One moment I am in the Garden of Eden... The next moment I feel like I am being pushed out of a car flying at 80 miles an hour. Were women so impossible to read, or did they receive daily nourishment from feasting on the foolhardy hearts of vulnerable young men?*

Ever so slowly, he forced one foot in front of the other until he reached the front of the restaurant where he treated his eyes to one more peek of the girl of his impossible dreams. His heart grew envious of the elderly couple that was now engaged in conversation with her.

What I would give to have a girl like Amber, thought Pete as he exited the Pancake House. *Too bad she is so out of my league.*

Chapter Fifteen

The first official day of school was a seven hour tug-of-war between two equally-resolute combatants: the natural exuberance of the start of a new school year versus the inevitable boredom of the obligatory rites and rituals of the educational institution.

In general, most students and teachers were optimistic for the new opportunities and challenges. In keeping with that spirit, the majority of students dressed up in the latest back-to-school fashions. A small percentage of students wore the same wardrobe as the previous year: the same dingy black-hooded sweatshirt, the same thread bare jeans and the same discount store tennis shoes. It had to be quite a challenge trying to embrace a new attitude while wearing the same unfashionable costumes. Yet it wasn't as if they had a choice in the matter.

The primary agenda was the communication of and installation of school policy. Mundane tasks such as roll call, talking through the syllabus, and lectures on rules and expectations dragged on and on and on.

Nevertheless, the opportunity to interact with new students amidst the formal structure of the day were much appreciated by Coach Allen and Coach Abraham, providing them with a brief respite from the mounting pressure of Friday night's game. Learning the correct pronunciation of a student's name or briefly explaining a few of the topics students would be learning about in the upcoming semester was a much welcomed break from stressing out about what they were going to do if Mike Owens, Jr. wouldn't be able to suit up Friday evening.

Lunch for Jim and Keith was spent reviewing practice plans and making last minute contingency plans on the special teams depth chart. Even if Owens was a green light for Friday night, they were going to want to limit his playing time to offense first and defense second. Hopefully, Mike had been diligent in icing his injury during the last 18 hours. If he was still hobbling at today's practice, they would have to rest him during practice and cross their fingers for the game on Friday.

The first official lunch of the school year was as bland as usual. The menu consisted of a dry, over-cooked chicken sandwich, a Dixie cup of fruit salad, a handful of tater tots and a carton of milk. Pete was glad that he had packed his own lunch. For one, the school lunch did not provide the amount of calories required to fuel his growing body. Secondly, the nutritional value of every item on the menu was highly suspect with the exception of the milk.

Sitting at a table at the far end of the cafeteria, he sat on the side that afforded an unimpeded view of the food line. He was eager to catch a first glimpse of the female population of the new school year. The first to join him was Roger Collins. Pete was surprised to see Roger with a packed lunch; he would have expected him to be the type of kid to pull out a five dollar bill every day to purchase a couple slices of pepperoni pizza or a plate of nachos from the ala carte window.

"Eating healthy this year, Roger?" asked Pete.

"Hey, junk food is extremely overrated. It sure beats standing in line for 15 minutes."

"True… how'd your classes go this morning?"

"I managed to stay awake. How about you?"

"The same… You got your eyes on anyone yet?"

"Of course," responded Roger, with a matter of fact tone of voice, "you should see this knockout in my U.S. government class. I caught myself drooling over her at least six or seven times. I actually had to wipe off the puddle on my desk with my shirt sleeve."

"Who was she?" asked Pete, his eyes as round as nickels.

"I think her name was… oh what was it again? Oh yeah… I think her name started with an M. I think it was Mm… what was it again? Oh yeah, I remember now. It was Melanie… her name was Melanie."

"Very funny."

Roger was laughing so hard that half the cafeteria could hear him.

Steve Wilcox and Craig Daniels were the next teammates to join them.

"Have any of you guys seen our sophomore Primadonna yet?" asked Steve.

"Not yet. I sure hope he's in school," answered Pete.

"He's in school alright. Wait till you see him."

"There he is in line, Pete," pointed out Roger. "He's not using crutches, is he?"

"Of course, and he's got his whole entourage following him," said Steve. "Is that his girlfriend carrying his tray?"

"Nah, Melanie's working in the kitchen. She earns a free all-you-can-eat lunch that way doesn't she, Pete?"

"I am going to kill you, Collins."

"I thought you were over her, Pete?" asked Craig.

"Over her? Are you kidding? Pete will never be over her. She's over three hundred pounds."

"You guys are hilarious," responded Pete. "You should have seen the babe I was sitting across from last night at the Pancake House."

"What was her name?" asked Steve. "Aunt Jemima?"

"Ha ha… why do I even sit with you guys?"

Pete was more than happy to give up all the attention once their sophomore teammate strolled by on his crutches.

"Hey Mike," asked Roger. "What's the word?"

The rookie running back slowly maneuvered himself around on his crutches so he could face his elder teammates.

"I'm going to be fine," answered Mike. "The doctor just wants me to stay off the ankle as much as I can today."

"You been icing the crap out of it?" asked Craig.

"Oh yeah. Coach Abraham made sure of that; he had me icing it during my first hour P.E. class. He told me he was going to get me another bag of ice for sixth hour. It's already feeling a lot better."

"Good to hear," said Pete. "It looks like you have plenty of help getting around."

Mike looked at the eight sophomores behind him, waiting to see where their hero was going to sit down for lunch. They were mostly JV players with a couple of cute sophomore girls thrown in the mix.

"You know how it is when you're a superstar," Mike replied.

"Sheish, someone get me a pin, so we can pop this boy's ego," said Roger.

At 2:45, the official Juddville High School bell rang for dismissal, and the football players immediately descended upon the locker room. Enthusiasm filled the air in anticipation of their first pre-game practice. Posted on the mirror above one of the sinks was the Special Teams depth chart.

For the most part there were very few surprises. Each player was responsible for knowing exactly what teams he was on and for what teams he was a backup. When Coach Abraham called for each team, you were expected to sprint promptly to midfield and join the huddle. If you weren't in the huddle and should be, you earned a post-practice gasser; if you came out onto the field when you shouldn't have, you also earned a gasser.

What was so ironic was the great pleasure Coach Abraham derived in writing down a player's name on his extra-curricular running list. Naturally, there wouldn't be an ounce of sympathy from the other players.

Typically, the offenders would be first year varsity players who had neglected to allot enough time to look over the depth chart thoroughly. Perhaps, they had been guilty of spending too much time saying goodbye to their girlfriend after school.

What also made pregame practice special was the privilege of practicing on Raymond Sanders Field; the use of the game field was generally reserved for games and pre-game practices—both Varsity and JV teams included. Since the JVs played their games on Thursday nights, their pre-game practice was conducted on Wednesdays. When the varsity was at home on Friday, the JV was on the road on Thursday. Tonight, the JV would be playing at Pennington. After the varsity practice, the varsity coaching staff would be high-tailing it to Pennington to watch the JV game and get an early preview of the Pennington offense and defense.

Needless to say, team spirit was sky-high after their abbreviated warm-up. When Coach Abraham blew his whistle and commanded the entire team to move themselves from the playing field to the Juddville sidelines, there was electricity circulating amongst the players.

The three varsity coaches congregated at the 40 yard line. Coach Abraham looked down at his copy of the depth chart and called out the first special team.

"Kickoff Team, on the double. Steve, get the placekicking tee."

The number one kicker had been recruited just over a week ago, and his audition had taken place no where near a football field. In dramatic fashion, Steve's size 12 Reebok had made quite an impact upon the groin of the notorious juvenile delinquent Josh Evans.

After Steve and three teammates had caught Josh and Adam Foster in the act of stealing a package from Pete's porch, Josh had foolishly pulled a knife on them. Steve reacted quickly with his powerful right foot.

The knife tumbled out of Josh's hand as he keeled over, wincing in pain. A Juddville police officer along with Coach Abraham just happened to be coming around the corner moments later to deliver the news to the O'Connor household that all charges against Pete had been officially dropped.

Officer Kane had listened to the players' story and then handcuffed Josh Evans who was still incapacitated by pain. After hauling him down to the police station for questioning, he was charged and released on a $10,000 bond.

Needless to say, Steve would never receive as much adulation after a kick as he earned from the one planted on Josh Evans. While the players sprinted out to the 40 yard line, the much-heralded kicker gathered his trusty orange tee and sprinted out to the 40 yard line. As Coach Abraham went through each name on the chart, he identified one missing player.

"Greg McDonald?"

A chorus of catcalls ensued.

"Way to go, Greg."

"Gasser number one, Greg."

"Great day for extra conditioning, McDonald."

"Let's move it, McDonald," shouted Coach Abraham. "We haven't got all night. You're a wedge-breaker, don't you remember?"

After four deep kicks inside the 10 yard line, Coach Abraham called for subs. Four players promptly reported to the huddle for four regulars who were more than happy to give their replacements the opportunity to sprint 50 yards downfield.

Next was onside kick, kickoff receive, hands receive, punt, PAT, and then a much needed water break. Punt return and punt block would be covered later in practice during team defense.

Greg McDonald only earned one more gasser, forgetting to report for PAT. Don Jacobs was also a no-show for PAT, so Greg was relieved that he wouldn't be running his Special Teams Gassers all alone.

For the time being, Mike Owens was held out of all special teams.

Throughout the practice he received three 15 minute ice treatments. When he wasn't getting treatment he was on crutches behind the offensive huddle.

Tommy Schultz was his emergency sub at fullback on offense. On defense, Jacobs moved up to weak corner, Nash shifted over to strong corner, Schulz slid over to strong safety, and David Riley was substituted in at free safety.

Coach Allen hated to make so many adjustments in the defensive secondary, but the players who were moving to new positions were all relatively smart, and he felt confident in their ability to carry out their assignments.

Furthermore, Plan A was that in 24 hours, Mike Owens would be healthy enough to play offense and defense. On defense, Mike would move back to free safety which gave Coach Allen much cause for concern. Clearly, Mike wasn't the brightest bulb in the pack; it seemed that he required a little more time than most to fully understand his assignments. Unfortunately, time was not on their side.

Team offense and defense were just walk throughs and went smoothly for the most part. David did a good job leading the offense, and Pete was the commander supreme of the defense, having memorized the entire scouting report on the Pennington Pirates as well as—if not better than—Coach Abraham. For every Pirate formation, the senior linebacker knew their favorite plays and tendencies. Furthermore, Pete had inspired every member of the defense to pursue to the ball at maximum speed. No one dared to disappoint the captain of the defense.

Pete even quizzed Mike Owens, making sure he was paying attention to the assignments for his new defensive position. Unfortunately, Mike didn't know what to do on over half the plays. During the water break at the conclusion of the defensive session, Pete took the sophomore aside.

"You better make sure you ice that ankle tonight. We're going to need you as close to 100% as possible tomorrow night."

"Hey, I'll be ready. You can count on it."

"Gotta have you for this one, Mike. Get that ankle wrapped up heavily with tape and pop a couple of ibuprofen. You are going to have to just suck it up for the team. This is a must win for us tomorrow night. Understood?"

"I hear you, Pete. Nothing is going to keep me off that field tomorrow night. Don't worry."

Water break was followed by punt return and punt block. Finally, the first offense was called back onto the field. Victory formation was rehearsed; the quarterback basically took a knee to reduce the chance of a fumble while killing off the remaining time on the clock.

After two reps, Coach Abraham blew the whistle and gathered the team at midfield.

"Listen up, men. We've come a long way in a short period of time. Over the course of three weeks, 29 individuals from a variety of backgrounds and levels of experience have been molded into one unified team. But we haven't been tested yet. Tomorrow night is our first test.

"Each one of you has a very important role. Those who are out on the field have a specific assignment each and every play. Carry out that assignment to the best of your ability with every ounce of passion that you can muster. Those of you who are on the sideline must support your teammates with relentless enthusiasm. Your teammates need to be able to hear you out on the field every single play.

"This game is essential to achieving our team goals—there is no doubt about that—but don't forget to have fun. Football is a game; it's meant to be fun. In my humble opinion, there is no game that is as much fun. Nothing comes close.

"When you get into the locker room, you'll find your game jersey and pants folded in front of your locker. Take good care of the Juddville uniform. Wear it with pride; it's an honor. On game days, you will be wearing it all day in school. Big Larry, make sure you don't get any ketchup and mustard on it at lunch."

"Hey, that would be a waste," retorted Osborne.

His teammates groaned.

"Bring it in, men."

"Team on three. One… two… three…"

"TEAM," shouted the Juddville Jaguars in one thunderous voice. In a matter of seconds, the game field was clear of the majority of players. The only exceptions were Mike Owens—hobbling off the field on crutches—and four players who were staying after practice to complete their extra-curricular conditioning.

The majority were basking in "the moment". It was the culmination of a dream which had begun way back in grade school when they were first exposed to the Juddville Football Tradition. "The moment" arrived when they officially received their "Blues", and would then be crystallized in 24 hours when they would be sporting their Juddville Jaguar uniforms under the lights of Raymond Sanders Stadium in front of thousands of crazed fans. It was every Juddville boy's dream.

Coach Abraham assumed the responsibility of supervising the extracurricular running while dismissing his assistants to head into the locker room to change clothes before heading up to Pennington to watch the JVs play.

Don Jacobs ran his bonus gasser along side Greg. After completing his obligatory run, Jacobs thought about waiting for McDonald to run his last gasser, but he couldn't wait to get into the locker room to receive his jersey.

Greg ran his final gasser along side Roger and Adam. Then it was just Coach Abraham and the two suspended players.

"Three more gassers, boys," said Coach Abraham. "You guys are getting in such good shape you could give the cross country team a run for their money."

For the most part the two athletes were evenly matched. Roger won the next two gassers, but Adam had more in the tank for the last one. Before leaving the field, Coach Abraham pulled them aside for a brief pep talk.

"Listen up, you two. I know this isn't easy for you to go through all our practices, to do all the extra conditioning, and then to not be able to suit up for tomorrow night's game. But I want you to understand that discipline is a very important tool in growing up. When we understand that there are consequences for our actions, we can learn from our mistakes. You are not the first on this planet to ever make a mistake, and you won't be the last. I want you to know I am proud of the way both of you have responded to your discipline this week.

"Tomorrow night, I am expecting more of the same from you. You will wear your jerseys on the sideline, and you will be an important part of this team. We will be depending on you to provide enthusiasm and to help in whatever way you can. In eight more days, your suspensions will be served, and then you'll both be competing for starting positions."

After shaking Roger's and then Adam's, he said, "I want you to know I'm glad both of you are a part of this team. If there is anything I can ever do for you… at any time, don't hesitate to call. You hear me?"

"Yes sir," responded Roger, his eyes beginning to water.

Adam nodded frostily.

"Now hustle in and get your uniforms."

As Coach Abraham gave the field one final look-over, he couldn't help but notice a dad standing impatiently over by the entrance gate. Keith didn't have the time nor the desire for a conversation with Mike Owens, Sr. right now. Furthermore, his adrenaline was pumping at full-force; there was nothing like the season opener staring him right in the face to get his blood flowing. Whatever it was that Mike, Sr. had to say better be quick and better be appropriate.

Coach Abraham briskly approached the reigning LFP (Least Favorite Parent). Extending right hands simultaneously, they gripped hands with enough force to crush a walnut.

"Ready for victory number one, Coach?" asked Mike, Sr.

"Hope so… we'll see tomorrow night though, won't we? You think your boy will be ready to play?"

"That's what I wanted to talk to you about, Coach. I would prefer if he would only play on offense for this one. He got hurt while he was playing defense, you know, and I don't think his future is going to be…"

"Mike, I hate to cut this conversation short," lied Coach Abraham, "but we're heading up to Pennington to watch the JVs."

"This'll just take a…"

"So we'll have to continue this conversation at another time. Make sure your boy stays off that ankle tonight, and make sure he keeps icing it. We are counting on him to help us tomorrow night on offense… and on defense. Good talking to you again, Mike."

Two minutes later, Keith was in the coaches' office, closing the door securely behind him.

"Was that my buddy standing out by the gate, Coach?" asked Jim.

"You mean Mr. Owens?"

"The same. Last memory I have of him he was marching out of that gate… in a bit of a hurry as I recall. Did he have some pearls of wisdom to share with us for tomorrow?"

"I just didn't have any time for chatting… not if we're going to make it to the JV game on time."

"How did you get rid of him so fast, Keith? Tell us your secret?"

"No secret," responded Coach Abraham, not finding much humor in the situation.

"See that, Coach Oliver. Keith's always keeping his cards pinned close to his chest," joked Jim.

Isn't that the truth, Coach Abraham thought to himself.

Jim couldn't help but feel his pressure gauge topping out as he collapsed into the driver's seat of his minivan at 10:00 p.m. Though the game had gone exactly the way the Juddville coaches had wanted, a 34 to 0 blowout was a tough act to follow. The JV Jaguars had their way with the JV Pirates, leading 28 to 0 at half time and then scoring on their first possession of the second half, but missing the extra point. Unfortunately, the running clock—mercy rule—did not go into effect. A 35 point spread in the 2nd half meant the clock only stopped for timeouts, injuries, penalties, or a score. A running clock would have reduced the amount of time required to finish out the game by as much as a half hour.

Nevertheless, it was a big victory for the jayvees. Who cared if the varsity coaches were denied the opportunity to leave a half hour earlier? More important was that every jayvee player contributed, and that every player ended up playing a significant number of minutes.

Unfortunately, the expectations of the Juddville faithful would now be even higher on Friday evening. The varsity coaching staff was expecting a tighter match up, however. For one, Coach Patterson had pulled up his five best sophomores to make his varsity team as competitive as possible, leaving the JV team with very little talent left in the cupboard.

Nevertheless, Coach Allen was genuinely happy for the JV team and for the program, for they were next year's varsity. As the jayvee game slipped into the back of his consciousness, his mind raced forward to the responsibilities of the next day. Lesson plans for the second day of class were all set to go.

The offensive game plan was printed and ready for laminating. Most offensive coordinators had in excess of 75 to 80 plays for a given game. This year's Juddville play sheet was composed of only 30 offensive plays, and only six of them were passes. Normally, this fact wouldn't bother him, but with the prospect of not having their number one running back on the field, Jim wasn't expecting to get much sleep that evening.

The twenty minute drive was a total blur. His mind was processing one scenario after another, round and round like a merry-go-round.

First play of the game? With or without Owens? Schultz would be his replacement, and that would change things a ton. Third and long, throw a pass or quarterback keep? With Riley at quarterback? Are you kidding me? Why not run the counter? It's not very polished, but it might be worth a try.

Fourth and inches at the goal line, inside trap or halfback power? Game's on the line. What's it going to be? Trap or power, what's it going to be, Coach? Call a time out? Time out!

Too late… Delay of game.

Jim pulled into his driveway, and his thoughts were now focused on only one thing: a cold Budweiser. Perhaps, a cold one or two might slow down his highly-charged brain. He went for the refrigerator as soon as he entered the kitchen. The house was quiet; the kids were certainly asleep by now.

He walked into the living room and sat in his favorite recliner. The house was spotless, and the remote was sitting in its preferred spot on the corner of the coffee table. He maneuvered the chair into a reclining position and took a long swallow.

Ah, that hits the spot, thought Jim. *Now for a few sports highlights…*

His mind at ease, he slipped off his shoes and let his worries drift off into Never Never land. All of a sudden, the sound of scampering feet, followed by Luke's head suddenly appearing on his left.

"Daddy, please don't hurt Freckles. He didn't mean it. Don't hurt him, please."

The next family member to appear was Mary with a sober look on her face.

"Hi, honey. Luke, you're supposed to be in bed. Tomorrow is a school day, and it's a game day. You've got to the count of five."

"Aw, Dad," whined his oldest son.

"Give me a hug first," said Jim. Luke jumped up on his dad's lap and received a vise-grip hug.

"How was school?"

"Oh, it was alright. I've already got homework though."

"That's a bummer. At least you've got recess." Jim was reluctant to send Luke off to bed, yet the realities of the next day kept pressing forward.

"Good night, son."

Luke hopped off his lap and sprinted for his bedroom; Mary followed him, deciding that this might not be the best time to give Jim the latest update on Freckles.

Jim's curiosity propelled him immediately out of his seat of comfort to the scene of the crime in his backyard. He went through the garage, turned on the spotlight, and froze in his tracks when he surveyed his ravaged lawn. Five holes—more aptly described as "pits"—had transformed his meticulously-manicured lawn into a ragged mine field that looked like it had been trampled upon by a herd of ravaging elephants.

"Where is that dog?" shouted Jim to no one.

Back into the house Jim walked with determination and purpose. To the basement he descended. Sitting forlornly in his cage, wagging his tail nervously, Freckles readied herself for the judgment to come.

Jim reached into the cage and grabbed his newly acquired mutt by the collar, dragging her up the stairs, through the kitchen, through the garage, and out to the scene of the crime.

Together they journeyed to each of the five pits. Into each pit Freckles's nose would disappear before getting forcefully smacked on the backside. The fifth and final pit resulted in a backhand to her mouth. Just when he was about to dropkick the dog, he heard a voice behind him.

"What are you doing to her, Jim?" asked Mary.

"Somebody's got to discipline this dog. Did you see what she did to this lawn?"

"Yeah, in case you forgot, I was here the whole time."

"And what did you do about it?"

"First, I tied her to a stake. Then I squirted lighter fluid on her and barbecued her. Then I filled up the laundry tub and dunked her under water for 30 seconds at a time."

"This isn't funny, Mary. Remember, it wasn't my idea to get this dog."

"It seems to me I clearly remember you giving your approval. If your memory needs refreshing, we can wake up Katie and ask her if you'd like."

"Forget it, Mary," pausing a few moments before continuing. "I am sorry... I guess the pressure of football and school is already beginning to get to me."

"Let's go inside, Jim. Maybe I'll join you for another beer if you don't mind."

"What about the yard?"

"Who cares? At least it's in the back where no one can see it."

"Good point, Mary."

"I better grab Freckles before you kill her."

"Hey, I'm just trying to teach her not to dig holes."

"Really? You might think about leaving the deepest hole unfilled... just in case we need it."

"You're a comedian tonight. Who taught you how to be so sarcastic?"

Under the cover of the night, Coach Allen followed his wife and his dog inside. Yet the fear of what might have been was sitting in his stomach like a cinder block.

Chapter Sixteen

When Pete awoke on Friday morning, the first thoughts of his day were completely shocking — if not embarrassing. And they occurred on a day that he had been looking forward to for nearly two years, a day when he would finally get his first opportunity to start for the Juddville Jaguars Varsity Football Team. He had truly believed that this day would one day come though he had always pictured himself as a running back, not as a guard. And he certainly hadn't anticipated the privilege and honor of being a team captain.

Yet on this exceptional morning, Pete's mind was focused on something altogether foreign to football. When he had rolled out of bed, his thoughts were not about the type of performance he intended to bring to Raymond Sanders Stadium that evening. No, somehow he had let his guard down, allowing for a most embarrassing and potentially dangerous intrusion.

Simply stated, his inner most thoughts had been hijacked by a girl named Amber. Over the past day and a half, his mind had gravitated towards her. Her hair, her eyes, her smile. And he must have replayed his recent encounter with her a hundred times. Despite Pete's best attempts to analyze and reanalyze their brief rendezvous at the Pancake House on Wednesday evening, he could not ascertain whether she had given him a stop-right-there red light or if she had given him a proceed-with-caution yellow light.

Over and over he dissected her words:

"I would love to give you my number, Pete, but I would have to make sure it's okay with Joey first."

To say that Pete was baffled by the contradiction of her words would be an understatement. First, he questioned the sincerity of, *"I would love to give you my number"*. Was Amber being truthful or was she just trying to be kind?

Her next statement had Pete completely befuddled. What on earth did she mean when she said, *"I would have make sure it's okay with Joey first."* Didn't that imply she already had a boyfriend, and if so, why in the world would Joey ever want to grant Amber permission to give her phone number to Pete?

Were girls always so mixed up? All the same, the frustrations caused by that brief conversation were completely overshadowed by those enchanting eyes. Did she smile like that to every guy she met, or was she intentionally putting him under her spell?

Lastly, was Pete to believe that she would keep her promise and show up at the game? Why would a girl from Juddville Christian Academy have any interest in attending a Juddville Jaguar football game? They didn't even play football at JCA. Nevertheless, she wanted to know his jersey number. For what purpose?

By the time Pete was out of the shower and dressed in his favorite blue jeans and his sparkling blue Juddville jersey, boasting his all-time favorite number 54, he still hadn't pushed Amber out of the forefront of his mind.

This has got to end, thought Pete. *I've got a football game to play tonight.*

As he entered the kitchen, there was an 8 ½ by 10 sheet of paper with a message written in black marker from his mom.

It's a beautiful day to beat Pennington. Good luck tonight, Pete.

Next to the note was the rust-covered cowbell. His mom was definitely geared up for tonight, anyway.

Pete popped a couple of Eggo waffles into the toaster and poured himself a large glass of orange juice; he drained it and then refilled it. While he waited for his breakfast to heat up, he grabbed a plate, a fork and knife, and found the Aunt Jemima syrup in the cupboard.

He remembered Steve's joke the day before during lunch. It was actually pretty funny. Amber was no Aunt Jemima, though. There she was again, magically reappearing in his thoughts.

"I'll be cheering for you, Pete."

The Abraham household was so serene that Keith could hear the grandfather clock ticking, the pace of its pendulum bound by its relentless, purpose-driven beat. He closed the Bible on his lap.

In Keith's experience, he had learned two ways to measure time. One was chronological. The grandfather clock and his Ironman wristwatch measured time as it moved in a forward progression. He knew that if it was now currently 6:00 a.m., and an hour of time elapsed, his wristwatch and living room clock should now read 7:00.

There was another way to measure time, however. Instead of moving forward, moving backwards. An hour glass worked in this way. Once it is tipped over, you have a limited amount of time. Once all the sand sinks to the bottom of the hour glass, time has expired. The clock on a football scoreboard works in a similar fashion although it allows for stoppage of time under certain circumstances—timeouts, injuries, and etc.

As Keith sat in his favorite chair and began to pray, he thought about his daughter Julia. How much time was left on the clock for his relationship with her? How much time did he truly have until she was gone?

Two weeks ago, Keith had already accepted the fact that her time at home had reached zero. All that had changed, however, at a Saturday night beer bash at Lakeside Park on the eve of her departure for Tyler Bible College. Now she was talking about going to live with Mary in the Big Apple. There was a huge difference between going off to college and going off to live in a frighteningly-large city like New York.

Oh Lord, I haven't been much help to Julia. I haven't been the father I should have been. Please watch over her. Guard her from evil. Lead her along straight paths. If it is Your will, let her stay with us a little while longer… yet not my will, but yours be done.

Roger strolled into the kitchen wearing a Nike tee-shirt and his newest pair of Levi's. His mother was propped up on a stool in front of their expansive L-shaped kitchen island, sipping on her freshly-brewed cup of Seattle's Best coffee. She had yesterday's Juddville Gazette spread out on the glistening black marble counter.

"Aren't you going to wear your jersey today, Roger?"

"I don't feel like I deserve to."

"You're still part of the team," said Kate. "I'm sure Coach Abraham will insist that you wear it."

Roger thought for a moment about the consequences that might come his way if he should bump into Coach in the hallway.

"Yeah, you're probably right," he was loath to admit. "I'd sure feel a lot more excited if I was playing."

"You're time is going to come, young man. And when it does, you'll hear my voice louder than any other voice in the bleachers."

"Thanks, Mom," in a rare moment of intimacy. "I guess Dad won't be showing up after all."

Pausing to look directly into her son's eyes, "I am so sorry, Roger. I know how much it means to you. Your dad…he loves you. He just marches to the beat of his own drum. He probably had something unexpected come up at work."

"Is he too busy to call?"

"I think he feels awkward calling here. The thought of talking to me or to Bill probably petrifies him. Can I get you something for breakfast?"

"Just cereal, I guess."

Kate lifted herself up from the bar stool and grabbed a bowl from the maple cabinet. Then she retrieved a box of Captain Crunch with Crunch Berries from the pantry. After filling up Roger's bowl with crispy golden and raspberry red morsels of sugar, she grabbed the gallon of 1% milk off the top shelf of the refrigerator.

"Say when," said Kate as she began to pour.

"When," replied Roger when the bowl had reached three quarters full.

"Daddy, did you hit Freckles last night?" asked Luke over his bowl of generic brand fruit hoops.

Jim was standing with his back to Luke, filling his travel mug with coffee. Because he was running late as usual, he was going to settle for a mug of coffee and an apple. The question hovered above the kitchen airwaves, waiting for a legitimate response.

"Did I hit her? " Jim asked in an attorney-like voice, his back still turned to Luke as he rinsed off the apple under faucet.

Turning to face his son, Jim confessed, "Well, I spanked her. That's for sure."

"But she didn't know any better, Daddy."

"She's got to learn somehow, Luke. In the meantime, you need to make sure you keep an eye on her when she's in the back yard so she doesn't get into anymore trouble."

"Okay, Dad..." his eyes staring down at his lap.

Changing the subject, Luke asked, "Are we going to win tonight?"

"I sure hope so," said Jim. "I sure hope so."

Mary entered the kitchen wearing her pink terry cloth robe and matching slippers.

"Do you want me to make you a lunch, Jim?"

"Sure, I'm in a hurry though. A couple of sandwiches maybe?"

"Coming right up."

With two to three minutes to spare, Jim sat down across from his oldest son while Mary prepared the first of literally hundreds of sandwiches for the coming school year.

Pretending as if he was conducting an interview, Jim reached out an imaginary microphone asking, "Luke, how does it feel to complete your first week of 1st grade?"

"Dad, it's not a week. It's only two days."

"Seems longer than that... doesn't it? I sure miss hanging out with you guys. You don't know how much I miss you and your brother and sister during football season."

"Don't worry, Dad. There's always off-season."

"Yeah, that's right, Luke. There's always off-season."

Hating to interrupt, but well-aware of the time, Mary interrupted, "One victory lunch, for Juddville's finest looking coach!"

Jim rose from his chair, walked over to Luke, and kissed him on the cheek.

"Have a great day, Luke. I'll see you at the game tonight."

"Bye, Daddy."

Mary walked him out of the kitchen, handing him his travel mug of coffee, "Don't forget this."

"You're too good to me," said Jim, embracing her tightly, reluctant to let go before giving her a goodbye kiss.

"Good luck tonight, Jim."

"Thanks, honey, we could use a little bit of luck on our side of the ball tonight. Give Kevin and Katie a big hug for me when they roll out of bed."

To say there was an overpowering current of electricity flowing throughout the hallways of Juddville High School on Friday would be to say there were a few extra calories in a slice of Reese's Peanut Butter Chocolate Cheesecake.

The students, teachers, secretaries, cooks, bus drivers, custodians, and principal were literally counting down the minutes to kickoff. Between classes, a stream of blue jerseys and cheerleading outfits poured out from one classroom to the next. Most of the student body — players and non-players — were wearing some type of Juddville attire. Many, in fact, proudly wore last year's Juddville State Champions t-shirt.

Most of the conversations revolved around plans for attending the home opener. Many debated whether this year's team had a chance to repeat as state champions. During third period, the band could be heard rehearsing the Jaguar fight song. The majority of teachers chose to leave their windows open to provide a spirited background for Friday's lesson plan.

Coach Abraham handed out textbooks and assigned an in-class reading assignment with a study guide to be completed for Monday. During the last ten minutes of class, he gave the students permission to put their books aside and talk about current events — specifically, Juddville football.

The cafeteria during lunch was a steady buzz of football fervor. Varsity players filled up several tables with their bold blue jerseys. Pizza and Gatorade was the lunch of choice for most of the boys. The JV players strutted around in their Juddville tee-shirts, more than willing to share exaggerated play-by-play accounts of the previous night's victory.

Pete sat at his customary table, and Roger was once again seated across from him. The captain spoke very few words and seemed to be concentrating intently on each bite of food. After eating his second peanut butter sandwich, he proceeded to his banana. Normally, this highly-esteemed football fruit would disappear in three bites or less. Today, he tried to chew his food more deliberately to aid in its digestion. Finally, he advanced to his shiny Macintosh apple. The first bite squirted juice out from the left side of his mouth.

"What is wrong with you today?" asked Roger. "You've hardly spoken a word."

"Just thinking about the game. That's all," replied Pete.

"You've got nothing to be nervous about. You're going to be kicking some serious Pennington Pirate booty tonight. You know that."

"I just want to do everything in my power to make sure we start out the season with a win," said Pete.

"You're sure there's nothing else. You seem awfully quiet."

"I'm sure."

"No girl...? You wouldn't be lying to me now, would you?"

Is it that obvious? thought Pete. *Friends for a week and Roger can already read me like a book?*

Sixth hour was released ten minutes early for the traditional Friday Pep Assembly. The hallways were jammed with rowdy football players and enthusiastic classmates. The band could be heard from the gymnasium, already belting out the school fight song.

The Juddville Jaguar cheerleaders — already in mid-season form — led the student body in a few favorite cheers, concluding with the class competition cheer. Generally, the senior class won, but this year the seniors were a little weak on enthusiasm. As a result, the juniors snuck up from behind to win the "spirit stick". Coach Abraham concluded the rally with a few inspirational words for his players and a few words of encouragement for the student body.

"Tonight is game one. Our boys have worked their tails off the last three weeks to prepare for this game. The motto this year is TEAM: Together everyone achieves more. That starts tonight for the players, the coaches, the students, and our community. Please come out tonight to support us in our mission to defeat the Pennington Pirates. Thank you for your support. Go Jaguars!"

The rally concluded with the players congregating in the center court of the gymnasium. In the middle of their huddle was the captain, wearing his #54 jersey with great pride.

"Let's really hear it now, fellas. TEAM on three. One… two… three…."

"TEAM!"

Chapter Seventeen

After the dust had settled and the corridors of Juddville High School had cleared, a much appreciated tranquility descended upon the building. All but a few teachers had packed up their things and were out the door by 3:00. The student parking lot was virtually empty.

The only activity on school grounds was the JV football team and the cross country boys and girls teams who were anxiously looking forward to completing their practices prior to the big game. The varsity players had vacated the high school, most having gone home for a light snack.

Pete was so pumped up after the pep assembly, like a large inner tube dangerously close to exploding if someone didn't a release a little bit of air. Consequently, he headed home to distance himself from all the pre-game hype.

As soon as he got home, he went right to the kitchen where a refreshing lemon lime Gatorade was waiting for him in the refrigerator. A note from his mom was next to the cowbell on the counter. He could hear his mother stirring in her bedroom.

She was listening to her favorite Oldies radio station, cranked up loud as usual. Right now she was singing along with Bob Seger to "Old time Rock'n Roll." Pete chose to hide in the kitchen as long as possible.

Two minutes later she came charging into the kitchen wearing Pete's white away jersey.

"Pete! It's game day. Can you believe it? I'm so excited I could do cartwheels around the whole park."

"Hi, Mom."

"Are you nervous, honey?"

"What do you think? Wouldn't you be?"

"Pete," said Cindy O'Connor, gripping both of his shoulders and looking him straight in the eye, "You are going to be great out there today. Just relax and have fun. This is the reward for all your hard work. Enjoy it. You hear me?"

"Yes, Mom."

She gave him a kiss right smack in the middle of his forehead.

"You need some time alone, don't you?"

"How'd you know?"

"Mom knows everything. You know that."

"I think I'll go lay down in my room for a bit."

Pete dismissed himself to the privacy of his bedroom. He sprawled out on his bed and stared at the ceiling. Somehow he wished he could just put his finger on the minute hand of Mr. Clock and spin it around a few times until it read 7:00 p.m. Reaching over to his bedside table, he turned on his portable CD player. His favorite CD was loaded: a mix of hard-core rock classics by Led Zeppelin, AC/DC, Pink Floyd, and Metallica.

Closing his eyes, he programmed his mind to defense. He was lined up directly over Pennington's right guard.

I-pro formation, a tight end and wide receiver to my left, imagined Pete. *Look for the sweep or the tight end running a corner with the split end running a hitch. Or better yet, how about a lead right up the gut. Come on, Mr. Fullback, introduce yourself.*

The playside guard double-teamed with the center on the nose and then chipped over to Steve on the weak side.

Step up and fill, was the manner in which Pete's mind and body were programmed to respond.

Three quick steps forward, hips low, elbows cocked, and SMACK went his hands underneath the shoulder pads of the trespassing fullback. The lead blocker wannabe's helmet snapped back as Pete ripped his left arm underneath him.

A small window opened in front of Pete. The quarterback had just handed off the ball to the tailback, and he was coming his way. Pete bulled his neck and readied the hammer.

CRACK!

Pete's shoulder pads sent tremors through the tailback's entire body.

Dozens of times, Pete repeated the scene in his head. Then he switched to offense.

The first play was his favorite, the 34 trap. He crouched down in his three point stance. His legs coiled like a powerful spring. On the second GO, Pete's right foot bucket-stepped and planted for take off. His pads were at mid-thigh level as he scraped behind the center, creating the perfect angle for ramming his right shoulder into the stomach of an unsuspecting defensive tackle. Left cleat, right cleat, left cleat pounding into the soft Bermuda grass. The moment of impact... Pete's hands pressed forcefully into the victim's rib cage.

"Finish," was the routine command of Coach Oliver.

Up, up, and over went the defensive tackle.

An hour or so later, Pete snapped out of his pregame visualization/mental preparation time and looked at his alarm clock.

4:30 p.m.

Time to get a move on.

All of Pete's gear was already in his locker, so he didn't have to bring anything from home. He had made sure of that. More water was what he needed, however; Coach Abraham had insisted that they fully-hydrate themselves during the 24 hours prior to game time.

Pete heard some laughter coming from the kitchen. His mom must have one of her friends over for happy hour; everyone had their own pre-game ritual.

Pete popped into the kitchen for a large glass of ice water.

"There he is… number 54 of the Juddville Jaguars… Pete Bring-the-Heat O'Connor," announced Cindy's friend Tina in her best broadcaster voice.

"Hi, Tina. Make sure my mom behaves tonight, would you please?" pleaded Pete.

"I gave up on that impossible task a long time ago, honey. There's no controlling your mother during a Jaguar football game."

Pete drained his water glass and went for a refill.

As he turned off the faucet, he noticed the label on the empty beer bottle sitting next to the sink: **Amber Bock**.

Sitting quietly all alone in his classroom, the door locked to prevent any outside interference, Keith opened his Bible. He read a couple of Psalms and then closed his eyes and began to pray. He lifted up each player on the team, each coach, and lastly, Carol and his two daughters, Mary and Julia.

For some peculiar reason, he felt a calm assurance about the outcome of the game. Although Pennington would be a much improved football team after hiring Greg Patterson—former defensive coordinator of Bellview, a state powerhouse from the other side of the state—realistically they were a year or two away from becoming a playoff contender. Nevertheless, they would be stingy, quick, and physical on the defensive side of the ball.

Anyone remotely close to the Juddville football program was well aware that there was quite a bit of uncertainty regarding the state of the Jaguar offense. With an unproven quarterback and banged up fullback, the offensive line was going to have to win this game in the trenches.

If anything, the line was better prepared with the assistance of Coach Oliver. As a whole, they were much more polished and cohesive as a unit than he had thought possible for this early in the season.

With a few minutes left to kill, Keith reminisced over a couple of highlights from the week. First, there had been the heated phone call with the superintendent regarding his handling of the Mike Owens, Sr. incident. Keith had, in his own mind at least, held his ground and refused to be manipulated or intimidated by Dr. Jones. The next highlight was the showdown with Julia's former boyfriend, one in which he was certainly not proud. He still could not pinpoint what had possessed him to visit Brian at his place of work to deliver such a tersely-articulated threat. Not surprisingly, his actions had received irrevocable condemnation from his wife and Julia.

Nevertheless, it was crystal clear to Keith that God had sustained him through these troubles.

Opening up his Bible, he turned again to his new favorite passage, 2 Corinthians 4:7-9.

"But we have this treasure in jars of clay to show that this all-surpassing power is from God and not from us. We are hard pressed on every side, but not crushed; perplexed, but not in despair; persecuted, but not abandoned; struck down, but not destroyed."

Grabbing a blank index card from the middle drawer of his desk, he copied the passage with his blue Bic pen. Then he placed the index card in his back pocket.

Without a doubt, he felt less anxiety than earlier in the week, for he was reminded of the fact that he was indeed human, and he would never ever reach perfection this side of heaven.

Rising up from his seat, he felt confident that God would supply him with all the grace he would need. And afterwards, he would give God the glory, for Coach Abraham was well aware of where his strength came.

Jim absolutely hated the down time between the end of the school day and the 7:00 starting time for home football games. He lived far enough from school that the option to drive home was impractical, not to mention that his kids and new pet Freckles would probably not provide the best atmosphere for him to get mentally prepared for Game One.

As a result, sitting in his classroom in the middle school was about his only option for killing time. His mind was usually racing a hundred miles per hour, and there was very little he could do to put it at ease. Reading was impossible; he would attempt to read a page and discover that he hadn't retained a single sentence worth of information by page end. It was too difficult to concentrate on a book when his mind was bombarded by an onslaught of concerns about the forthcoming football game.

As a result, Coach Allen could not come up with a valid reason for turning down Jimmy Harrison's invitation to workout at the local gym before the big game. Initially, he doubted his ego would be able to handle working out with a former UFL tight end. Back in the day, he might have been able to hold his own in the weight room, but that was before having three kids. Jim was lucky if he was able to fit in one workout a week during the summer. Furthermore, his shoulders couldn't put up with the wear and tear of a rigorous weight training routine anymore.

Jimmy assured him, however, that they would go light and that his days of heavy lifting were over as well. One thing that was becoming increasing difficult to do was to lie to Jimmy. Every time he attempted to come up with an excuse, his new friend would see right through it. The main reason he couldn't say "No" to Jimmy was because he thoroughly enjoyed being around him.

When Coach Allen entered the Body Shoppe, it became immediately apparent that Jimmy had already arrived. He was surrounded by eight other lifters asking for autographs. Jimmy made eye-contact with Jim, and then politely dismissed his admirers.

"Here's my partner now," said Jimmy, winking at Jim. "Can't keep him waiting now can I? Coach Allen's got a big game tonight."

The Jimmy Harrison fans turned their heads towards the Juddville Offensive Coordinator. "Hey Coach, all systems ready to go?"

"I sure hope so," responded Coach Allen, knowing that just about any prediction he made could come back to haunt him.

"I'll go change in the locker room quick, Jimmy. Remember, you promised to take it easy on me."

Ten minutes later, Jimmy and Jim were two sets into the bench press. After their third set of 10 repetitions, they shifted to lat pull downs. A minute at the drinking fountain, and they were pumping 40 pound dumbbells for three light sets of incline flyes. Taking full advantage of their close proximity to the dumbbell rack, they moved on to dumbbell rows with 70 pounders.

After Coach Allen completed his last set of rows, he looked over at his workout partner. Thus far, Jimmy had barely worked up a sweat. Jim couldn't say the same. His Juddville Jaguar Big Lake Conference Champion tee-shirt was already soaked from front to back.

"The hardest part is over now, Jim. How much time you got left?"

"Oh, allowing 15 minutes to shower, I'd say no more than 20 minutes."

"In that case, we might want to superset some core in between sets of biceps and triceps."

"You lead the way, Jimmy. I'm not going to have much of an arm to throw to our DBs during pre-game. Any chance you'd like to help us out on the sideline tonight?"

"I thought you'd never ask," answered Jimmy. "Anything I can do to help..."

"Alright, what's up next?"

"Skull crushers."

"My favorite... after you, my friend."

Chapter Eighteen

The atmosphere in the locker room was tense; hardly a word was spoken while the players dressed into their game pants and tee-shirts. The reporting time was 5:00 in the meeting room; the first 30 minutes the players would be treated to the latest UFL highlight video. For the most part, the highlights consisted of a defensive back taking out a vulnerable receiver slanting across the middle, or a defensive end ripping through an offensive tackle en route to decapitating a helpless quarterback. Mixed in with the vastly imbalanced number of tremendous defensive hits were a few amazing performances on the offensive side of the ball, like a quarterback standing tall in the midst of severe pressure to deliver a perfect touchdown strike to a wide out who slipped away from his defender, or perhaps, a running back who carries not one, not two, but three would-be tacklers into the end zone for a game breaking touchdown.

After programming their minds with images of jaw-breaking collisions and death-defying receptions, the Juddville Jaguars were stoked for battle. On the white board, Coach Allen reviewed the blocking schemes for the inside trap and halfback power versus the 4-4 defense along with the anticipated stunts and defensive modifications they might see. Coach Abraham reviewed the primary offensive formations of the Pennington Pirates along with their basic tendencies. Finally, Coach Abraham called out each of the seven special teams, and there were no mix ups — not even Greg McDonald.

At exactly 5:55, all specialty personnel reported to the field to practice long snaps, PAT, punts, and kickoffs. Quarterbacks took snaps from the centers and warmed up their arms by throwing short routes to the backs and receivers. The rest of the players — primarily linemen — were waiting in the wings in the locker room until 6:10.

Since Coach Oliver was an offensive and defensive line coach, he stayed in the locker room with the beefers. Coach Allen and Coach Abraham were out on the field supervising and giving last minute coaching details to the specialty personnel. Coach Oliver kept the linemen focused in the locker room by reviewing pass protection responsibilities should the need or the opportunity to pass present itself.

At 6:05, the visiting Pennington Pirates were ready to hit the field. In a single file line, they walked down their sideline to the 50 yard line, crossed the field to Juddville's sideline and then turned left towards their goal line. They were dressed in pearl-white pants and jerseys, with black and yellow stripes. Their helmets were bumble bee yellow with a black stripe down the middle, matching their black face masks. On the sides of the helmet was a pirate logo that looked more like a drunken sailor than a soldier of the sea.

At midfield, Coach Abraham greeted Coach Patterson, and for a couple of minutes they exchanged pleasantries while refraining from revealing any information of consequence. For example, there would be no updates on the health of any key players, such as the status of Juddville's starting fullback who was currently stretching in the end zone with the rest of the running backs and receivers. Much to the relief of all the blue-blooded Jaguars, Mike Owens had experienced significant healing in his ankle. The swelling had subsided, and his foot had been meticulously taped by the team doctor. While the team was watching the UFL highlight video, Dr. Peters was running Mike through a series of mobility tests in the privacy of the gymnasium. Though not 100%, the sophomore back was certainly healthy enough to suit up for his first varsity game.

In perfect-synchronization, the Jaguar linemen joined their teammates on the field at 6:10, led by Pete O'Connor who looked like he was chomping at the bit to light someone up. The captains counted off the players by fives before assuming their places in the front to lead their team down the visiting sideline, across midfield and down the home field sideline. Each group spread across the field on a different yard line, starting with the four captains on the goal line, then groups of five on the 5, the 10, the 15, the 20, and the last three on the 25.

The Jaguars' captains led the team through a spirited warm-up, making sure to stretch out the major muscle groups while stirring up their enthusiasm. The three coaches were huddled together on the thirty yard line reviewing last minute details when an enormous shadow converged upon them.

"Jimmy," yelled Coach Allen, in the direction of the 6 foot 8 inch oak tree advancing towards them.

"What a pleasant surprise," said Coach Abraham, extending his right hand to welcome Juddville's most distinguished alumnus.

"Hi, Coach. Been a long time since I've stood on this field."

"Too long. Any chance we could get you to suit up tonight? I think we could find a spot for you."

"I don't think I would be of much use to you. I don't move quite like I used to."

"He's not as strong either," joked Jim, who was still feeling the after effects of their pre-game workout.

"Ha…" laughed Jimmy. Looking in Coach Allen's direction, he breathed in deeply, pretending to take a whiff. "I thought you said you were going to shower before the game, Jim. Or is that a new cologne you're wearing?"

"You're a regular comedian, aren't you?" Then Coach Allen became serious, "I invited Jimmy onto our sidelines tonight, Keith. Another pair of eyes always comes in handy, don't you think?"

"You're always welcome here, Jimmy. Don't hold your breath waiting for us to pass, though."

"Some things never change."

"That's right. I'm sure you remember our philosophy, don't you."

"How could I ever forget? Only four things can happen when you throw the ball: an incompletion, an interception, a sack, or a completion. Only one of them is good."

"You forgot a few, Keith," added Coach Allen, "You can add a holding penalty and the clock stopping on an incompletion, as well. The way some teams are passing the ball these days — with all the incompletions — the games aren't getting over till nearly 10:30."

Noticing that the youngest member of their coaching staff was being unintentionally ignored, Jim corrected the mistake.

"I'm sorry, Gary. I forgot to introduce you. Jimmy, this is Gary Oliver. He played for us a couple years back. He's doing his student teaching this fall, and we are extremely fortunate to have him helping us out. Gary's doing an outstanding job coaching our linemen."

"Nice to meet you, Gary," said Jimmy, with a firm Jaguar-to-Jaguar handshake.

By design, the last stretch was the loudest. As the 27 Jaguars performed their jumping jacks, each time their hands touched above their helmets they spelled out J-A-G-U-A-R-S. Loud and proud their voices echoed through the ears of the visiting Pirates.

On Pete's command they rushed towards him like a stampede of horses.

154

Hands began to clap, slowly at first as everyone joined in the rhythm, then faster and faster until the following command:

"Break down."

"Hit!"

"Break down."

A louder, "Hit."

"What's the name of the game?" asked Pete.

"Hit!" responded his 26 teammates dressed for battle.

"I said, 'What's the name of the game?'"

"Hit!"

"Bring it in," shouted the captain. "TEAM on three. One... two... three..."

"TEAM," hollered the Jaguars, all fired up and foaming at the mouth for battle.

Dividing into two groups, the quarterbacks and running backs went with Coach Allen. The offensive line went with Coach Abraham and Oliver. The linemen warmed up with blocking drills and form tackling while the backs practiced hand offs with a minimum of blocking and form tackling.

At 6:45, the team huddled at the 40 yard line to run a handful of offensive plays against a scout defense wearing yellow beanies over their helmets. The five players not in the drill—in addition to Adam and Roger in their game jerseys and shorts—spread out behind the offensive huddle.

The first play called by Coach Allen was no surprise: a 34 trap. Jim breathed a sigh of relief as he watched #34 Mike Owens shoot out of his stance, receive the handoff from Riley, and accelerate through the gigantic hole created by the offensive line. Next, the offense ran the halfback power to both sides, followed by the 36 trap. Finally, Coach Allen chose to finish pre-game with a play action pass.

"22 Halfback Power Pass on two," said Jim. "Good fakes now backfield."

David called the play and wiped his hands off on his pants as the team jogged up to the 30. He was planning on hitting the wide open tight end on the delayed "out" route.

"Blue 19... Blue 19... Set... Go..."

The quarterback pulled out from under center, but there was no football in his hands. The other 10 players were all poised in their stances, waiting for the second Go.

"Run it again from the line of scrimmage," commanded Coach Allen, with more than a little irritation in his voice. "Come on, Riley. Get your head in the game."

"On two... on two..." said David, as the mounting pressure began to feel like he was carrying a Sumo wrestler on his back.

"White 48… white 48… Set… Go… Go…"

Daniels snapped the ball crisply into David's hands. The defense watched as #11 reverse pivoted to his left as #34 sprinted by him. The quarterback reached out to #24, halfback Rob Bast, but as he did so, he bobbled the ball. Thinking twice about scooping the ball up and attempting to execute the rest of the play, the signal caller remembered what he had been coached, wisely opting to just dive onto the ball, cradling it close to his body where the defense had no chance of stripping it away from him.

"Huddle up, offense," bellowed the authoritative voice of Coach Abraham.

Coach Allen's first instinct was to march right up to his quarterback, grab hold of his facemask, and give him an earful. He held back, however, glanced over at Jimmy, and shrugged his shoulders.

"We can't go into the locker room like this," declared Coach Allen before changing the play. "22 Halfback Power. Execute the play correctly, men. Just like we have been doing the last three weeks."

This time the offensive play looked more like the offense the Juddville faithful had expected to see, both Owens and Riley carrying out their fakes to perfection.

"That's more like it," shouted Coach Abraham, clapping his hands enthusiastically. "Now hustle into the locker room. Hubba, Hubba!"

Twenty-seven Jaguars suited up in metallic blue jerseys and matching helmets sprinted towards the home team locker room, followed by the coaches, and honorary guest, Jimmy Harrison. Roger Collins and Adam Foster—acting as managers—collected the water bottles off the bench, making sure each one was filled before leaving the field.

A tunnel of fans formed the path to the home team's locker room. A large contingency of Juddville mothers, wearing their sons' away jerseys, stood clapping their hands emphatically. Junior varsity and middle school players in their home jerseys yelled encouraging words to the upperclassmen, but they were not to be outdone by the Rocket Football League Jaguars who were showing off their brand new jerseys as they proudly slapped hands with their varsity heroes en route to the locker room. The intensity of the players and coaches was deeply evident.

"Coach Abraham," from somewhere in the vicinity of the concession stand. "Coach Abraham…"

Keith looked to his left.

"Hey Coach Abraham, you want a piece of me now?" beckoned the one person who had been an enormous pain in the ass to his family and his team.

Standing alone, his arms extended out from his body, hands open, and palms facing forward. A clear invitation for a fight, but Coach Abraham wasn't biting.

"That's Brian Taylor, isn't it?" asked Coach Allen, taking three steps toward him and then shouting, "Why don't you go crawl back under your rock."

"Back off, Jim," said Coach Abraham, putting an open hand on his assistant's chest. "This isn't the time or place. Just ignore him."

All of a sudden, one of the mothers, proudly adorned in her son's #54 jersey, strutted right up to the agitator, holding up a rusty cowbell and waving it menacingly in his face.

"You shut your mouth, scum bag, before I shove this cow bell where the sun doesn't shine. If you think your face was messed up after my boy got done with you, you ain't seen nothing yet."

"You tell him, Cindy," jeered her friend Tina. "I've got your back, girl."

Brian's face grew pale as a crowd began to surround him. His boldness quickly gave way to cowardice.

Encouraged by her friend Tina and by the horde of Jaguar fans gathering around her, Cindy O'Connor moved even closer, cornering Brian Taylor against the fence.

"Why don't you get the heck out of here?" a sudden rage flaring up in her blue eyes, "You're not wanted here. This is no place for a rapist!"

All of a sudden a uniformed Juddville police officer stepped into the fray. He seemed to recognize the young man as well as the Juddville mom.

Mrs. O'Connor was well-aware of the officer's identity.

"Officer Kane, this young man was harassing the coaching staff as they were walking off the field."

"Yeah officer, the players and coaches were on their way to the locker room, and he called Coach Abraham out, challenging him to a fight."

"All right, all right... everyone can go find their seats," ordered Officer Kane, "I'll handle this from here."

"Kick that pervert out of her," yelled Tina. "He is a troublemaker. He's not here to watch a football game."

"All right, that's enough. Everyone disperse. I'll handle this."

"You do that, Officer Kane," responded Tina, "Just don't arrest the wrong person this time."

Officer Kane turned his head sharply, pointing his finger at Cindy and her friend. "You listen here, ladies. If you want to see this football game, I suggest you both go find your seats immediately. I've heard enough from you two."

Backing away from Officer Kane and Brian Taylor, Cindy lifted her cowbell, clanging it wildly with malevolent intent. As they turned and headed to their seats, the two ladies broke out in hysterics.

"Now I see why Pete asked me to make sure you behaved," laughed Tina.

"Someone's got to stand up for what's right," said Cindy.

"Hey, I'm with you, sister. I've got your back," assured Tina.

"Now let's go get our popcorn before the game begins."

Coach Abraham paced back and forth at the far end of the locker room as players took advantage of the last opportunity to empty their adrenaline-pumped bladders. He was well aware that his mind should be zoomed in on football right now, but he couldn't stop thinking about his awkward confrontation with Brian Taylor. Part of him wanted to forego his coaching responsibilities and rip Brian to shreds like a lawnmower running over tissue paper. Deep down inside, though, Keith couldn't help feel at least partially-responsible. What Brian had attempted was not really all that much different from what he had done earlier in the week when he had decided to make a personal visit to Brian's place of employment.

While the players finished taking care of their last minute bodily needs, David Riley sat on a bench in the corner all alone. In a few short minutes, everyone in the stadium would find out whether the unproven signal caller was up to the challenge. Every thirty seconds or so, he would wipe the relentless perspiration from his hands onto his game pants. The blood was pumping through his heart at record pace, and the barrage of erratic thoughts racing through his mind was making him so dizzy he feared he might pass out.

Bowing his head, he repeated a phrase that his dad had often prayed.

Be still and know that I am God. I will be exalted among the nations. I will be exalted in the earth.

Over and over, David repeated this verse in his mind. And then he added a line of his own:

I will be exalted among the Jaguars…

"Alright, men. Grab a knee," commanded Coach Abraham. The upper classmen led the way instinctively extending an open hand to the left and the right, holding hands with their teammates as their coach prepared to pray. Under normal circumstances, you could never get one of these young men to hold hands with another man. But this occasion was of extraordinary significance.

"Dear Lord, we are so thankful for the game of football. We are so thankful for the extraordinary opportunity to compete in this contest tonight. Give us strength, give us perseverance, and give us enthusiasm, O Lord. Put a hedge of protection around each player on both sides of the ball tonight, keep them safe from injury. In the name of Jesus, we pray."

"AMEN," agreed 29-strong Jaguars, plus three coaches and one distinguished alumnus.

Chapter Nineteen

Two-by-two marched the Jaguars in an intense procession to their end zone. The band was playing the Juddville fight song. The visiting Pirates were already huddled by the visitor's bench. A huddle formed around Pete, David, Steve, and Jeff.

"This is what we play for," exclaimed Steve. "We busted our asses for this. Now it's time to party."

"No mercy," screamed Pete. "All you got… every play… nothing less."

David had a faraway look in his eyes; his mind focused on the task at hand. *Be still and know that I am God,* he repeated over and over.

Jeff Nash sent them out onto the field. "TEAM on three… One, two, three…"

"TEAM!"

The revved-up Jaguars sprinted through the "Go Jaguars" banner held up by the fearless cheerleaders. The Juddville faithful rose to their feet, vigorously clapping their hands for their team.

The players formed a huddle at their sideline, jumping up and down as if on a trampoline. Shrieking whistles and a handful of clanging cowbells erupted from the bleachers.

"Jag…uars…. Jag…uars…!" chanted the football-crazed enthusiasts.

The team captains from the both teams met with the officials on the 50 yard line for the coin toss. The Pirates were led by quarterback #10, Seth Howell; receiver #83, Alex Matthews; and Ben Bisson, offensive and defensive tackle #72. Enemy eyes stared each other down as they exchanged handshakes.

After a few reminders about sportsmanship, the head referee asked the visitors if they would be calling "heads or tails".

"Tails," answered quarterback Seth Howell.

The coin flipped end over end en route to the plush green grass of Raymond Sanders Stadium.

Staring up at the captains and head official was the shiny profile of our nation's first president.

"It's heads," announced the referee, making it official. "Juddville, what do you elect to do?"

"We will defer," responded Pete.

"Okay, Pennington, would you like to receive?"

"We want the ball."

The head referee pantomimed to the anxious crowd that Juddville would be kicking off and Pennington would be receiving.

Moments later the captains rejoined their teammates on their sideline for the national anthem. The players removed their helmets and stood in a single file line, facing the flag pole near the stadium entrance.

A sophomore soprano standout belted out the words without a hint of trepidation:

"O say, does that Star-Spangled Banner yet wave o'er the land of the free and the home of the brave?"

At the completion of the anthem, a roar of patriotic enthusiasm erupted from the crowd of football-hungry fans, ecstatic over the birth of a new football season. The kickoff and kickoff receive teams hustled out onto the field.

"Welcome back, Football!" shouted Dr. Pete Wilcox, wearing his Juddville Jaguar hat with great pride. Cindy O'Connor was clanging her cowbell at a maddening pace.

Steve Wilcox positioned the orange tee on the 40 yard line. An official handed the brand new Wilson leather football to him. He placed the ball upright with a slight tilt backwards. Measuring his steps back from the ball and then setting his feet, he lifted his hand, ready for the go-ahead whistle.

The referee raised his hand and blew his whistle.

Steve lowered his right hand to his side and began his descent upon the ball. Ten hungry Jaguars—five on a side—trailed him by a distance of 1 to 2 feet.

The ball blasted off Wilcox's Size 12 Reebok, and the kickoff team pursued the pigskin with reckless abandon. Head hunters Pete O'Connor and Jeff Nash were leading the pack.

A wedge of five blockers was forming on the 20 yard line; their attention focused behind them on their returnman, #83, Alex Matthews. He caught the ball just inside the 5 yard line, secured it under his right arm pit, and sprinted towards the wedge forming in middle of the field. The timing of the wedge was too slow, however.

Consequently, they were ill-prepared for the ensuing collision. Pete O'Connor broke through the middle of the wedge with ease, but lost his feet in the process. Nevertheless, Pete drew most of the wedge's attention, freeing up Nash and Jacobs from the outside.

Pete scrambled back on his feet. Matthews had started in his direction but had since angled away. Jeff Nash was the closest Jaguar to the ball, and he was closing in for the kill.

Matthews's first intention was to try to bounce it out to the left sideline, but he decided at the 15 yard line that he was never going to make it. So he opted to cut back towards the middle and try to find a running lane behind what remained of the wedge. He didn't account for O'Connor who was back on his feet and prepared to flatten the untested receiver.

Leading with his left shoulder, Pete crashed into the mid-section of the returnman, ripping his arms up through the tackle, dropping Matthews flat on his back.

As Pete hopped up off the ground, he could hear the opponent moaning like a constipated sea lion. He was rolling back and forth like a windshield wiper, apparently having had the wind knocked out of him on the very first play. Within a few moments, however, Matthews was back on his feet, jogging to the offensive huddle for the next play.

There was a reemergence of cowbell amidst the freakish howl of the Juddville faithful.

"Wooo, hooo!" exclaimed Cindy O'Connor, jumping to her feet and slapping a high five with Tina.

A gorgeous, 18 year old with golden-brown hair—sitting two rows in front of Mrs. O'Connor—was also jumping up and down on the aluminum bleachers, praising the very same Jaguar. Her two companions stared at her in wonder, unsure how to interpret her exuberant reaction.

The umpire spotted the ball on the 15 yard line as both teams huddled for the next play.

"Base defense, ready…"

"BREAK!"

The Juddville defense appraised the Pennington offense as they broke from the huddle. Fully-recovered from the previous play, Matthews flanked out to the left on the tight end side, while #3 split out on the weak side. The fullback and tailback aligned in the I-formation while the quarterback took a pre-snap read of the Jaguar defense.

Fifty-two, Cover 2, thought quarterback Seth Howell, *how predictable.*

On the snap of the ball, the quarterback reverse pivoted and pitched the ball to his right. The tailback, Ronny Jackson #20, reached out, caught the ball with his fingertips, cradled it under his armpit, and headed for the right sideline.

"Sweep," hollered Pete.

Jeff Nash—recently converted to cornerback—flew across the line of scrimmage, shedding the wideout's block. The fullback was chugging straight at him. Jeff ripped into the fullback with his right arm, forcing the play to his inside.

Given no other option, Jackson planted his right foot, cutting sharply upfield. He lowered his shoulder and held his breath in anticipation of the forthcoming hit.

As expected, #54 was scraping down the line of scrimmage, licking his lips in anticipation. Pete lowered his shoulder and exploded with every ounce of power he could generate. In the process, however, he had dropped his head, causing him to take his eyes of the running back. The result was a poor tackling angle, allowing the running back to stiff arm Pete.

Stretched out flat out on his belly, the captain of the defense had failed to bring down the Pennington running back. The only hope now was for one of the safeties or the backside corner to run him down.

Unfortunately, the secondary was slow to react. As the runningback juked to the outside, strong safety Schulz could not shed his block. Mike Owens—playing free safety because of his tweeked ankle—pursued exactly as Coach Allen had instructed him. Yet even with all Mike's speed, he was not going to be able to run down Ronny Jackson; there was just too much ground to makeup.

The last hope of the Jaguars was backside cornerback, Don Jacobs who was normally a strong safety. Unfortunately, he chose an angle far too aggressive, leaving him with no chance to prevent the visiting Pirates from putting the first points on the scoreboard.

The sparse crowd on the visitor's side rose to their feet and cheered on their team with wild amazement. The rest of the offensive unit chased their running back into the end zone, lifting him off his feet as they pounded his helmet and shoulder pads with unbridled enthusiasm.

The beleaguered home team huddled in the end zone as they awaited the call from Coach Abraham. Their heads were hanging low, none lower than #54, the starting inside linebacker and captain of the defense.

The result was an 85 yard touchdown run. Pete lifted his head and snapped out of his momentary trance of self-pity. He waited expectantly to see if Pennington was going to kick or go for two.

Unsurprisingly, the Pennington kicker, #83, positioned the black tee on the 10 yard line. Pete looked to the sideline and saw Gary Osborne sprinting onto the field.

"Owens, off. Goal line defense," barked O'Connor. As Gary neared the huddle, he relayed Coach Abraham's call to Pete who made the call to his teammates who were huddled in the end zone.

"Sixty… Double Blast Man. Let's block this, fellas."

Pennington came out of their huddle with a pronounced bounce to their step, quite pleased with their early lead. They lined up in PAT formation.

The backup quarterback, #13, was the holder.

The defensive line lined up in their gaps; inside linebackers, O'Connor and Wilcox, prepared to blitz B gap.

On the snap of the ball, the defense exploded from their stances. The right offensive tackle down blocked, denying Pete an opportunity to reach the kick. Steve, however, had about a 12 inch seam on the left side of Pennington's line.

Wilcox swiveled his hips and blasted by the slow-to-respond tackle. All of a sudden, he was five yards deep staring directly ahead at the black kicking tee just two yards in front of him.

The snap was accurate, and the holder placed the ball firmly on the tee, spinning the ball so the laces faced forward. The kicker began his approach.

Steve stretched out like Superman, crossing his arms and casting an ominous shadow upon the holder. The ball thudded off of his right forearm, falling harmlessly to the ground. Steve was the first to pounce on it, and the referee whistled the play dead.

Pete was the first to congratulate his linebacker partner. The defense took a moment to regroup on the Juddville sideline.

"Alright defense, #20 is a good athlete. He didn't suit up for their scrimmage," said Coach Abraham, looking straight at Pete. "We've got to wrap him up, and we can't drop to our knees. Just play how we taught you. We'll be fine. No more scores!"

Then shifting gears, "Kickoff return, let's break one right off the bat. Everyone sustain their blocks. Returnmen, make sure you cover up the ball with both hands when you're in traffic, and no turnovers!

"Middle return… Ready… Break."

The coaching staff held their breath as the kickoff return team sprinted out on the field. The front seven was composed primarily of reserve players. The Kickoff Receive Team had always been where the weaker or less experienced players received their playing time. Usually, the backup running backs were also out on the field during this time, as well.

Nevertheless, if the coaching staff did their jobs, by mid-season this particular unit could become quite adept at providing favorable field position for the offense or even taking the ball the distance themselves. Often times, the kickoff receive players who excelled in their roles would earn looks on other special teams — once they learned to accept the fact that they were required to sacrifice their bodies and play extremely physical.

Pennington's Alex Matthews kicked the ball to the Jaguar 15 yard line. Tommy Schulz caught the ball and followed his lead blocker to the wedge. Covering the ball with both hands, he followed the wedge upfield. He saw two yellow helmets closing in on him from his left, so he veered to his right. Unfortunately, the wedge broke apart almost immediately, and #64 came out of no where.

Tommy braced himself for a collision and went down to the ground without much of a struggle. The ball was spotted on the 26 yard line.

Pete was on the sideline gulping down one last sip of water before returning to the field for Juddville's first offensive series. That was when he committed Cardinal Sin #1: never look up at the bleachers during a game.

Perhaps, he was still in a momentary daze after missing a wide open tackle that led to the opening score for Pennington, or perhaps he was experiencing early symptoms of dehydration. For some inexplicable reason, Pete looked up into the stands where his mother always sat during his junior season, the season where Pete spent the majority of the game standing on the sidelines.

He certainly had no intention of waving to his mother — he probably just needed to make eye contact. His eyes scanned the crowd for a woman wearing a white #54 jersey. There she was with her friend Tina. Just as he was about to turn to sprint out on the field, his head snapped back in astonishment as he noticed a familiar face sitting two rows in front of his mother.

Oh my gosh, there's Amber.

She was wearing a canary yellow tank top that accentuated her bronze skin, and her smile was as dazzling as the morning sun. In one brief moment, Pete had been taken hostage by Amber, leaving him spellbound, impervious to his immediate surroundings.

All of a sudden, Roger smacked him on the helmet.

"Pete, wake up. You're on first offense. Get your fanny out there, you big dummy!"

He felt like someone had just dumped a bucket of ice water over his head. As he sprinted out to the offensive huddle, he felt a resurgence of jitters. When the Jaguars broke from the huddle and jogged up to the line of scrimmage, Pete was having difficulty concentrating on the play. His mind was swimming.

What was it again? Oh yeah, 34 trap. What else could it be?

"Blue 18... Blue 18... Set... Go..."

The left guard bucket stepped with his right foot and drove his hands right into the left hip of the center who was still in his stance, along with the other nine Juddville offensive players.

A whistle sounded. The first yellow flag was tossed into the air.

"Dang it!" shouted Pete, pounding his right fist into his thigh pad as the referee marched five yards off for illegal procedure.

The Jaguars rehuddled, only five yards deeper.

First and 15. Not exactly the best way to start the first offensive drive of the season.

This time David chose to go on "One". Mike ran the inside trap to the opposite side and picked up three yards before getting hauled down by the playside linebacker.

Second and 12. For most offenses, a pass would be in order. Coach Allen called a pretty conservative game, however. Rolling the dice according to his way of thinking would be letting the quarterback keep the ball and run it around the end.

Therefore, David took the snap and pivoted counter-clockwise. Owens sprinted by, faking an inside trap and filling for Pete who was pulling to the right. David turned his back to the defense and executed a great ball fake to left halfback Rob Bast who was dragged down by the inside linebacker and overly-anxious safety.

Jeff Nash hooked the outside linebacker, and Pete was leading the way around the end, running straight at the cornerback. David put the ball on his hip and ran to daylight, sprinting upfield 20 yards before getting knocked out of bounds by the backside corner.

The Jaguar quarterback was ecstatic as he turned to run back to the huddle—until he noticed the yellow flag out on the perimeter of the field. The line judge was walking towards the referee, signaling a holding penalty.

Coach Abraham was 10 yards out onto the field. "What number?"

The line judge turned back towards him and held up five fingers, followed by four.

"Are you kidding me?" he yelled as he turned back towards the Jaguar sideline.

—

165

"Simpson…" shouted the Juddville head coach. "Simpson, get out there for O'Connor at left guard."

Reserve guard Craig Simpson sprinted out to the Juddville huddle which was now all the way back to the 10 yard line.

Since the holding call was a spot call, the 10 yards had been marched off from the 30 yard line. Consequently, it was now 2nd down and 16 from Juddville's own 20 yard line.

"Pete, what's wrong with you?" asked Coach Abraham as his captain reached the sideline. "Out of three offensive plays, you've committed two penalties. Are you feeling okay?"

"I'm fine, Coach. It won't happen again."

Coach Abraham patted him on the shoulder and said, "Alright get back out there on the next play, and let's start playing Juddville football. You hear?"

"Yes, sir."

Unfortunately, the next play was a halfback power to Jeff Nash. Simpson missed his block on the defensive tackle in A gap, and he penetrated into the backfield, tackling Nash for a two yard loss. Now the Jaguars were facing a near-impossible 3rd and 18, from inside their own 20.

"Pete, run the next play in," said Coach Allen. "34 trap."

Pete hustled back out on the field, slapping Simpson's hand as he sprinted by him. He relayed the play to David and reclaimed his spot in the huddle.

Pennington was looking for a pass, backing off their linebackers a few steps to get to their hook zones, so there was some decent running room for Mike. Pete flattened the defensive tackle with his trap block, but the safety came up and dragged Owens down on the 25 yard line, forcing Juddville to punt.

Craig Daniels hovered over the football and prepared to snap the ball to punter Bryan Cox. The Pennington Pirates were lined up with five men on each side of the ball, clearly going for the block, having only one man deep to catch the punt.

Bryan called out the punt cadence.

"Set…"

As soon as Craig was ready—about two seconds later—he snapped a perfect spiral back to Bryan. He caught the ball right at his numbers, bobbled the ball momentarily, panicked, and then shanked the ball off the side of his foot. The errant punt traveled on a low trajectory to the 30 yard line of Juddville, bouncing out of bounds, into the hands of #8, Roger Collins, who normally would have been the first team punter under more favorable conditions.

"Defense, it's time to make a stand," shouted Coach Abraham. "We've got to stop them right here."

The Juddville defense huddled on their 30 yard line. Pete called the play.

"Weak blast, Cover 1. Swarm to the ball. Ready…"

"Break!"

Pennington came out in a new formation—one that wasn't in Juddville's scouting report. They had three immediate receivers to their right: a wide receiver, a wide slot, and a tight end. On the weak side they had a tight end. In the backfield was a lone halfback, with their quarterback under center.

"Trips left," called out Pete. "Cover 3… Cover 3…"

Seth Howell called out the cadence as he processed the defensive adjustments of Juddville. He noted the strong corner take two steps back. He observed the strong safety shift towards the strong side, sneaking up to within five yards of the line of scrimmage in the process. No movement from the free safety, however

Number 34 was still lined up over the tight end on the weak side. Seth could hear the Juddville coach barking out instructions from the sideline.

"Slide over, Mike. You've got deep middle," shouted Coach Allen.

Perceiving an opportunity to grab another quick score, the Pirate quarterback hurried his cadence before Juddville could make any adjustments. Just as the ball was snapped into the talented quarterback's fingertips, Coach Abraham was frantically calling out to the nearside official for a time out. But it was too late.

As #10 received the snap, he sprinted out to his right. #83 Matthews came sprinting inside as if to execute a crack back block on the strong safety, but then he abruptly turned upfield and ran a post route to the wide open middle third of the field. The tight end ran a 5 yard out, and the slot receiver ran a corner route.

Howell followed his halfback #20 to the right. His eyes were on the tight end. Pete had dropped back to the hook zone, and Wilcox was blitzing through B gap on the weak side, but the quarterback was sprinting away from him.

Pete took one step forward before he recognized #83 cutting upfield behind him.

Owens will have him, thought Pete. But as he turned to look, he saw Mike stuck over on the weak side, oblivious to his middle third responsibilities.

Howell set his feet and threw a bullet to his favorite receiver. Owens read the play about two seconds too late. Matthews caught the ball with fully-extended hands, secured the ball and bolted for the end zone only 15 yards away.

Mike made up ground and managed to get his hands on #83 at the five yard line. Pete was also chasing from behind.

Matthews broke loose from Mike's grip, but not before Pete came crashing into him at the two yard line. Unfortunately, the force of his tackle propelled the receiver into the end zone for another Pirate score.

Because of the Pirates' failure to convert on their first PAT opportunity, they elected to go for two. They broke out of the huddle in an I-pro formation, with #83 split out on their left side. Cornerback Don Jacobs was lined up on their star receiver's inside, looking for the quick slant. On the strong side was tight end #80 and wide receiver #3.

"Watch the slant," yelled Pete, to weak corner Don Jacobs.

Howell took the snap, looked to his right, and then back to his left, zinging a perfect strike into the numbers of #83. Jacobs's helmet arrived at the exact same time as the ball, and the ball squirted out, bouncing harmlessly to the ground.

"Awesome hit," yelled captain Steve Wilcox. "Now let's get back into this game."

With 8:02 left in the 1st quarter, the Juddville Jaguars found themselves in a hole, trailing 0-12.

After a mediocre return by Tommy Schulz, the Jaguars started to settle down. The offense managed to earn a first down on some hard-core running by Mike Owens, but they stalled at their own 45 and had to punt. This time Cox got off a decent punt, and the ball rolled all the way to the 8 yard line.

Pennington ran the ball up the middle the next two plays, gaining a total of three yards. On the next play, they tried the sweep again. This time, Jeff Nash fought off the lead blocker and tripped up #20 after a minimal gain. The sideline let out a big sigh of relief because the safety was slow to fill and there was little to no interior pursuit from the Jaguar defensive line and linebacking corps.

Facing a 4th and 5 from their own 13 yard line, the Pirates had no option but to punt. Now it was Juddville's turn to line up in punt block formation. Sophomore Mike Owens was the deep return man. Juddville overloaded on their left side. It was Greg McDonald who broke through.

The snap skipped two feet short of the punter. He reached down to pick it up. As soon as he lifted his head, he saw #59 McDonald zeroing in on him.

Taking one quick sidestep to his right, he tried to get the ball off before the rush collapsed on him. He was too late; Greg got his hands up and steamrolled the punter before he could punt the ball away.

The ball scurried into the end zone. Greg was tangled up with the punter. The next person on the scene was Pete. He sprinted towards the ball. It was rolling steadily towards the back of the end zone. By the time he was halfway into the end zone, it only had a yard to go.

Pete dove for the ball, trying to recover it in the end zone for a touchdown, but he was a half-second late. His fingertips touched the ball just as it was crossing the end line.

The referee put his palms together above his head, signaling a safety. The first two points of the season for the Jaguars. The score was now 2-12, and the Pirates would be kicking the ball back to Juddville.

The Juddville faithful rose to their feet, sensing the momentum swinging in their direction. Pete easily identified the clang of his mom's cowbell, but he dared not look up into the stands; the thought of becoming entranced by Amber's eyes absolutely terrified him.

The Pirates lined up on their 20 yard line and prepared to kick off. This time they opted to punt the ball; an option afforded them after giving up a safety.

This time the punter got all of it, and the ball sailed over the unsuspecting heads of Juddville's deep backs, rolling all the way to the five yard line. Tommy Schulz retrieved the ball and ran to daylight. He found some running room on the Juddville sideline, finally getting knocked out of bounds at the 35 yard line.

Coach Allen put the ball in the hands of Mike Owens on two consecutive inside traps for a first down, followed by a 48 halfback power to Jeff Nash who broke loose for a 15 yard gain.

The teams switched sides at the end of the first quarter. Juddville was eager to drive the ball down the field for their first touchdown of the season. Both teams gathered at their respective sidelines for a 60 second break between quarters.

Coach Allen stood in the middle of the offensive huddle.

"Men, we have already played one 12 minute quarter of this season, and we haven't scored an offensive touchdown. We've got a good drive going. Let's keep pounding the ball down their throats. Sustain your blocks and carry out your fakes and we will score. Score on three.

"One... two... three..."

"SCORE!"

Chapter Twenty

The Jaguars started the 2nd quarter on the opponent's 38 yard line. The offensive line and backfield were finally beginning to click. With a 1st and 10, nearly every Juddville fan in Raymond Sanders Stadium was 100% certain of what play Coach Allen was going to call next. And the same could be said for Coach Patterson of the Pennington Pirates.

He was convinced that the Jaguars would run an inside trap to #34, Mike Owens. And he was exactly right.

Both inside linebackers ran an inside stunt through both A gaps, simultaneously crunching the sophomore runningback just as he was receiving the handoff. The ball fell to the ground where it was inadvertently kicked five yards behind the line of scrimmage.

David Riley—risking life and limb—dove for the ball. The next four players on the pile were wearing Pennington jerseys.

The referee blew his whistle.

The Pirate foursome scratched and clawed, pinched and pulled, but couldn't get the ball from David. In fact, the referee had to give a warning to Pennington's linebacker #51 to "tone it down a bit".

One-by-one, the Pirates were pulled off the pile until only David remained. As if committing an act of defiance, he lifted the ball above his head with both hands and then handed it to the referee, snarling at the Pennington defense in the process. Then he sprinted over to the hash mark on the Juddville sideline and waited for the next play.

Coach Allen questioned his own sanity as he decided upon the next play. With a 2nd down and 15 to move the chains, the defense would be on the lookout for a pass or some sort of trickery, yet they had to respect the run, being that it was only 2nd down.

"19 Boot on one... Ready... Break!"

As the Jaguars hustled up to the line of scrimmage, David discretely reminded the other running backs to carry out their fakes.

"Red Twenty-two...Red Twenty-two...Set...Go..."

The Jaguar quarterback received the snap cleanly and opened up counter-clockwise as Owens sprinted by filling for left guard O'Connor who was pulling to the left. David turned his back to the line of scrimmage, giving an exaggerated fake to left halfback Rob Bast, who cradled his arms and took off for the right sideline as if his life depended on it.

Then Riley put the ball on his left hip and galloped towards the left side of their formation. O'Connor had secured the edge, cutting the outside backer's legs out from beneath him.

Bryan Cox, the left tight end, released upfield and ran a deep corner route. The playside corner was trailing him by no more than three feet. Right end Dan Hardings, blocked down for a quick count before beginning his drag route across the field. Fortunately, he had no trouble avoiding the inside linebackers because they both had blitzed.

As David was making his way to the left sideline, he sensed pressure from behind. One of the blitzing linebackers had not been fooled by Rob Bast's faking, but all he could do was make a last ditch effort to dive for David's shoestrings.

The Jaguar quarterback stumbled and began his descent to the ground. With extraordinary balance and coordination, however, he reached down with his right hand, pushed himself back up, regained his balance and continued to the open field.

Squaring his shoulders in the manner in which he had been taught, David read the routes in front of him. Cox was closely covered and unfortunately was out of his range. That left one other option besides running it.

Streaking across the center of the field with no one around him was Hardings. David took three more strides and tossed a "touch pass" to his tight end. Hardings caught the ball, secured it under his left arm pit and turned upfield.

He crossed the 40 yard line and the 35 before getting pummeled by the Pirate safety #40 at the 30 yard line — just two yards shy of a first down. As the Jaguars retreated to the huddle, Pete turned to his quarterback and gave him a high five.

"Nice ball, David," complimented the senior captain.

David hustled over to the near hashmark to get the next call from Coach Allen, who was pacing back and forth, feverishly scratching his head. He was in an intense conversation with the JV coach on the other end of the headphones. Jim wanted to run the ball inside again, but the feedback from the press box was that the Pirates were overloading the inside on almost every play.

"We just ran David to the outside on the last play," commented Coach Allen. "I hate to go to that well too often."

"Run the 11 Keep, Coach. They are not respecting David's ability to run. We killed them on that play last night."

Jim didn't have time to remind Coach Dewitt of the obvious fact that Coach Patterson had also been at last night's JV game.

"Alright, it's third and two. We still have another down if it doesn't work," said Coach Allen.

The play was called out to David who quickly sprinted to the huddle. The Jaguars were still in the huddle when the back judge held up his right arm to signal 10 seconds remaining on the play clock. By the time the Jaguars broke from the huddle, he was opening and closing his hand, counting down the remaining five seconds.

"Hurry up, David," shouted Coach Allen. "You're not going to get the play off."

Three, two, one... The back judge blew his whistle and threw his yellow flag.

Delay of game.

Coach Allen raised his right hand to the bill of his hat and was about to curse when he felt a strong hand upon his shoulder.

"It's okay, Jim," said Jimmy, his new-found friend. "You've still got two downs."

"You're right," acknowledged Coach Allen, not accustomed to hearing from his new friend in the heat of battle.

He called out a different play this time, and it was the one he had wanted to call previously. Unfortunately, Mike Owens was stopped dead in his tracks by the playside linebacker after gaining only three of the seven yards needed for a first down.

"Coach Oliver, our right tackle is not getting off the ball. He hasn't made his block on the linebacker once. Do we have anyone else that can do the job?"

"He's the best we've got right now, Coach," responded the rookie line coach, feeling the same frustration as Coach Allen.

"Let's call a time out," suggested Coach Abraham, recognizing the importance of this next play.

Coach Allen concurred, and time was halted.

The Jaguars desperately needed a touchdown before half. With a 4th down and 4 yards to go, on the Pennington 32 yard line, this offensive possession was one that they could not afford to waste.

After a brief discussion amongst the coaching staff, the play was called in the huddle along the Juddville sideline. The Jaguars sprinted directly for the line of scrimmage, hoping to catch the Pennington defense off guard with a quick count.

David received the snap and reverse pivoted to his left. Mike sprinted by and cut the linebacker who was blitzing like a freight train through A gap. David turned all the way around and handed the ball off to Bast and then carried out his fake around the right end.

Bast took three steps with the ball and planted his right foot to turn up field. He saw his pulling guard #54 leading up through the hole. Hardings and Osborne had caved their men down inside, creating a natural running lane. Rob put his shoulder down as he crossed the 30 yard line, fully aware that he needed only two more yards for a first down. The safety was filling, but his approach was too high. There was no way he could stop Rob from reaching the first down.

Rob collided with #40, getting underneath the tackler's pads and driving his legs until he was finally brought down at what appeared to be the 26 yard line. The line judge on Juddville's sideline saw things differently, however.

His right foot was back on the 28 yard line. The Juddville faithful were up on their feet, boisterously voicing their displeasure at the unfavorable spotting of the ball.

The umpire marked the ball according to the line judge's assessment, and called for the chain gang to come out on the field for an official measurement.

The Juddville Coaching Staff held their breath as they stretched out the chain.

A chorus of boos echoed upon the field as the referee held up his hands to show the 2 inch deficit of the Juddville offense.

"That's the second time you've screwed us," shouted Coach Allen.

The line judge turned his head sharply towards the Juddville sideline. Then his right hand reached for his yellow flag as if he was Clint Eastwood reaching for his Smith & Wesson. His eyes cast a cold stare in the direction of Coach Allen, baiting him to "make his day" by making one more disparaging remark about the quality of the officiating.

Coach Abraham put both hands on Jim's shoulders, pushing him back to their sideline, creating as much separation as possible between his assistant and the agitated official.

"Let it go, Jim," said Coach Abraham. "We can't afford another flag right now."

"That was a terrible spot. He screwed us out of two yards."

"I know, Jim. Let it go. We'll get it back. We'll be fine."

On their next three possessions, however, they failed to earn a first down and were forced to punt. The home team found themselves down 12 to 2 at half time, and the Juddville fans were getting restless.

The majority of fans had expected their team's development to be slightly behind last year's state champion team at this point in the season, but no one had expected them to be trailing the lowly Pennington Pirates by two scores.

As the sea of Juddville metallic blue jerseys trotted off the field towards the locker room, there was a buzz of mumbling and expressions of disbelief throughout the stadium.

"What kind of offense we running this year? We can't even move the ball on Pennington. Ain't there any runningbacks in that high school?" asked Andy Sommers, a die-hard Jaguar fan for over a half century.

"I thought that O-line was going to open up some holes this year," said Jack Hendrickson, his long-time sidekick and sounding board.

There was one fan who was not the least bit dismayed. Wearing her white #54 jersey, she was on her feet, rattling her cowbell like it was providing CPR for her beloved Jaguars.

"Come on Jaguars, you can do it. We believe!" shouted Cindy O'Connor at the top of her lungs.

The players were immune to all of this, of course. They high-tailed it to their locker room at record speed. As the coaches conferred outside of the locker room, chaos reigned within.

"Come on line, you've got to open up some running lanes," whined Mike Owens, Jr.

Pete, normally the first one to come to the defense of the O-line, hung his head in humiliation. His mind was currently analyzing everything he had done wrong that half: the penalties, the missed tackle, the failure to recover the blocked punt before it rolled out of the end zone.

Greg McDonald was the next to voice his displeasure.

"We are playing like a bunch of pussies. They're kicking our asses right now. Offense, you're stinking up the whole field. You can't expect the defense to do all the scoring!"

An unexpected voice rose from the corner of the locker room.

"Be still," said the Juddville starting quarterback. "Listen to us right now. We can't be pointing fingers. We've got to stay together and believe in our team… believe in each other… and believe in ourselves."

The silence was deafening. David continued, "Does anyone really believe that Pennington is the better team? Of course not. Everyone just settle down and wait for the coaches to come back in and get us back on the right track."

"David's right," said Captain Steve Wilcox. "Everyone just shut the heck up and think about how things are going to go differently in the second half. We are not going to lose this football game!"

While the team sat in silence, Roger and Adam walked around the locker room handing out freshly-sliced oranges for the players to gnaw on as they psyched themselves up for the second half. At the same time, water bottles were passed around to try to replenish the fluids lost during the first half of this humid August evening.

A minute later, the door slammed open. Coach Abraham was the first to take the floor.

"All right listen up, men. Did Pennington do anything on offense that we didn't prepare you for?"

Jeff Nash bravely raised his hands. "Well, we didn't spend much time against trips this week, Coach."

"You're absolutely right, Jeff. So here's how we will adjust against trips. First, we're going to move our secondary back to their normal positions. Mike, you're back to strong corner, and Jacobs to strong safety. Tommy, back to free. David, if Mike needs to a breather, you'll go to corner. But Mike's going to suck it up aren't you, Mike?"

"Yes, sir," accepting the fact that Coach Abraham hadn't given him any choice in the matter.

Coach Abraham continued, "If they come out in trips again," pausing a moment to draw it up on the whiteboard, "here's how we'll adjust. We'll go Cover Three Sky. Don, you'll play off the number three receiver 5 yards, and if you read run, you bring force immediately and contain the runningback. If it's pass, you've got the strong flats. Mike, you'll drop to deep outside 1/3; and Tommy, you've got deep middle 1/3. Jeff, you've got deep 1/3 on the weak side. Whichever outside LB is on the weak side has got weak flats. Look for the back or the tight end to run a screen. Remember #83 is their favorite receiver, so keep an eye on him at all times. If they come out in I-Pro, we'll stay in Cover 2 unless you hear a Cover 1 call. Alright?"

"Listen closely. We are much better than we played that half, and we're going to show everyone this half. Do you understand me?"

"Yes, sir!" responded 29 Jaguars in unison.

"Coach Allen?"

Accepting the marker from his long-time coaching partner, Jim walked to the board. He drew up Pennington's 6-2 defense.

"Okay, now what are they doing that is giving us problems?"

Osborne raised his hand. Coach Allen nodded his head.

"Coach, I can't get to their linebacker. He's gone by the time I get there."

Coach Allen thought for a moment. His initial thought: *Why don't you get your fat ass out of your stance quicker?*

But he knew that would be inappropriate and completely ineffective at the moment. Then a new thought emerged:

"David, what count have you been going on?"

"We've been going on 1, Coach. Except for the first series when we jumped offsides."

175

"No wonder, we can't get to the linebackers," Coach Allen responded with extreme irritation in his voice. "We completely lose our advantage when we go on the same count every play. From now on you mix it up, David."

"Yes, sir."

Meanwhile as Coach Allen was drawing up the blocking schemes for the inside trap and halfback power vs. blitzing linebackers, one of the players was beginning to shake. Roger Collins happened to be sitting next to him.

"Pete, you okay?" whispered Roger.

His inquiry was ignored. He continued to shake, not born of fear, but sheer rage. His mind was involuntarily flashing back to images from his past that were causing him to become so incensed he was about to go over the edge. Roger was the one person in the room at the moment that had witnessed the damage Pete could do when he was pushed to the point of no return.

Nevertheless, he grabbed hold of his teammate's arm. "Pete, Pete... you need to chill out. You've got to be able to think when you're out there."

Pete turned to his teammate, the junior who never seemed to shut up. There was a ring of truth in what he said. Football was a game where you had to channel your emotions, not let them control you.

He had to admit he had lost control in the first half. Two penalties on one drive. A missed tackle where he tried to take the ball carrier's head off rather than wrap him up.

"You're absolutely right, Roger," Pete finally acknowledged, taking a deep breath.

"Remember, this is supposed to be fun. Just relax, would you? I know you're going to go out there and light people up. I just know you are. So do me a favor. Enjoy it, would you? I sure know that I would if I had the chance."

Feeling relaxed, and especially grateful to Roger for his unexpected encouragement, Pete responded, "Your time is going to come... You know that, Roger? Your time is going to come. Just like it says in that Led Zeppelin song."

"Led who?"

"You're kidding me, Roger. Don't tell me you have never heard of Led Zeppelin."

"Who is he?"

"You're killing me, man."

Coach Abraham reclaimed the floor as Coach Allen erased his scribbling from the white board.

176

"Listen up, men. We start off the second half with the ball. Kickoff return, make sure to cover the ball up with both hands. Offense, march the ball down the field and stick it in the end zone for our first touchdown of the season. Then everyone will know the game is on. We've got to play as a team, though. Remember our motto: Together Everyone Achieves More. Bring it in now. Team on three. One… two…three…"

"TEAM!"

A revved up Jaguar team exited the locker room. An alley of fans was formed leading all the way to the field. There was a multitude of youth and middle school players wearing their Juddville blue jerseys. Hands were clapping furiously along with exuberant shouts of support.

"Come on, Jaguars. Put those Pirates away," shouted a 4 ½ foot youth football player wearing his treasured #11 Juddville jersey.

A deep voice overshadowed all. "This is your time, Michael. You've got to take this game on your shoulders. Show us all what you can do, son."

Mike Owens chose not to acknowledge his dad's presence. He knew his dad meant well, but could he be more embarrassing? In all honesty, the sophomore runningback was somewhat relieved that his dad hadn't gotten kicked out of the stadium yet.

Pete was one of the last to leave the locker room. He had helped Adam and Roger pick up all the discarded orange peelings strewn across the locker room floor.

The tunnel of fans had begun to disperse to their seats, but there was one brand new Juddville fan that hadn't moved an inch. She was wearing her alluring canary tank top and sleek black running shorts, accentuating her shapely, athletic legs. A smile was beaming from her face.

"Pete! Pete!"

Walking at a brisk pace, #54 turned and looked straight into Amber's eyes.

His stone cold demeanor melted instantaneously into a warm-hearted smile.

She reached out and grabbed his right forearm.

"Hi, Amber."

"Go get 'em, Pete! Knock them silly!"

Pete laughed. "Alright. I will!"

As he trotted onto the field, his heart felt like it was about to burst — in a good way. He no longer felt nervous. He felt giddy; he felt like Christmas morning, ready to open the largest gift under the Christmas tree that just so happened to have his name on it.

"Who was that?" inquired Roger, catching up to Pete.

"Huh? What are you talking about?" said Pete, playing dumb. "I didn't see anyone."

"Yeah right. Now I see how it's going to be. You keep your girlfriend a secret so your good friend Roger can't make a play on her."

"Whatever. Leave me alone. We've got a game to win."

"No problem, Pete. We'll have to take this up later... after our first W."

Chapter Twenty-one

Coach Allen was in panic. Never had he envisioned having to claw their way from behind in their first game. The first half was over; nothing could be done about that now. If they could just score a touchdown to start out the second half, momentum would shift back to the Jaguars.

He turned to Jimmy who was standing on his right, "What do you think, Jimmy? What do we need to do to put the ball in the end zone?"

"Stick with your game plan, Coach. I'd keep wearing them down with your running game, and then come back with the play action pass. I think your quarterback has the confidence if you need to throw."

"You think so? He did make a decent throw on that bootleg. That play was one block away from a touchdown."

"Yeah, I would come back to that again. Do you have a counter or reverse?"

"Sure, we haven't repped it a lot in practice, but I think we could catch them over-pursuing. That's a great idea. Don't let me forget about that play, Jimmy."

"I won't. I got your back."

"Are you sure you're up for that? If things don't go our way in the second half, I might need a bodyguard to get out of here in one piece."

"Think positive, Jim. Think positive."

Coach Abraham had the kickoff receive team huddled around him. There was passion in his voice. There was intent in his eyes. And more importantly, there was belief in his heart.

"Bring it in, men. Let's start this half off by busting one. For that to happen, we've got to sustain our blocks. Middle return... Middle return... Ready?"

"Break!"

The eleven proud members of the receive team sprinted onto the field.

Cindy O'Connor was on her feet, clanging the rust off her cowbell. Her friend Tina was by her side, a pair of fingers in her mouth expelling an ear-splitting whistle. Their spirit grew contagious as the Juddville faithful rose to their feet. The student body was bouncing up and down on their feet, generating a football fervor throughout the Juddville bleachers.

Alex Matthews of the Pennington Pirates teed up the football on the 40. Deep for the Jaguars were Jeff Nash and Mike Owens, the latter replacing Tommy Schulz.

The ball sailed to the Jaguar five yard line. Mike fielded the ball and cradled it securely under his right arm and followed Nash to the wedge. He found daylight to the left, and he accelerated through the gap. There was nothing preventing him from going the distance except for the kicker, #83, who was Pennington's best overall athlete. He was sprinting towards him at an advantageous angle of pursuit.

Consequently, Mike made a sharp cut back against the grain, hoping to surprise Matthews. The cut backfired, however, as the kicker was able to dive at his feet and make a shoestring tackle.

Nevertheless, the sophomore running back had advanced the ball to their own 49 yard line which was great field position for the Jaguars to begin their first offensive series of the second half. Coach Abraham was pleased that his last minute substitution—Owens for Schulz—had paid dividends. Hopefully, it also signaled a sign of things to come for his sophomore running back.

On the first play from scrimmage, Coach Allen surprised everyone. He called a 22 Power Pass.

"Blue 48... Blue 48... Set... Go... Go... Go..."

A whistle blew and a yellow flag flew in the air from the hand of the line judge. Linebacker #51 jumped off sides, running over #54 of the Jaguars in the process.

Steve Wilcox grabbed Pete's hand, lifted him off the ground, and said, "Great job, Pete, way to earn our offense an easy 5 yards."

The Jaguars rehuddled. David looked over at the sideline. Coach Allen signaled to run the same play. Once again Riley called for a long count.

The Jaguars lined up in T-formation, and David quickly began the cadence.

"Red 19... Red 19... Set... Go... Go..."

Daniels snapped the ball crisply into David's hands. David reverse-pivoted to his left. Mike sprinted by and filled, cutting the defensive tackle at the knees. Riley turned and faked to Bast who stutter-stepped like he had the ball. After his fake, Rob joined Pete on a double-team on the outside linebacker, creating a solid wall of protection for David to rollout behind.

Nash was flying downfield, wide-open on a Go route while tight end Hardings was breaking free from the cornerback on a simple out route. Both receivers were viable options for Riley.

Nevertheless, the most favorable option for David was to secure the ball under his right arm and take advantage of all the green in front of him.

"Go!" yelled David, signaling to his blockers that he was crossing the line of scrimmage and that they now had the green light to block downfield.

Pete pushed the outside backer off to Bast and proceeded downfield. Hardings turned inside and hooked the cornerback. Nash worked to the outside of the safety who was in hot pursuit.

David veered towards the sideline, feeling pretty secure behind the personal escort service of O'Connor. As they crossed the 40 yard line, Pete looked to the inside and observed linebacker #51 giving chase. The memory of a recent cheap shot came to mind, and he pounced upon the linebacker, dipping his hips and ripping his hands up through #51's shoulder pads.

David broke into the wide open as Hardings had no problems neutralizing the under-sized cornerback. The safety, #83, had David in his sights and was rapidly closing on him, but he did not see Jeff coming from his blind side.

Nash was just able to get his head in front, and the safety never saw him coming. The safety went down hard, and David continued to run at full speed for the end zone.

He crossed the 30, the 20, the 10, and was finally knocked out of bounds at the 3 yard line by the backside cornerback, Ronny Jackson — the same player who had score Pennington's opening touchdown.

Riley went down hard out of bounds but popped up immediately. Pete was the first teammate to congratulate him, but the celebration was cut short as they both realized that they still hadn't put the ball in the end zone.

Riley jogged over to the near hash mark to receive the next play from Coach Allen. David relayed the play to his teammates, and the offense broke from the huddle with heightened enthusiasm.

"White 19… White 19… Set… GO!"

David received the snap and handed the ball off immediately to Mike Owens who found a seam between O'Connor's trap block and Steve Wilcox's down block on the back side linebacker. Mike kept his legs churning as he crossed the 3 yard line, the 2 yard line, and the 1. He was finally dragged down at the goal line.

The sophomore runningback was smothered by both defensive tackles, both linebackers, and the safety. No signal was given yet as each player had to be pulled off the pile one at a time.

The line judge spotted the location of the ball and worked back to where Mike's knee first made contact with the ground which he assessed to be the six inch line.

Mike Owens, Sr. led a chorus of boos in the bleachers.

"Are you blind, ref? That was a touchdown, you moron!"

Second and six inches. Again Coach Allen called David all the way over to the sideline.

"15 Keep. Find an opening and dive into the end zone, David. Make sure you protect the ball."

David sprinted out to the huddle and called the play. He nervously wiped his sweaty hands onto his game pants as they broke from the huddle.

"Watch the quarterback... watch the quarterback," barked linebacker #51.

No, you better watch the guard lined up in front of you, Pete thought to himself.

"Red 36... Red 36... Set... Go... Go!"

David leaned into the center and received the snap cleanly. He stepped to his left, drove his shoulder into the backside of Pete who was bulldozing #51 five yards deep into the end zone. A defensive tackle grabbed onto David's jersey, but he was already two yards into the end zone.

The Juddville fans erupted into a tumultuous applause — with the exception of one disgruntled fan, however.

"What are you doing, Coach? That should have been Mike's touchdown. The ball should have gone to Mikey!"

Cindy O'Connor's head snapped around and stared at Mike, Sr. Then she did what any normal person would do under the circumstances. She lifted her cowbell directly into his face and shook it defiantly.

Then she stated the obvious, "Who gives a rip as long as we scored?"

She turned to her friend Tina and gave her a high five before resuming their cowbell and ear-piercing whistling duet.

Mr. Owens folded his arms across his chest, fuming mad that his son wasn't getting the glory he deserved.

Juddville's PAT team sprinted onto the field to kick the point after. Wilcox set the tee on the 10 yard line while David called the play in the huddle.

"PAT on snap. Ready?"

"Break!"

The Jaguar special team unit rushed to the line of scrimmage and set up in three point stances. Craig wrapped his hands around the Wilson pig skin.

Riley barked out the cadence, "Set."

When Craig was ready a few seconds later, he snapped a perfect strike back to David who fluidly set the ball down on the black tee, spinning the laces forward.

Steve took three quick steps toward the ball and punched it through the middle of the uprights. His teammates congratulated him, and they sprinted to the sideline, super-pumped that they had decreased their deficit to just three points.

With 10:46 left in the 3rd quarter, the scoreboard read Juddville 9, and the Visitors 12. Pennington's next possession was a three and out, but their punter was the beneficiary of a 17 yard roll at the end of his punt — the result of Mike Owens's failure to come up and fair catch the punt.

Therefore, Juddville started their next possession back on their 22 yard line. The first play was predictable: a 34 trap. Pennington's defensive tackles were pinching A gap hard. Pete ended up trying to hook block the tackle. Owens, seeing no running room up the middle, tried to bounce it out wide. The outside linebacker got a hold of his jersey, and #51 came out of nowhere and leveled him.

The net result was a loss of 2 yards, yet potentially much worse as running back #34 was still lying on the ground. The referee blew his whistle for an official's timeout, and Coach Abraham trotted out to check on the condition of his sophomore back while backup Tommy Schulz sprinted onto the field to join the Juddville huddle.

Team physician, "Doc" Phillips, walked out to the field to offer his assistance. This week's managers — Roger and Adam — ran water bottles out to the Juddville huddle as the Pennington managers were allowed to do the same.

As Dr. Phillips started to examine Mike's ankle, the young runningback started to become restless and tried to get up on his feet.

"Just a moment, son, let's just make sure you're okay before we send you back in."

After a few quick tests, Dr. Phillips had decided that no serious damage had been done to Mike's ankle. Coach Abraham and Doc Phillips helped Mike onto his feet and assisted him to the Juddville bench in order to take a closer look at his ankle.

Meanwhile, Juddville struggled on their next two plays and was forced to punt. Coach Allen walked over to the bench to check on the status of his starting fullback and cornerback.

"Is he going to be alright, Doc?" asked Jim.

"It looks to me like there isn't any further damage to the ankle. I'm just going to retape it. Then he'll be good to go."

Bryan Cox got all of his foot and then some into his punt, the ball sailing all the way to the Pennington 17 yard line before rolling out of bounds.

The Pirates decided to attack Owens's replacement while they had the opportunity. On the first play, Howell took a 3-step drop, planted his right foot and threw a perfect strike to #83 on a hitch route.

David closed on him and wrapped his arms around both ankles, keeping the gain to 5 yards. The next play, they chose to pick on Riley again.

This time they decided to go for the homerun.

Three stutter steps by Matthews and then a sharp cut to towards the sideline.

Fade, observed David.

Reaching out with his left hand, David punched the receiver in the shoulder, grabbing a fistful of white jersey and then shoving him off-stride.

Matthews regained his balance, broke free from David and sprinted upfield. Safety Don Jacobs playing over the top in Cover 2 was able to get to the sideline by the time the ball was in flight.

Just as Matthews's hands lifted up to catch the perfectly thrown spiral, Jacobs rammed his shoulder pads into the receiver's sternum.

The ball squirted free from the receiver's hands and fell to the ground for an incompletion. The Juddville faithful rose to their feet, howling with approval. Their cheers changed to jeers when a yellow flag appeared in the vicinity of where the pass was broken up.

The officials conversed and the referee signaled defensive holding on #11. Coach Allen went berserk.

"You're kidding me," he shouted, about to walk out on the field.

An extra-large hand gripped him tightly on the shoulder, stopping him dead in his tracks. Jim winced and turned around abruptly, only to be looking up at Jimmy who was eyeballing him with an awkward grin on his face.

"Let it go, Coach. Your kids need to see composure right now."

Coach Allen paused a moment before responding. He remembered that it was his idea to invite Jimmy onto the sideline.

"Thanks, Jimmy. You're absolutely right," admitted Coach Allen with a straight face before breaking into a weak smile. "But could you take it easy on the shoulder, please?"

By this time, Mike's ankle was retaped, and he was ready to rejoin the battle.

Coach Allen put his hands on the sophomore's shoulder pads and started to direct him out onto the playing field.

"Get back in there, Mike," said Jim, about to release his grip but then adding, "Do you think you can play press coverage with that ankle?"

"Sure, Coach. I'm fine… really."

"Alright, tell the safeties that nothing gets behind them."

As David Riley trotted off the field, his head was hanging low. Coach Allen and Jimmy immediately headed in his direction.

Jimmy beat Coach Allen to the punch.

———

"Hey David, that was a horse sh... I mean a horse crap call," said the former UFL player. "Don't let it get to you."

Coach Allen couldn't help but chuckle at Jimmy's choice of words. Then he added, "Yeah, David. That was a horrible call. Water up and get ready for our next possession. It's time to score again, don't you think?"

"Yes, sir."

The next play Pennington returned to their trips formation. Number 20 was the lone running back with a tight end and two wide receivers overloading the right side. The last time they had come out in this formation, they had hit #83 on a deep post route for a touchdown.

Pete recognized the formation immediately and changed the pass coverage to Cover 3. Strong safety Don Jacobs rolled up close to the line of scrimmage—four yards off the tight end and 3 yards wide—Mike Owens backed 7 yards off the widest receiver, and free safety Tommy Schulz cheated over about halfway between the center of the field and the hash mark.

Linebacker Pete O'Connor was lined up on the weak side anxious to execute the stunt that Coach Abraham had just signaled. Even though it was 1st and 10 on the Pirates' 37 yard line, the Jaguars were expecting pass, and Pete was hoping to get to Howell before he had to time to throw the ball.

On the snap of the ball, however, Howell reverse pivoted and pitched to #20. The tight end got a decent hook block on outside backer Craig Daniels, allowing the right guard to loop outside of his block. The wide receivers tied up the corner and free safety, so it looked like safety Don Jacobs was going to have to take on the guard's block and bring down the running back with little help from his teammates.

Pete O'Connor had other intentions, however. While the nose tackle slanted to the right, Pete scraped right off his behind and came flying untouched through the playside A gap. The ball was already in the hands of #20, so Pete rerouted his path to the outside, giving him the perfect angle to make the tackle.

This time the senior linebacker kept his head up and his eyes on the target. Leading with his right shoulder, he ripped his arms up and around the runner, lifting him off his feet before dropping him flat on his rear end. The result was a crushing blow and a 4 yard loss. Equally important was the effect on the Juddville fans. They were up on their feet, riding the wave of momentum, hungry for a defensive stop in their opponent's territory.

"Defense, Defense," chanted the Jaguar faithful. "Defense, Defense."

184

Second and 14 on the 33 yard line, Coach Abraham was expecting pass, probably out of the I-pro formation. He signaled Cover 2 with an inside strong stunt. This time he called Steve Wilcox's number for the blitz.

As expected, Pennington lined up their tight end and wide receiver to the right. Owens faced up on #83, pressing him tightly, just a yard separating the two. Safety Don Jacobs was eight yards deep over the tight end. Jeff Nash lined up tight on the weak side receiver. Free Safety Tommy Schulz played 10 yards deep over the weak side tackle.

On the snap of the ball, Seth Howell began his 3-step drop. His fullback blocked the edge to the right while his tailback ran a swing route to the left. The quarterback's focus was on his favorite receiver Alex Matthews. On his third step—at the very moment he had been prepared to throw—he noticed that Matthews was late in getting to his slant route.

Mike Owens had jammed #83, punching his hands underneath his shoulder pads, completely disrupting his timing with the quarterback. Howell grew antsy, scrambling to the right, eyes still glued on Matthews, expecting him to break free at any moment.

He never saw Wilcox coming. Defensive tackle Jimmy Smith had been going C gap the entire game, but on this play he pinched down to B, drawing the offensive tackle with him.

Time was precious. The Pirate quarterback read the safeties sitting in deep ½ coverage. If he didn't hit Alex soon, his receiver would be running right into a safety. The tight end had been jammed by the outside linebacker and was having grave difficulties just getting off the line.

Seth Howell brought his arm back to throw, having decided that he would just have to trust Alex to get to the spot on time.

Crunch!

He hadn't even had time to bring his arm down to protect himself. The ball fluttered towards #83 but bounced a good 10 yards short.

Pennington's sideline held their breath as Seth Howell slowly rose to his feet. He was hunched over and in obvious pain, appearing to be favoring his ribs.

Coach Patterson immediately called for a timeout. Seth forced himself to stand upright as his coach came out on the field to check on his condition.

"I'm alright. I'm alright," said the highly-touted quarterback. "My rib pads absorbed most of the hit."

The rest of the Pirates huddled around their coach. He was doing his best to rally the troops, fully aware that the Jaguars were licking their lips, preparing for the kill.

With 3rd and 14 in their own territory and a quarterback still stinging from the last play, there weren't too many options. Juddville was bringing a ton of pressure, sending a linebacker on every play.

Meanwhile, Coach Abraham and Coach Allen were giving final instructions to the Juddville defense, reminding the safeties to keep everything in front of them.

"Don't be surprised to see them run the ball, though," said Coach Abraham. "Their quarterback's a little banged up right now. Swarm to the ball."

The head official broke up the Pennington timeout, and the coaches jogged off the field.

The Pirates came out in a 2 by 2 formation: a split end and slot to the left, and a tight end and wide receiver to the right.

"Stay in Cover Two," called out Coach Allen. "Everything in front of you, safeties."

Neither linebacker would be blitzing on this play; both were dropping to their hook zones on a pass read.

On the snap of the ball, Seth took a 5-step drop. Lone back #20 took two steps to his right, setting up as if to pass block. Pete and Steve dropped to their zones. The outside backers, defensive tackles and nose tackle were rushing hard like freight trains, each determined to be the next to get a piece of the "star" quarterback.

Howell set up a yard behind #20, in awfully close proximity to the runningback if he were to throw the ball. All of sudden, with the ball in his off-hand he reached around in front of his halfback who hadn't moved a muscle, placing it snuggly into his bread basket.

Simultaneously, the Pennington linemen transitioned from pass blocking to aggressive run blocking, driving their man to the outside and creating a huge inside running lane.

"Draw! Draw!" hollered Coach Abraham with extreme urgency in his voice.

Pete O'Connor, eyes on the quarterback the whole time, had sensed something fishy. He was the first to notice the handoff to #20, and he was now in full pursuit of the speedy back.

After accelerating through the hole, Jackson cut sharply to his left towards the Pennington sideline. The corners and safeties had all been run off by their receivers, so it was basically one-on-one: O'Connor versus Jackson.

Pete corrected his angle, realizing that he would have to give up some ground in order to make the tackle. The speedy halfback had already crossed the 30 yard line and was in full gear as he approached the 35.

Fully-aware that it was now or never, Pete dove for #20, swinging his right arm like a club at his ankles. Down went the runningback, face first into the luscious Raymond Sander's Stadium turf. The Juddville crowd breathed a deep sigh of relief before cheering with reckless abandon as the Pennington punting unit ran onto the field.

Pennington got off a decent punt and held returnman Mike Owens to a minimal return, forcing him out of bounds at the Juddville 36 yard line. Juddville failed to gain ten yards in their next three plays. With a 4th down and 1 on their own 45, the Jaguar fans and the Jaguar players wanted to see the home team go for it. But Coach Abraham would have none of that, opting to send his punt team out on the field to gain control of the battle for field position.

A perfectly executed pooch punt by Bryan Cox resulted in the ball rolling harmlessly out of bounds at the Pennington eight yard line. The Pirates had enough time to run one fullback dive up the middle for a measly one yard gain before time ran out for the 3rd quarter.

Chapter Twenty-two

With near-perfect synchronization, the Jaguars unsnapped their helmets, lifted them high to the sky, and shouted with one determined voice, "FOUR!!!"

This was the quarter that they had busted their butts for. This was the quarter where the entire game was on the line.

Pete grabbed one last hit from a water bottle and was unable to fight the temptation to take another look up into the stands. His mother was easy to spot, her cowbell clanging furiously, in his white #54 jersey.

His eyes glanced down two rows to where Amber had been sitting during the first half. Much to Pete's surprise, the seat was vacant. There was another girl—whom Pete did not recognize—right next to where Amber had been seated, but there was no Amber.

Surely she couldn't have left. Not from a game like this, thought Pete.

"Defense," called out Coach Abraham. "Bring it in. We need to keep them pinned down here to give our offense good field position. Play assignment football and swarm to the ball.

"Team on three... one... two ... three."

"TEAM!"

The Juddville defense hustled onto the field. It was the final quarter, 2nd down and 9 from the Pirates' nine yard line.

The first play was an off-tackle run to the left; #20 picked up two hard-earned yards before being dragged down by defensive tackle Joey Miller and Pete O'Connor. With a 3 point lead and the ball deep in their own territory, Coach Abraham was quite certain that Pennington would play it safe and run the ball again.

The Pirates broke out into their 2 by 2 formation with Ronny Jackson as the lone back. The last time they were in this formation they ran the draw play, and their halfback almost broke loose for a touchdown.

This time, however, they ran a halfback counter to the right side, pulling the guard and tackle from the tight end side. Pete read the play immediately and followed the guard all the way to the hole, delivering a punishing blow to the halfback for a one yard loss.

Pennington's punt team trotted out onto the field. Coach Abraham called for a punt block.

Sensing that the home team was not setting up a return, one boisterous fan rose to his feet and exclaimed, "Come on, Coach. Go for the return. You're wasting talent. Michael could walk into the end zone easily from this distance."

Simultaneously, Cindy O'Connor and her friend Tina turned around and stared.

Then Tina grabbed Cindy's cowbell and pointed it at the obnoxious father saying, "Sit down and shut up unless you want to eat this cowbell."

"I can say what I want," his voice beginning to tremor, "it's a free country isn't it?"

Out in the huddle, Pete cautioned his teammates "Make sure you don't run into the punter if you don't get a piece of the ball."

The lone returnman was Mike Owens, standing with his heels on the 45 yard line of the Pirates. The snap from the center was a rope, and the punter had plenty of time to get the ball off. The punt was a line drive towards the Pennington sideline. Owens sprinted over to cover it, but he could not get there in time. The ball bounced on the 45, crossed the 50, and stopped rolling on the Juddville 41 yard line.

Even though the Jaguars would have preferred to have blocked the punt, they were content to start their next drive with decent field position.

The first play was a halfback power to Rob Bast who cut back against the grain and picked up 8 yards. Coach Allen felt confident in his team's ability to move the ball on the ground. With a full quarter to play, he wanted to eat up as much clock as possible while avoiding anything risky that might shift momentum back to the visiting Pirates.

Their next play was the same play but to the other side of the formation. Nash ran the ball hard, lowering his shoulder and plunging ahead to gain two and a half yards for a first down.

"Move the chains… move the chains," chanted the Juddville faithful, up on their feet, sensing their team was about to finally take the lead.

1st and 10 on the Pennington 48 yard line. Coach Allen was hesitant to call another off-tackle halfback power, and he was reluctant to give the ball to Mike on the inside trap. They hadn't had much success with the inside trap all game long, and he was hoping to come back to it after they hammered away a few more times at the perimeter of the Pirate defense.

There was one play that had been successful each of the previous times they had run it, so Coach Allen played by the numbers and called for David to run the ball again.

The Juddville offensive coordinator held his breath as the Jaguars jogged up to the line of scrimmage.

"Red 48… Red 48… Set… Go… Go… Go!"

Riley took the snap cleanly and reverse pivoted to his left, faking a handoff to Owens. Pete was pulling to the right. David rode the fake to Bast, snapping the ball out at the last moment before hiding the ball on his right hip as he sprinted towards the Juddville sideline.

Nash hooked the outside linebacker. Pete pulled around the edge and set his sights on the cornerback who was in retreat mode though pursuing at an angle that forced David to cut inside. Pete drove the corner into the chain gang while his quarterback tucked the ball under his arm, cutting straight up the numbers.

The safety #83 had bit on Bast's fake so David had some serious running room. He crossed the 45… the 40… the 35… the 30… and was brought down at the 27 by the safety, Alex Matthews, who had managed to make up a serious amount of ground, demonstrating to every fan in Raymond Sander's Stadium that he had a superior set of wheels.

Coach Allen was growing more confident in the offense by the minute. He looked up at the clock and read, "10:14."

The next play the Jaguars went back to Nash on the halfback power to the left side of the formation. They only picked up two yards because left halfback Bast was having a difficult time J-blocking their outside linebacker. There was very little space for the right guard Wilcox to lead up through the hole. Fortunately, Nash was not opposed to creating his own hole if needed.

Second and eight, and the Jaguars ran the halfback power to the right where Nash had been abusing the outside linebacker all night. Bast received the handoff took three steps, planted with his right foot and followed Pete up the enormous hole. Safety #83 dragged Rob down at the 15 yard line.

At this point in the game, there wasn't a single Juddville fan sitting down. Cindy's right arm was numb, so she had to switch the cowbell to her left hand.

Juddville was moving the ball with purpose, but #34 had not touched the ball on this drive.

"Come on, Coach.   Give the rock to #34.   Let him put it in." Fortunately, Mr. Owens's voice was drowned out by the riotous roaring and foot stomping tremors of the Juddville faithful.

David came over to the hashmark for the next play; he could barely hear Coach Allen's voice because of all the noise. He turned and sprinted back to the huddle. His confidence was soaring; he felt like a kid on a playground.

The Jaguars broke from the huddle and jogged up to the line of scrimmage. The Pirates were bent over, hands on their knees, fighting for their next breath.

Safety Alex Matthews cheated over to the right side of Juddville's formation, expecting to see the off-tackle power that had proven so successful on this drive.

David took the snap, quickly handed off the ball to Owens, turned counter clockwise and executed an incredible fake to Bast. Then he put his right hand on his hip and sprinted for the sideline. Bast was tackled by both the inside linebacker and outside linebacker, and David was chased by the playside cornerback all the way to the sideline.

The Pirates' sideline was jumping up and down, absolutely certain that they had tackled Bast for a loss.

The roar from the home team bleachers suggested a different outcome, however. The Juddville fans were familiar enough with the Wing-T offense to know that in order to shut down the Jaguars, you better tackle every single back — most importantly, the fullback running straight up the middle.

Standing in the end zone, holding the ball high above his head was #34, Mike Owens, Jr. It was the first official touchdown of his varsity career, and it couldn't have happened at a better time.

"I told you to give him the ball, Coach. I told you to give him the ball," shouted Mr. Owens.

Cindy chose to ignore the comments of Mr. Ignoramus this time, however. She knew that the touchdown was more the result of her son's punishing trap block and some outstanding faking on the part of quarterback #11 and halfback #24. Furthermore, there was a long season ahead of them. She was going to have to learn to ignore the obnoxious one or start bringing a roll of duct tape.

The PAT team hustled onto the field, and Steve Wilcox's kick split the uprights, making the score 16 to 12, in Juddville's favor, with more than 8 minutes left to play. Nevertheless, the Jaguars had their first lead of the season, and now it was the defense's game to lose. Coach Allen breathed a huge sigh of relief.

Steve Wilcox received the football from the official and set the ball purposefully on the tee. The young kicker wanted nothing more than to boot the ball into the end zone for a touchback. The rejuvenated kickoff team was huddled behind him, starting to believe that victory was within reach.

Unfortunately, Steve shanked the ball towards the Pennington sideline where it bounced out of bounds at the 22 yard line. The line judge threw his flag and blew the whistle.

Pennington chose the option of taking the ball on the 35 yard line rather than forcing Juddville to rekick. On the first play they ran a sweep to the weak side of their formation, and #20 picked up 4 yards. On the next play, Howell hit his favorite receiver Matthews on a hitch route, earning just enough yardage for a first down.

To begin the next series of downs, the Pirates ran the ball on a fullback trap; it was #44's first carry of the day and would most likely be his last. Pete read the guard pulling, and he scraped right behind his nose tackle into the hole, meeting the fullback with his shoulder, lifting him off his feet and dropping him flat on his back for a 1 yard loss.

With a 2nd and 11 on the next play, Juddville was expecting pass, and Coach Abraham rolled his corners up and ran Cover 2. Owens jammed #83 Matthews, and he could not get off the line of scrimmage cleanly. Howell's throw went sailing out of bounds over the receiver's head.

On third and 11 from their own 44 yard line, the Pirates came out in their tight end trips formation. This time their three immediate receivers ran off their coverage while their halfback swung out to the right on a bubble route. Strong safety Jeff Nash had flats coverage, and he tackled Jackson as soon as he caught the ball, limiting him to a four yard gain.

With the ball on the Pennington 48 yard line, Juddville was on the lookout for a fake punt, but the Pirates chose to play conservatively with over 6 minutes left on the clock.

The Pirate punter got off a monstrous punt, and they were able to down the ball on the 2 ½ yard line. Coach Allen sent the play in from the sideline, and the Jaguars formed a tight huddle backed up deep in their own end zone.

On the first play they ran a 22 halfback power to Rob Bast. This time their outside linebackers were slamming into C gap, and their defensive ends were looping into D gap. Tight end Hardings missed his block on the defensive end. Nash caved the outside linebacker down into C gap, but there was so much congestion, Pete was unable to lead up the hole. As a result, Pete redirected to the defensive end, pushing him back a foot at most, leaving a slim running lane. Bast panicked, however, and tried to bounce it outside.

Safety #83 Matthews came up and took Bast's legs out from underneath him, resulting in no gain for the Jaguars. Coach Allen was pacing back and forth, yearning to move the chains while eating up some clock, but he was deathly afraid of turning the ball over and giving the Pirates fortuitous field position.

On second down, David ran a QB sneak straight up the gut. It looked like he had more running room on the right side, but he chose to follow left guard O'Connor. The quarterback went down without much struggle after a measly three yard gain.

With third and seven, no one expected to see the ball in the air, and Coach Allen played it conservative and called a 36 trap. O'Connor and center opened up a gaping hole inside, Wilcox made the hole even larger, trapping their defensive tackle who had over-penetrated, making Steve's block relatively easy.

Owens received the quick handoff and bursted through the line of scrimmage. It looked like he was off for the races, but Matthews dove at his ankles and tripped him up on the 13 yard line. The line judge on the Pennington sideline spotted the ball back on the 12 where he had judged Mike's knee to have gone down.

The Juddville faithful were incensed and wasted no time expressing their hostility towards the poor officiating.

"Go home, zebras!" yelled a pair of Juddville old-timers.

"Get your eyes checked, morons!"

The head official blew his whistle for an official's timeout to get a measurement.

The chain gang hustled out to the middle of the field. As they stretched out the chains, the sparse crowd from Pennington rose to their feet and cheered appreciatively. The ball was marked a foot short. Juddville had no option but to punt the ball. With just over four minutes of clock remaining, it looked like the visiting Pirates were going to get the ball back with excellent field position.

Punter Bryan Cox set his heels on the goal line as Craig Daniels prepared himself to snap the most critical snap of his career. The Pirates were sending 10 players to block the punt; the snap was going to have to be perfect.

The ball zipped back to Cox on a perfect line. He caught the ball and unleashed all of his might into the leather ball. The ball turned, sailing down the field with a perfect spiral, flying over the head of the returnman, Ronny Jackson. The ball bounced on the 41 and rolled five more yards to the Pennington 36 yard line.

Coach Abraham congratulated his punter on the sideline.

"Way to boot the ball, Bryan! That was a clutch punt if I ever saw one."

The Pirates started their next possession with 4:11 on the clock. On the first play, they came out in I Pro Right, with #83 to the strong side. Coach Abraham expected to see nothing but passes now; he signaled in Cover 1 Free to his secondary.

Coach Oliver screamed out to his defensive linemen, "You've got to put pressure on the quarterback. If you can't get to him in time, get your hands up and tip the ball."

The first play was a hitch to Matthews. Owens brought him down in bounds, limiting the gain to 5 yards. The clock was ticking

"Keep everything in front of you," shouted Coach Allen. "Nothing gets behind you, safeties!"

On second down, the Pirates came out in a 2 by 2 formation with two wide outs and two slot receivers. Matthews was split out wide on Juddville's side of the field.

Coach Allen yelled out to his secondary, "Switch to Cover 4. You each have quarters."

Once again, the wide outs ran 5 yard hitch routes while the slot receivers ran deep corners. Howell threw a dart to his receiver of choice who gained 11 yards—due to the soft coverage called by Coach Abraham—before running the ball out of bounds and stopping the clock at the Juddville 48 yard line.

With 3:29 on the clock, the Pirates had plenty of time to score the go ahead touchdown. They came out again in their 2 by 2 formation. This time they ran Jackson off-tackle.

Big Larry Moore got a hand on him and tugged the runningback slowly but surely to the turf. Pete was first on the pile, followed by outside linebacker Daniels, limiting #20 to a measly one yard gain.

Ever so slowly, the Jaguars lifted themselves up from the pile. The umpire tried to hurry them up, but Big Larry was taking his sweet old time. By the time Pennington broke from their huddle, the clock was under three minutes.

The Pirates broke out into their 2 by 2 formation; Howell took the snap, dropped back three steps and threw another hitch to #83. Matthews caught the ball and picked up 7 yards, but he was unable to get out of bounds.

"You're playing 'em too soft, Coach!" cried out Mike Owens, Sr. "We're giving the game away!"

A growing number of Juddville fans were beginning to share that opinion. With a third down and one on the Jaguar 40 yard line, the pressure was intensifying on both sides of the ball.

"Come on defense. We've got to stop them," shouted David, at the top of his voice.

The Pirates brought their tight end back onto the field and lined up in I-pro left. On a quick count, Howell received the snap and plowed behind his right guard for three yards and a first down. Once the ball was spotted and the chains reset, the clock resumed.

With the ball on Juddville's 37 yard line and 2:24 remaining, Coach Patterson realized his offense needed a breather if they hoped to finish this drive and score the go-ahead touchdown, so he used his second timeout.

On the opposite sideline, Coach Abraham conferred with his defense. "Nothing big, secondary. Keep everything in front of you, and try to keep the ball inbounds to keep the clock running. D-line, we sure could use a sack right now.

"Listen, men. We've got to believe. We've got to believe in each other. We've got to believe that we will put a stop to this drive. Everyone takes care of his own assignment, and we taste our first victory. Get your hands in here. Team on three. One… two… three."

"TEAM!"

The Pirates broke from their huddle and spread out in their 2 by 2 formation. This time #3 was slot on the same side as their "Go to" receiver, Alex Matthews. Given the strength of Howell's arm, the Pirates were certainly close enough to the end zone to hook up with one of their receivers on a deep route.

In the midst of the most dramatic, most critical juncture of the game, a pivotal observation was made on the sideline by a most unlikely source. It wasn't made by Coach Abraham, Coach Allen, or Coach Oliver. Nor was it made by the former UFL legend Jimmy Harrison either.

"Coach Allen, Coach Allen…" shouted Roger Collins, running frantically towards him while pointing out to the field. "Number 83 took his glove off during the time out."

After spotting the Pirate receiver on the field, Coach Allen concurred, "You're absolutely right, Collins!"

Then he ran down the sideline to the 25 and shouted out to Mike Owens and Don Jacobs, closest to the Jaguar sideline, "Watch out for the double pass. Watch out for the double pass."

On the first count, halfback Ronny Jackson ran in motion to the left. The ball was snapped on the third count. Howell took a three-step drop and threw the ball out to #83 who had dropped back five yards behind the line of scrimmage.

Matthews caught the pass cleanly—technically, it was a lateral since the ball traveled on a backwards plane—while Jackson ran straight at Owens who was coming up to defend Matthews.

Slot receiver, #3 ran a deep corner route. Don Jacobs, alerted to the trick play by his sideline, fully anticipated the "double-pass".

Matthews had plenty of time to throw the ball, but his target was guarded tightly, so he attempted to make lemonade out of a lemon.

Breaking to the sideline wasn't an option as Juddville's corner, #34, had outside leverage, so Alex had no other choice but to try to cut back to the inside.

By the time he reached top speed, he was 7 yards behind the line of scrimmage, providing the defense with ample time to close on him. As he reached the original line of scrimmage, #54 was hot on the trail. Matthews looked back to the outside as he crossed the 35 and noticed the cornerback shedding his block.

CRUNCH.

The linebacker had reached him sooner than expected, tackling him below the waist, wrapping his legs up so tightly that he had no chance of breaking free. Although he had gained six yards, the clock was still ticking, and it was now second and four from the Juddville 31 yard line.

By the time the Pirates had broke from their huddle and sprinted to the line of scrimmage, there was 1:57 remaining.

The quarterback crouched under center and barked out the cadence. One "hut", two "huts", and nose tackle Greg McDonald jumped offsides, colliding into the center.

A chorus of groans erupted from the Juddville sideline as the visiting Pirates had become the beneficiary of a most desperately needed first down. Furthermore, the clock stopped for the defensive penalty, as well.

The referee spotted the ball on the 26 yard line and waited for the sideline crew to reset the chains. The tight end returned to the field for Pennington, and they came out of their huddle in an I-Pro Right formation.

On the third hut, Howell took the snap, reverse-pivoted and pitched the ball to Ronny Jackson running a sweep to the right side of their formation. Jacobs flew up and took on the fullback. Owens was getting held by Matthews and couldn't break free. Jackson got to the corner and gained eight yards before getting knocked out of bounds on the 18 yard line, stopping the clock with 1:49 remaining.

Sensing that his bend-but-don't-break strategy was failing miserably, Coach Abraham realized that an aggressive defensive call was long overdue.

The Pirates came out in I-Pro again. This time they ran play action. Howell faked a handoff to Jackson and turned to look to his tight end who was wide open on a seam route. What the star quarterback didn't expect was #54 coming at him like an armored tank.

Before Howell could blink, the linebacker's facemask was buried in his sternum, laying out the quarterback flat on his back. Miraculously, he was able to maintain control of the football.

But the damage had been done. The ball was marked all the way back on the 24 yard line, it was 3rd and 8, and more importantly, the clock was ticking.

The Pennington sideline was a scene of mass confusion. Coach Patterson was in a heated discussion with his offensive coordinator. After 10 seconds had transpired, the head coach called a timeout; they had none remaining.

Roger Collins and Adam Foster ran water bottles out to the defensive huddle as Coach Abraham reminded his troops of their responsibilities.

"Secondary, keep everything in front of you. Nothing gets behind you. D-line and outside backers, bring pressure, and don't let the quarterback break contain. Two more stops are all we need."

Pennington came out in trips to their sideline with #83 all by himself on the weak of the formation. Jackson was the lone runningback.

"Coach, let's call a time out. We need to double cover Matthews," said Coach Allen.

"Time out… time out!" screamed Coach Abraham to the side judge.

The coaches went back onto the field and made adjustments.

"Mike, I want you to man up on #83. Tommy, you give him help over the top. On the trips side, Nash and Jacobs play quarters and O'Connor, you cheat over and take the flats. And Pete, keep one eye on the tight end and one eye on their halfback. Wilcox, you're firing B gap."

Pennington broke out of their huddle in the same formation. Howell took the snap and dropped back five steps. He lofted a beautiful spiral to the corner of the end zone to his favorite receiver on a fade route. The Pirates' Tommy Schulz was in the right place at the right time, leaping up and spiking the ball harmlessly to the turf. The clock stopped on the incompletion.

With only 1:17 remaining, the Pirates had one more opportunity to get a 1st down. They broke out of their offensive huddle and line up in their 2 by 2 formation. The Jaguars lined up in a soft Cover 4.

Before the quarterback's hands were under center, Juddville called a timeout. Coach Abraham wanted to make sure his defense was armed and ready.

The Juddville crowd was going berserk: hundreds of feet — loud as thunder — pounding the bleachers, ear-piercing whistles, and a cowbell clanging at a feverish pace.

"Jaguars…Jaguars…"   shouted   the   Juddville   faithful, "Jaguars…Jaguars…"

Coach Abraham brought his defensive unit into a tight circle around him. "We have an opportunity to finish this game on the next play… an opportunity to seal the deal and earn our 1st win. We finish strong. You hear me? Finish strong.

"Finish on three. One... two... three."

"FINISH!"

Fourth down and eight yards to go for a 1ˢᵗ down. Ball on the 24 yard line. 1:17 on the clock.

Pennington spread out in 2 by 2. Owens lined up on #83 Matthews; Schulz played 10 yards off slot receiver #3. At the last second, Owens crept up into press coverage — only two yards separating him from their star receiver.

On the snap of the ball, #3 streaked upfield and cut to the right corner. Matthews took 3 steps and ran a slant. The ball arrived in Matthews hands at the same time as Owens's helmet.

The ball ricocheted up into the air. Linebacker #54 was dropping to his hook zone and saw the ball suspended in mid air. Pete accelerated, reached down, and caught the ball at his ankles. Regaining his balance, he sprinted towards the opponent's end zone that was all of 80 yards away. Pete could see the quarterback out of the corner of his eye, but there was no way that Howell would catch him.

He crossed the 30, the 40, the 50. There was nothing but green in front of him. His ears went deaf. His heart was thumping like a bass drum.

At the Pirate 40, Pete felt an intense burning in his lungs. Out of the corner of his eye, he could see a white colored jersey closing in on him. It was #83, the fastest player on the Pennington Pirates.

As Pete reached the 20, he felt contact at his ankles, causing him to go down at the 17 yard line.

The crowd went crazy as Pete rose to his feet. First on the scene were Owens, Nash, and Jacobs, patting him obsessively on the shoulder pads, jumping up and down in sheer ecstasy. The rest of the defense was soon to follow. The celebration was cut short by Coach Allen who was frantically trying to get the offense out on the field before incurring a delay of game penalty.

The Juddville offense sprinted out on the field with 1:03 remaining.

"Victory formation," David called out in the huddle. The Jaguars jogged up to the ball and lined up toe-to-toe, one halfback to the left of the quarterback and one to the right, with Owens lined up 10 yards directly behind David to serve as "safety".

On the first count, Daniels snapped the ball to David who backpedaled 5 yards, dropped down on his right knee, and immediately popped back up onto his feet. A quick whistle by the referee.

The umpire spotted the ball on the 22. On the next play, David allowed the clock to reach 0:27 before taking a final knee.

The Juddville faithful counted down with great expectation.

"Five, four, three, two, one."

Chapter Twenty-three

Bedlam…pure, unadulterated bedlam. It was as if the young Jaguar team had never experienced victory before. Coach Abraham and Allen set their headphones down on the bench and gave one another the customary congratulatory hand shake and victory hug.

"Knew we had them the whole time," quipped Coach Allen.

"Ha… once we scored the go ahead touchdown, the defensive stand was just a formality, right?" retorted Keith.

"I think I might have aged five years tonight," admitted Jim.

"Congratulations, coaches," said Jimmy Harrison, offering his huge right hand to Keith, followed by Jim. "And thank you for the opportunity to be on the Juddville sideline again. I had a ball!"

"Thanks, Jimmy," responded Keith. "You know you are always welcome on our sideline and our practice field, as well."

Coach Abraham went searching for a water bottle before joining the traditional post-game handshake.

As he tipped back the water bottle and squirted a healthy dose of cold water down his parched throat, he cautiously looked up in the stands for Carol. He found her sitting next to Mary Allen and their small children. Catching her attention, he signaled thumbs up, the official Abraham post-game ritual.

Finally, Coach Abraham joined the handshake line, right behind rookie assistant, Coach Oliver.

Tapping him on the shoulder, he said, "Congratulations on your first victory, Gary."

"Thanks, Coach. Are they always like this?"

"Most of the time? Yes. Once in blue moon, you get an easy one, but those are few and far between."

"That was intense. The defense sure came up big when we needed them to."

After shaking the Pennington players' hands, Coach Abraham shook hands with the opposing coaches. It was always such an awkward occasion. One coaching staff was ecstatic, the other dejected. Sure, there was a lot of pretense involved: the winning coach pretended to be humble and gracious, and the defeated coach attempted to suppress the disappointment while trying to appear doggedly-optimistic.

The reality of football, however, was that neither coaching staff would have much time to dwell on the game that had just transpired. Instead, their minds would automatically begin focusing on their next opponent.

"Good game, Coach," offered Keith to the new Pennington Pirate head coach. "Your team played well. That defense is going to give a lot of teams fits this year. And that quarterback and receiver of yours... they're going to put up a lot of points, along with that shifty halfback."

"Thanks, Keith. Your team played with a lot of spirit. That #54 was all over the place. And that sophomore back of yours, he can play some defense too."

"Good luck next week, Gary."

"You, too. I see your next one's going to be a big one," pointing his head back in the direction of three Billington scouts who were carrying two video cameras and a couple of clipboards as they descended the visiting bleachers.

"Thanks, for reminding me," said Keith, his lips curled up in a forced smile.

The victorious Jaguars were already huddled in their end zone, anticipating the traditional post-game prayer and wrap-up. As Coach Abraham neared the end zone, he was met by quarterback David Riley on the 10 yard line.

"Coach, would it be okay if I said the prayer?" uncertain as to how Coach Abraham would respond to his request.

"That would be great, David."

Coach Abraham got on a knee and grabbed hands with Coach Allen on his left and David on his right.

Starting out a bit timid, David began to pray, "Dear God, thank you for a great victory tonight. Thank you for keeping us safe and for allowing us to enjoy the game of football. Be with us this weekend. Keep us safe. In the name of Jesus, we pray."

"Amen!" his teammates joined in unison.

The first parent onto the field was Mike Owens, Sr. His girlfriend stayed off the field, out of the spotlight, a safe distance from the unpredictable — often times, volatile — actions of her latest fling.

"Way to go, son. You played a heckuva game."

"Thanks, Dad," said Mike, Jr., giving his father a grizzly bear hug.

"You ran hard, Mike. Too bad your coach didn't give you the ball more. I only had you down for 10 carries for 51 yards."

"Who cares about stats, Dad? We won the game. That's all that matters, isn't it? And I made a couple big plays on defense too."

"What are you talking about, boy. That's nonsense. Of course, it matters how many yards you got. How are you going to get a scholarship with only 51 yards rushing?"

"You don't understanding anything about being on team, do you, Dad?"

"Course, I do. We Owens are a team. In my book, that's the only team that matters."

"Really, Dad? Then why did Mom leave?"

"Watch your mouth, boy!" jabbing his finger into Mike's chest.

Grabbing his dad's hand and pushing it downward, "I'll see you later, Dad. I'm going out for some pizza…to celebrate with my other team. Can I have some money?"

"Sure," holding out a twenty. "We'll talk some more about the game later."

Mike Jr. snatched the bill with his right hand and headed straight to the locker room.

"Daddy, can you throw me a pass?" begged Luke, appearing suddenly from behind him.

"Daddy, throw me a pass, too," begged Kevin.

"Hold on, will you? I've got to give my best gal a big kiss if you don't mind."

As Mary and Jim embraced, all of his anxiety dissipated. The play calls, the personnel moves, the officiating, everything that had been bombarding his mind just floated away like the smoke from a bonfire.

"I love you, Mary."

"I love you, too, Jim. That was a great game. Are all your games going to be like that this year?"

"I hope so… I'll take a win whatever way it comes."

Looking behind him, he remembered two people he wanted to introduce to Mary.

"Honey, I want to introduce you to Coach Oliver and Jimmy. Come over here a minute, guys. I want to introduce you to my family."

As they were formally introduced to Mary, the three children hid behind Coach Allen. The oldest boy Luke began tugging on his dad's pant leg.

"Daddy, is that Jimmy Harrison?" asked Luke as his eyes traveled all the way to the top of the former UFL player's 6 foot 8 inch frame.

"It sure is, Luke. Why don't you say 'hello' to him."

Jimmy reached way, way down and snagged the ball out of Luke's hands and said, "Go long, Luke. And you're next, Kevin."

Tilting his head straight back so he could see all the way to the top of the former UFL star's head, Luke asked, "How'd you know our names?"

"Because your dad never stops talking about you; that's why. Now let's see what kind of hands you've got."

Luke turned and ran a fade route to the end zone. Jimmy led him perfectly. Luke caught the ball in front of him and the cradled the ball safely into his bread basket with both arms.

"I'm next," reminded Kevin. "I'm next."

Coach Allen took advantage of the opportunity to swoop down and pick up his daughter Katie standing all alone chewing on a mouthful of popcorn. Her eyes lit up and she planted a buttery kiss on his cheek.

"Daddy, your skin is all rough. Did you forget to shave?"

"No honey, it's a superstition not to shave on game day."

"What does stuperstitching mean?"

"Oh, it just means Daddy was lazy this morning. Did you have a fun time tonight, Katie?"

"Yes, Daddy. I'm going to be a cheerleader."

"Really, honey? We'll talk about that when you get older."

"Daddy, can we go home now? I'm tired. Can you read me a bedtime story tonight?"

"You betcha, darling… I can't think of anything I'd rather do more."

Pete was one of the last to leave the field. As a captain, he felt obligated to help Roger Collins and Adam Foster carry all the gear off the field. There was an orange water jug, two water bottle trays each holding eight bottles, the ball bag, the portable phones, the towel bag, the first aid kit, the helmet repair kit, and the tool box. Without any help, they would have had to make at least three or four trips.

On his last trip out he was met by his mom at the outskirts of the playing field. She came up and gave him an enormous hug. He hadn't seen her so happy since the night that the assault charges had been dropped against him. Her friend Tina was standing by her side.

"Great game, Pete. You were awesome!"

"Thanks, Tina. The team really finished strong in the second half. I think all of our conditioning paid off."

Pete's attention turned to his mom. "I think your cowbell made a big difference, too. Your arm must have gotten quite a workout."

"Not nearly as much as my lungs. That was one exciting 4th quarter, Pete." Then changing subjects, "You coming straight home tonight?"

"I don't know… Why?"

"It looks like you have someone waiting to talk to you, and boy is she a knockout."

"What?"

Pete looked over at the gate and saw the girl with golden brown hair. The lights of Raymond Sanders Stadium seemed to have directed their attention solely upon her. She smiled and waved, and he was mesmerized once again by her alluring beauty.

Completely out of his comfort zone, Pete started walking like a zombie in Amber's direction without offering any type of explanation to his mother.

He had no idea what to say, and he felt somewhat self-conscious about his sweaty, filthy condition. Yet surely Amber wouldn't expect him to smell any differently after engaging in one of the most physical battles of his lifetime.

Nevertheless, he knew he wanted to draw near… to take a closer glimpse… to willingly become enchanted by her charm and magic. When he was within ten feet of her, she ran up to him and gave him a light kiss on the cheek.

"That was the best football gave I've ever seen, Pete," her stunning face a mere six inches from his face.

Pete inhaled her fresh perfume and wished he had the boldness to kiss her on the lips to see if she tasted half as sweet as she smelled.

"I wasn't sure if you stuck around for the whole game. I didn't see you in the stands when I looked up in the last quarter," confessed Pete, embarrassed that his thoughts had been anywhere but on the football field.

"Oh, yeah. That was when I had to…" then her face turned slightly red, as she looked to the ground.

Pete noticed an abrupt change in her demeanor.

All of the sudden, she regained her focus and said, "Pete, I want you to meet someone. I want you to meet Joey."

She ran over towards the parking lot where another girl was standing… another girl who was holding something extraordinary in her arms.

After completing his obligatory interview with the Juddville Gazette reporter, Coach Abraham had shaken hands with a throng of well-wishers. There was Superintendent Dr. Paul Jones, his principal and his athletic director, as well as a number of former players and parents. Finally, Keith searched for the one whom he desperately needed to see. There she was… waiting patiently in the background for her turn to congratulate "The Coach."

"Carol," sighed Keith, taking her in his arms.

They held one another for several seconds; Keith was waiting for her to say something, but she just seemed to squeeze harder.

He let go and looked deeply into her eyes. Her face looked uncharacteristically pale, and her eyes were wet with tears. It was clear to Keith that she was trying her best to hold something back.

"What is it, honey?"

"Read this," she weakly replied, handing him a note written in Julia's distinctive handwriting.

By the time Roger Collins hauled his last load of sideline gear from Raymond Sanders Stadium into the locker room, there were only a handful of players remaining. He headed directly for his locker and grabbed his cleats for tomorrow's workout. The only ones left in the locker room were Osborne and Moore, Riley and Bast, and Foster.

"Great game, David. You really showed a lot of poise out there tonight," said Roger.

"Thanks, Roger. I can't wait till you're back in one more week. We really need you."

"You guys did fine without me," responded Roger.

"Aw, let's all have a cry for Roger," mocked Big Larry.

"Don't you have a bucket of the Colonel waiting for you somewhere, big guy?"

"I sure hope so. What are we still doing in here anyways, Ox?"

Noticing the cleats in Roger's hands, David asked, "You running tomorrow?"

"Yeah, I was thinking about it."

"Mind if I join you?"

"That would be great. The more the merrier."

Big Larry interrupted, "Now I know it's time to split. All this crazy talk about running tomorrow. Are you guys nuts or what?"

"Somebody must have taken a blow to the head," responded Gary on their way out of the locker room.

The only ones left now were Foster, Riley and Collins.

Roger looked at Adam pointedly and said, "Stay away from O'Connor's locker, Adam, if you want to live to see your next birthday."

Adam's gaze continued to burn a hole through the tiled floor. He was sticking around only because he had something to tell Coach Abraham.

"Don't worry about Foster. He's a Jaguar now. Aren't you?" said David.

Adam nodded weakly, his eyes still staring downward.

"Well, I've got to go, David. What do you say…12:00 tomorrow?"

"See you then," responded Juddville's starting quarterback.

As Roger walked out to the parking lot, he was so astonished that he was convinced his eyes were playing tricks on him.

———

Standing beside Roger's burgundy sedan, his father asked, "You taking good care of my old wheels, son?"

"Dad?"

"Hello, Roger."

If Pete's jaw sunk any lower it would be breaking through the soil in China.

Even so, Amber was quite used to the reaction.

"This is Joey," said Amber with a somber look on her face. "He's 14 months old."

Pete's head was in a swim. He had absolutely no clue that the girl of his dreams was in fact a mother. Was he hallucinating or suffering from severe post-game dehydration? Virtually in shock, Pete had yet to say a word.

Finally, Pete stuttered, "I thought…"

Relieving him from the agony of having to finish his sentence, Amber interjected, "that Joe was my boyfriend? Nope. Joey's dad is out of the picture. He is a freshman at Wilburton College on the east coast. His parents send me a check once a month. But Brian has never even seen Joey."

"Really?" responded Pete. Then his mouth began to go on auto-pilot. "He doesn't know what he is missing."

"This is my best friend Brianna. We graduated together last year. Now we're roommates."

"Hi, Brianna. Nice to meet you."

"You played a great game, Pete."

"Thanks."

Then Pete did something that was way out of character, somewhere along the lines of wearing a suit and tie on the first day of school.

He asked, "Can I hold him?"

"Sure, he's wide awake right now. I don't think anyone could have slept through that final quarter."

Pete held the infant out in front of him and stared into his eyes. Such innocence… such wonder… such beauty.

"He's definitely got your eyes," said Pete, "and a smile that could melt the hardest of hearts."

Amber and Brianna quietly observed the interaction between the two males. Then Brianna leaned over and whispered into her friend's ear. Amber's chocolate brown eyes widened.

The only thing that Pete knew right now was that he wasn't ready for the most fantastic night of his life to end. It didn't make a whole lot of sense right now, but he was going to follow his instincts. Someone had mysteriously crossed his path. Someone remarkable. True, she was carrying some baggage — if you had the audacity to call Joey baggage — but one mistake does not a lifetime make.

Pete was going out on a limb. Surely, Amber had gone out on a limb just coming to his game.

"Are you doing anything tonight, Amber?"

She looked at her friend Brianna and giggled.

"Funny you should say that. Bri just offered to watch Joey for me tonight," a smile like the morning sun emerged from Amber's face.

"I'm starved. You want to go get something to eat?"

"I'd love to!"

"Let me go shower a second, and I'll be right out," said Pete, with a feeling of giddiness bubbling throughout his entire body. He started to run at ¾ speed to the locker room, but then turned and yelled back to Amber's roommate.

"Nice to meet you, Brianna!"

Then he resumed his run to the locker room, so revitalized he could hardly believe that he had just played almost every play of a varsity football game.

The last time Roger had seen his father was Christmas. For the most part, he looked the same. His blond hair was slicked back, and his face clean-shaven. He was always dressed like he was on the job, the consummate professional, and tonight he was wearing a navy blue pin-striped suit. Underneath, he wore a pearl white, long-sleeved shirt with a burgundy silk tie. "Over-dressed" was a concept unfamiliar to him. Most distinctive, however, was the familiar scent of his dad's cologne — a woodsy, musky smell.

"I didn't think you were coming, Dad… and to be honest, I was kind of hoping you wouldn't."

"Hop in, son. Let's go get a bite to eat. You got time for that?"

"I guess so."

As Roger sat in the passenger seat of his dad's new Lincoln Continental, he allowed his body to sink back and experience the cool, luxurious feeling of leather seats.

"What brings you back to Juddville? I thought you hated this town," said Roger.

"When did I ever say that? Can't be that bad if my son lives here," said Mr. Collins, electing to lay it on thick from the get go.

"Come on, Dad. I'm 17 now."

As they pulled out of the high school parking lot, Mr. Collins noted an unmistakable tone of resentment in his boy's voice. Roger wasn't the easy sell he used to be. He used to worship the ground he walked on. It never used to be much of a challenge to get Roger back in his corner, no matter how many times he had broken promises.

"So are you going to tell me why you weren't suited up tonight?"

"It's a long story, Dad. Basically, I violated the training rules and got a two game suspension."

"Drinking?"

"Yep."

"Did you learn your lesson?"

"Yeah, you don't know how miserable I felt being on the sidelines, unable to get in the game. The worst part was knowing how badly I let down the team."

Mr. Collins was silent as he listened to the honest confession of his son; he was amazed by how much he had matured since the last time he had seen him.

"Roger, I've been a pretty pathetic father. You're not the only one who has been on the sideline. And believe me, son, I know I've hurt you. It wasn't your fault your mother and I couldn't get along."

"When the fighting got so bad between your mom and me, I did the only thing I have ever known how to do. I ran."

Roger sat in silence.

Mr. Collins was hoping his son would give him some type of reaction, some sign that he at least partially understood his actions. Nevertheless, he wasn't so naïve to believe that forgiveness was forthcoming anytime soon.

"You know even though you were on the sidelines the whole game, you still had a huge influence on the outcome of the game. I saw how you pointed out to your coach that the opposing team's receiver removed the glove on his throwing hand. That was pretty darn observant of you, Roger. That play could have easily been the difference in the game."

Mr. Collins looked over at his son and thought he saw a miniature smile emerge from his face.

"What are you hungry for, Roger? Pizza or steak? Better yet, how about some seafood?"

After reading over Julia's note the second time, the message still wasn't sinking in. Keith was sitting in his car next to Carol, still parked in front of the Raymond Sanders Stadium though all of its lights were now turned off. The Juddville faithful had either gone home or to their favorite establishment to celebrate the first victory of the season.

Once more, he painfully reread the letter:

Dear Mom and Dad,

I can't live in this town anymore. I am sorry I screwed up your plans for my education, and I deeply regret all of the pain and embarrassment I have caused you.

Dad, you will always be my hero. I don't hold any grudges towards you. You did what you had to do to make Juddville a winning football team. Maybe things would have been different if I was a boy and one of your players.

I have to get away from Brian Taylor and from every place that holds a memory of him.

Mary is excited to have me come live with her. She says it will be easy to find a job. She's already got a promising lead at a clothing store.

Please don't worry about me. I am a big girl now. Too big for the Abraham home and too big for the town of Juddville. I purchased a one-way bus ticket to New York City. I will call you on Sunday.

Love always,

Julia.

P.S. Hope you won tonight, Dad. I'm sure you did (you always do). Go Jaguars!

Keith read the post script out loud to Carol and then wept uncontrollably. Then he folded up the note and placed it in his front pocket. Then he remembered back to earlier in the day and pulled out an index card from his back pocket. He had actually memorized what was written on the card, and he decided to share it with his wife though he didn't know how much good it would do now.

"This is a verse I copied down earlier today."

Carol took the index card from Keith's hand. It was a bit wrinkled, but the writing was still legible.

She began to read aloud, "But we have this treasure in jars of clay to show that this all-surpassing power is from God and not from us…"

An abrupt knock on the driver's side of Keith's window.

Keith rolled down his window. It was quite dark out, but he could see well enough to recognize Adam Foster.

"Hi, Adam," said Coach, trying to conceal his annoyance of yet another intrusion.

"I just wanted to ask you if there was anything else you needed me to do."

"All set, Adam."

Then deciding to offer his Billington transfer a little bit of encouragement, Coach added, "You did a good job tonight. One down, one more to go. Before you know it, you'll be suited up and eligible to play."

Adam looked down at his feet; his greasy brown bangs were thick, impermeable curtains unwilling to unveil what was hidden behind them.

Just as Coach Abraham was going to wish him a good night and speed him on his way home, Adam cleared his throat and spoke in a clear, articulate voice.

"Coach, I just wanted to say thanks... for giving me one more chance."

Acknowledgements

I want to express my appreciation to my personal editors: Sam, Barb, and Matt. Thank you for your constructive feedback and encouragement.

I would also like to thank John and Marilyn for their generous contribution to this project. In addition, I want to thank my good friend and lifetime mentor, Coach Jack Schugars.

Made in the USA
Monee, IL
26 July 2021

74282903R20118